CHRISTIANITY:

A Criminal Investigation of the Motivation, Structure, Growth, and Threat to Rome

by

Dr. Rocco Leonard Martino

BLUENOSE PRESS
WWW.BLUENOSEPRESS.COM

Please visit: www.roccoleonardmartino.com

Published by:

BlueNose Press, Inc.
www.bluenosepress.com
Printed in the United States of America
Published March, 2015

Novels by Dr. Rocco Leonard Martino

The Resurrection: A Criminal Investigation of the Mysterious Disappearance of the Body of the Crucified Criminal Jesus of Nazareth

9-11-11: The Tenth Anniversary Attack

The Plot to Cancel Christmas

Nonfiction Books by Dr. Rocco Leonard Martino

Applied Operational Planning

Allocating and Scheduling Resources

Computer-R-Age with Webster V. Allen

Critical Path Networks

Decision Patterns

Decision Tables with Staff of MDI

Dynamic Costing

Finding the Critical Path

Heat Transfer in Slip Flow

IMPACT 70s with John Gentile

Information Management

Integrated Manufacturing Systems

Management Information Systems

MIS Methodology

Personnel Management Systems

Project Management

Resources Management

UNIVAC Operations Manual

People, Machines, and Politics of the Cyber Age Creation

Rocket Ships and God

Reviews of
Christianity: A Criminal Investigation . . .

"I have read over Christianity: A Criminal Investigation of the Motivation, Structure, Growth, and Threat to Rome by Dr. Martino. There are no doctrinal problems with it."
-Rev. Robert A. Pesarchick, STD, Academic Dean, Theological Seminary and Professor of Systematic Theology, St. Charles Borromeo Seminary

"A very readable story, this could well be the basic text for a formation program. All Christian principles presented in a relaxed manner through the marvels of a fascinating narrative."
-Professor John J. Schrems, PhD, Professor Emeritus, University of Pennsylvania

"Christianity" is to Dr. Martino's previous historical novel, "Resurrection," as the Acts of the Apostles is to Luke's Gospel. Although the genres are different, in each case the second opus builds masterfully on the first. Highly imagined, well described scenes, populated by compelling characters, real and fictional, present a plausible understanding of the beginnings of Christianity in Rome - a historical fact confirming the ongoing presence of the Risen Christ in His Church. Readers, even more so, of this book will be especially drawn to Quintus, the quintessential military officer and the embodiment of ethics, who even after a lifetime of experience investigating the faith in Jesus Christ is unable to grasp the ultimate significance of the Resurrection. Mark, with a prominent role in the story, will record Jesus saying: "This is the time of fulfillment. The kingdom of God is at hand. Repent and believe in the gospel." Readers, with the grace of God, can grow in their faith, reading about Quintus struggling to go beyond his Roman mindset, to achieve what he sees in these first Christians, *metanoia* – their determination to advance the kingdom of God, a new creation – what Paul wrote to the Corinthians: "So whoever is in Christ is a new creation: the old things have passed away; behold, new has come."

-Paul Peterson, Professor of Theology, Archdiocese of Philadelphia

"Christianity" is a fascinating story and a must read for anyone seeking a deeper understanding of what it means to be in relationship with Jesus and one another-particularly those who question the value of "organized religion." Especially poignant for our times is the discourse between Quintus, representing the longing and searching in all of humanity, and Luke the Physician. Luke offers a reflection on Peter and Paul's life, which serves as a reflection of the immense love of God to allow imperfect humans, through the "Church" experience, to convey the presence of an ever-loving God. Even the quizzical Quintus can't help but express, "I have a sense of awe that I cannot explain." A wonderful, imaginative read for everyone!

-Mario R. Dickerson, MTS, Executive Director, Catholic Medical Association

"A refreshingly unique perspective on the beginning of Christianity. The characters' testimony of events from a different approach makes the reader delve yet again into the basis of their belief or non-belief."

-Anne Condello, Avid Reader

TABLE OF CONTENTS

PREFACE

AND

ACKNOWLEDGEMENTS

This book was difficult to write, I lived it for almost two years. I researched it for twenty months and wrote it in four, most of which were involved with the staging and storytelling. The dialogue all came easily since the characters were old friends from all the research. I often felt I was rapidly becoming a Biblical Scholar in my search for the facts.

All my life I have been fascinated by the two great miracles of the Christian religion. These are, of course, first, The Resurrection of Jesus; and second, a continuation of the first, the survival and growth of Christianity during the first century. When I decided to write about these two great miracles, I chose the mechanism of fiction as a means of linking the episodes in the Scriptures into a cohesive and integrated story.

My model was the "Passion Play" concept immortalized so grandly and effectively by the good people of Oberammergau, Germany. The Passion Play had a great impact on me when I first saw it during the 350th

Anniversary Celebration in 1984. It was enhanced when I saw it again in 2000. The scream of the actress playing the Blessed Mother, "mein sohn" (my son) often reoccurs in my memory. Watching that play made me realize the biblical characters were real people who felt pain and joy just as you and I. Hence I chose the vehicle of a novel as a means of not only telling a cohesive story, but also in creating memorable 'scenes' that would make the story real.

I see a great need to make the Resurrection and the Birth of Christianity as something real for all of us. It helps immeasurably to feel the truth of what is told. In the previous companion novel: *The Resurrection: A Criminal Investigation of the Mysterious Disappearance of the Body of the Crucified Criminal Jesus of Nazareth,* I attempted a totally logical proof of the Resurrection of Jesus. I was challenged to do this by our son Paul. From the reviews received, including those from learned Biblical scholars, I believe I succeeded in making the resurrection a matter of fact and not just a matter of faith. In this book, I attempted not only to tell the story of the growth of Christianity in the First Century, but also to include the basic truths of Christianity.

This book is centered in Rome, during the reign of the Emperor Vespasian who ruled from 69 to 79 AD. The setting for this book is early in his reign.

At that time, Rome was riddled with cross currents and struggles for power. Vespasian was the fourth emperor in a year. The other three were either murdered or forced into suicide. Vespasian, the general in command in suppressing the revolt of the Jews in Judea, seized power backed by the might of his Germanic Legions. His son Titus destroyed Jerusalem, and the Temple, to end the revolt in Judea. Emperor Vespasian then named his son

Titus to head the Praetorian Guard, cementing his hold on power in Rome. He ruled wisely, and was popular with the people. Early in his reign, the question of the Christians came to his attention. This book depicts that controversy.

There were many who favored a continuation of the persecution initiated by the Emperor Nero. This persecution, terrible, cruel, brutal, and extensive in its impact, also saw the execution of both Peter and Paul. Many favored a continuation of this persecution; while some favored allowing the Christians to live in peace. There was even a glimmer of the idea of union that led three hundred years later for Rome to establish Christianity as its official religion.

The approach taken in this book is to remain as true as possible to what is known and cataloged in the Scriptures and other extant historical texts. Extensive use has been made of the Epistles of Peter and Paul, with numerous quotations included in the text. These quotations are taken from the New International Version of the Bible, accessed through BibleGateway.com. The objective was to illustrate the direction given to the early church by these two great leaders, Peter and Paul. Both were driven by their firsthand knowledge of the teachings of Jesus. Both were martyred for their faith.

The central character, or hero, of this story is Quintus Gaius Caesar, now a Senator, and previously a Tribune and Deputy Prefect of the Praetorian Guard. It was Quintus whom the Emperor Tiberius placed in charge of the Investigation into the disappearance of the body of Jesus from the tomb. It was Quintus' investigation and report to Tiberius that is the basic story in the earlier book *The Resurrection: A Criminal Investigation....*

In this book, Quintus is commanded by Vespasian to recommend one of three possible solutions for the problem of the Christians. They were to be exiled, they were to be executed, or they were to be allowed to live in peace. Quintus, with the help of members of the Praetorian Guard, and knowledgeable witnesses such as the physician Luke, and the Tribune Cornelius (formerly a Centurion), sets in motion a wide-ranging investigation of Christianity. Is it a religion, is it a threat to Rome, can it survive, and what is attracting vast numbers to join?

Quintus sets out to establish the answers to these questions. His investigation includes a detailed study of the Epistles of Paul and Peter, and long interview with Cornelius, the first Gentile baptized in the new religion; extensive and direct interaction with the physician Luke, companion and chronicler of the activities of Peter and Paul; an assessment of the lives and work of Peter and of Paul; and extensive interviews with Cornelius, with Linus the successor of Peter; and with Cletus and Clementus, the potential successors of Linus.

A fictional opponent to the Christians, Senator Sarto, was invented to give poignancy and suspense to the story. He was representative of the many who sought to continue the persecution of the Christians.

Research for this book was extensive. Many sources were used. The Internet was used extensively for finding and producing such references. The basic problem associated with developing a cohesive history of that time in the history of Christianity is the paucity of information available. However, sufficient facts were uncovered through this extensive research to validate the storyline presented in this novel.

I am indebted to my wife Barbara for her support through all aspects of this difficult undertaking. She not only read the proofs, but suffered with me in the struggle through the changes and soul-searching I went through in terms of how to present the story logically and correctly.

I am deeply also indebted to Paul Peterson and Dr. John Schrems who read, commented and made editorial recommendations for this book; to Anne Condello and Amy Sammons who typed and assembled this book; and, as promised, to my granddaughter Maria Francis Martino who added numbers to the pages in the manuscript.

Most of all, I am indebted to the Holy Spirit for guidance, fortitude, and that spark of insight which guided me in writing this book, and which I hope will make it interesting and valuable to you, the reader.

DEDICATION

This book is dedicated to the three pillars of my life - my father, Domenico Martino; my brother, Jiacomo James Martino; and my Aunt Mary, La Zia, Maria Mencarelli, née Martino, my father's youngest sister. These three cared for me and protected me most of their lives. When my mother died I was eight years old, and my brother was eleven. My father, always Pop to me, asked his parents in Italy to send their young daughter Maria to take care of his two boys. They consented and soon this young 18 year old showed up. What a baptism of fire she had with two young, rambunctious and mischievous boys. She became sister, mother, protector, cookie cook, and companion in mischief. The four of us all grew up together, missing Mom terribly, but challenging each day as an adventure. They are all gone now, but they live on in my memory and in the person I am - molded and protected by them in their lifetimes, and even now.

Chapter One

The Christians

"Exterminate the Christians and banish the Jews from Rome! That's that must be done." The statement, uttered in the ringing tones of conviction by Senator Antonius Caesar Servo, seemed to hang in the air.

Emperor Vespasian was perturbed and angry. The wrangling before him was solving nothing. Rome was seething with unrest. The people were unruly and rebellious. Ambition, power, and the struggle to survive were the roots of the problem. The Christians, as they were called, seemed at the core. Were they the problem, or were they the scapegoat? Were they being used as a ploy by those seeking to grasp full control and power in Rome? Where was the real threat to his power?

He was a silent spectator in his Council Chamber of a heated dispute on how to define and then resolve this issue. Two of the most powerful senators in Rome, Senators Antonius Caesar Servo and Maxim Valerius Acquinas, were in heated disagreement. Senator Servo was no friend of Vespasian. He had contended for election as Emperor but had lost to Vespasian in the Senate vote.

Senator Acquinas, on the other hand, had always been one of Vespasian's strongest supporters.

The Emperor was seated on a raised dais at one end of his large Council Chamber. Sunlight streamed through the open doors leading to the balcony overlooking the Augustine Square, a balcony from which the Emperor often looked out over Rome. The Senators stood solidly before him.

The argument concerned the tenuous security of Rome. The Empire had just survived a tumultuous year following the death of Emperor Claudius. Four separate Emperors had waged civil war. With the end of the war, and the deaths of the contending Emperors, a troubled peace had come. Vespasian, backed by his Germanic Legions, had seized power as Emperor. The Senate then confirmed Vespasian as Emperor with a mandate to restore order in the Empire and in Rome. Such restoration was sorely needed. The Senate further challenged him to bring the finances of Rome into balance. As Rome's foremost general of the time, Vespasian was known for his ability to bring discordant elements of the population to live together in harmony and thus maintain order, backed at all times, of course, by the military might of his Legions and those of Rome. He was determined to rule firmly, quashing the least sign of potential challenge to civil order before it became unmanageable, and a major threat to security.

Recently he had become aware of a new religious sect reported to him as becoming an unsettling factor in the civil order of Rome. The members of this sect were called Christians, taking their name from the teacher they followed, one Jesus the Christ, a Jew from Nazareth in Galilee. This Jesus had been executed by the Roman Procurator of Judea, Pontius Pilate, in order to placate the religious leaders of the Jews. Pilate's objective had been to

14

maintain civil order in Judea. That objective had failed. Whether because of Jesus or not, Judea had proven increasingly ungovernable in the years following the execution of this Jesus. The ultimate revolt required major military force to suppress it. Vespasian had led that force which brought the revolt under control. The Christian sect had originated in Judea, and its first followers were Jews. Having conquered Judea, Vespasian was fully aware of the industry, intelligence and fortitude of the Jewish people. Even with the might of Rome behind him, and the seasoned Legions under his command, victory had been difficult. The Emperor's son, Titus, had been brilliant in executing the campaign plan. When Vespasian became involved in the War of the Four Emperor's, it was Titus who carried on, winning the final campaign in Judea, and destroying Jerusalem and the Temple in the process. It had not only been brutal but was only decided with reinforcements from Rome. Still it had been a brilliant military success.

That success had been a major factor in the Senate's confirmation of him to be Emperor. Now Vespasian faced a possible major disruption to the peace of the homeland due to a sect of the same Jews he had conquered in Judea. These Christians were potential troublemakers. Vespasian's recent predecessor, Emperor Nero, had identified the Christians as causing the great fire that had swept Rome, a fire that had destroyed over half the city. Nero had persecuted the sect, attempting to stamp them out with widespread executions. He had failed. The Christians almost seemed to proliferate in the blood of their martyrs - those who were executed for their beliefs. That tenacity created both admiration and concern in the mind of Vespasian. That had led him to call this meeting.

The Christian issue was not new. It had divided the Jews in the past and led to disturbances throughout the

Empire, even in Rome. Emperor Claudius had banished the Jews from Rome in order to quell that disturbance. The Jews had returned; and the Christians had not been exterminated. The decision before Vespasian to maintain order was to select one of three courses of action - banish the Jews from Rome as Emperor Claudius had done, execute the Christians to extinction as Nero had attempted, or to find some way to control the Christians and so maintain Pax Romana - the Peace of Rome - even in Rome itself.

Vespasian had a grudging respect for the Jews and was fearful that the Jewish population of Rome could become an unsettling factor in his quest for order throughout the Empire and especially in Rome. This Christian splinter sect could very well be the spark to ignite a rebellion. The dispute between the two Senators this day was on that very point. The issue was how to prevent turmoil, and how to enhance the control and governance of Rome and of the Empire. Both issues were paramount in the mind of the Emperor when he had summoned the two Senators before him. He knew they would disagree, and take strong opposing positions. In addition, Senator Servo was not a neutral - he was no friend of Vespasian. Any suggestion he might have would be self-serving, perhaps contrary to the best interests of Rome. There was always the ulterior motive to embarrass Vespasian and perhaps depose him as Emperor, with Servo then vying to replace him.

Senator Acquinas, on the other hand, was a strong supporter of Rome, seeking what was best for Rome, even if contrary to the interest and desires of the Emperor. He was a thoroughly honest man.

16

Vespasian was vexed. He sought opinions, no matter from what source, in order to assess the best course of action for both Rome and his reign as Emperor.

Senator Antonius Caesar Servo was an imposing figure. He stood tall, and erect, but somewhat corpulent, no longer the athletic lean soldier of his youth. He always held his head up high, making sure to gaze over the heads of all those around him, whom he obviously considered lesser in all respects. He was a product of many years in the Legions. As the first born of a historic Roman family, he had entered the military to seek fame and fortune before taking his family's place in the Senate. His entire bearing exuded success based on strength and self-confidence. He tolerated no challenge to his opinions and pronouncements. While acknowledging the role of the Emperor as the Head of State, he was not reluctant to voice an opinion in opposition to that of the Emperor, although he was sufficiently politically astute not to overplay his hand. He left no doubt of his opinion that he would make a better Emperor than anyone else.

Senator Servo was silent for a moment as he very carefully collected his thoughts. Then he repeated his strong challenge, looking in the direction of the Emperor, but not making eye contact. "Sire, I think you should exterminate the Christians and banish the Jews from Rome once more."

Before he could continue, Senator Maxim Valerius Acquinas interjected, "That is pretty extreme, Senator Servo. Are you manufacturing a solution for a problem that does not exist?"

Senator Acquinas had always been a strong supporter of the Emperor, and had been a leader in the Senate of those voting to elect Vespasian as Emperor. He was not as tall as Senator Servo, but equally lean and wiry.

17

He too had served with distinction in the Legions, especially in Gaul and in the conquest of Britain. He had been a bulwark of strength in working with the conquered peoples and establishing the rule of Rome. His command technique was to enroll the conquered people as allies of Rome, working as a team, and not as conqueror and vanquished, while still imposing the rule of Rome. He respected their religions and their mores, insisting only on law linked to 'What is good for Rome is good for all'. He was extremely popular with the people and was a bulwark of strength for the Emperor.

Senator Servo was startled at the interruption, but not surprised. He thought little of Maxim, even though he respected his power. Despite this, his tone of voice displayed open derision of Acquinas' opinion. Barely controlling his sudden anger, he virtually spat out the words: "If you give me an opportunity to complete my statement, Senator Acquinas, then perhaps you might understand."

The Emperor looked up, startled at the intensity of the reply, and the thinly veiled insult, but he was not surprised. It was only a question of time before he expected a strong disagreement between the two Senators. It suited his purpose to hear them out before committing to a course of action. He shifted his glance quickly to Senator Acquinas to gauge the impact of Senator Servo's insult. He saw no visible reaction. He was gratified at the self-control of Acquinas. He sat back pleased, and continued to remain silent.

Ever the politician, Acquinas remained poker-faced at the implied rebuke. Inwardly he seethed. Servo was evil. There was always some hidden agenda in everything he said or did. Acquinas' intent was to quash Servo like a pesky insect. First, however, he had to allow his fellow

18

Senator to continue to vent in the hope of finding flaws in his argument. He stared intently at Servo but remained silent.

Servo too suddenly became silent. Then, with a twitch of his shoulders as if to signify his disinterest in other opinions, he abruptly went on.

"We have a complex situation here in Rome. The Jewish population in Rome is larger than that of Jerusalem itself. They are a significant factor in the industry and commerce of Rome. They have come to dominate much of the merchant activity in Rome as well as becoming significant figures as physicians, scribes, and advocates. There is a strong possibility, that they could influence the elections in Rome with their wealth and power."

As he spoke, Servo moved his eyes between the Emperor and Acquinas, gauging the impact of his words. He was comforted when he detected a flicker of acceptance and agreement in both. He chose his next words carefully to exploit this opening. "Hence we cannot tolerate any disturbance or division between what is good for Rome, and what is the desire of the Jews." Then letting his voice rise into a thunderous level, he added sternly. "If there is a difference, the Roman way must prevail!" With a sly glance at the Emperor, he added "Thankfully they have no Legions to command."

Grudgingly, almost imperceptibly, Acquinas nodded. Servo was certainly crafty. First the truth and then the half truths and then the big lie with the hidden purpose.

The Emperor frowned. He was surprised that Acquinas seemed to be weakening. He waited patiently.

Noticing the impact of his words, Servo paused briefly. A slight smile touched his lips. Sensing victory, he suddenly looked directly at the Emperor, and continued.

"Sire, as you know, the Jews have now become divided. Some of them have become supporters of a man we executed as a criminal, a man named Jesus. Some of them look on him as the Christ and the Savior of the Jewish people. Pontius Pilate labeled him "King of the Jews". Others, including the religious leaders of the Jews, condemned him as a charlatan, a trickster, and a fraud. These Jewish leaders manipulated Pontius Pilate into executing the Jesus. Then the body disappeared from his tomb and the story was circulated that he had risen from the dead. They attributed divinity to this man." In the tone of his voice, Servo telegraphed his disbelief of these claims. He was almost sneering as he continued. "His followers multiplied, but still were at odds with their traditional religious leaders. Dissension became strong between the Christians and the Jews who rejected Jesus as a fraud. That dissension was evident everywhere, especially here in Rome. It was that very division that was a factor in the decision of the Emperor Claudius to banish the Jews."

Senator Servo seemed to sigh before continuing, "No matter what the cost, the security of Rome demands that we do it again!" He paused, and then began again, in a slow, deliberate, decisive tone of voice, couching his words to appeal to the Emperor's history. "Sire, now that you have conquered Judea, our immediate goal must be to secure control of the Jews of Rome." Again a meaningful pause. "In my opinion, Sire, that is impossible, mainly because of the Christians."

Looking directly at the Emperor, Servo continued in a strong, commanding tone, "I recommend that we banish the Jews." With a sudden gleam in his eye, he added, "Confiscating their wealth could be of great benefit to the Treasury of Rome!"

20

As Servo completed his statements, his chin seemed to jut out, adding emphasis to his words. Even his stature became more erect.

With a slight smile, but with a cold icy stare, Acquinas looked first at Servo and then at the Emperor, saying nothing. His body, however, seemed to quiver as if held in tight restraint. It gave the impression of tightly controlled anger. Hopefully the Emperor would see through Servo's stratagems.

The Emperor broke his silence. His words came out in a staccato burst. "Senator Servo" he began, "you are certainly consistent in your approach. You marshal history as if it is proof, bending it to suit your purpose. Your last words have shown me that you seek the wealth of the Jews under the pretext that they may have committed sedition and treachery against Rome. You would banish all Jews, and all Christians, without any evidence whatsoever to justify your actions. A dispute between two people is not evidence of revolt against Rome. In the same way, a dispute between two factions of the Jews is no crime against Rome. To vilify a religious sect because their founder was a Jew is ridiculous. Pax Romana - the peace of Rome - has succeeded by recognizing and respecting the right of people to have their own religious belief. It is wrong to condemn without cause. Rome is built on law, and the use of our military to enforce those laws. The Jews of Judea revolted, and that revolt was put down. You will recall Senator that I led that successful restoration of the power of Rome. As Emperor, I will do the same anywhere the will of Rome is challenged." Here the Emperor slowed his words, adding emphasis to each word as if a gauntlet was thrown down. "But hear me, Senator Servo, I will not condemn or confiscate unless treachery is proven."

The Emperor became silent for a moment. Then raising his right arm towards Acquinas he asked, "And you Maxim, what is your opinion?"

Thank the gods, thought Acquinas. The Emperor had seen through Servo's machinations. Acquinas was quick to respond, and with a vigor in his tone and words completely in contrast to the cold, measured and imperious presentation of Servo.

"Sire," began Senator Acquinas, "While many of the historic facts presented by my esteemed colleague are true, not all of them are. Furthermore, I differ in my interpretations and conclusions."

The Emperor had difficulty in maintaining a poker face, but the expression in his eyes as he looked at Acquinas seemed to say, "Go on! Go on!"

"First of all, confiscating the wealth of the Jews would be an empty benefit. We would lose much more in the future from the loss of their industry and taxes. Second, banishing or executing such a large number of our citizens would create, not lessen, turmoil." Here he stopped and looking directly at Servo, added as an aside, "Yes, my friend, many Jews are citizens of Rome". Then he turned directly to look at the Emperor and continued. "Finally, Sire, the Christians were created as a problem by Nero to hide his own error and crime. Until then, they were accepted by us and were a valued part of Rome. Their general approach is one of separating their religious beliefs totally from their involvement in the government of Rome. Their Founder, this man Jesus, was reputed to have often stated 'Render unto Caesar that which is Caesar's and unto God that which is God's.' It was Nero who made them a target of persecution to mask his own blunders and crime in burning over half of Rome. Until then the Christians had been peaceful citizens of Rome, in no manner being a threat to the order of Rome."

Senator Acquinas paused for a few moments to let his words take effect. He noticed a heavy scowl on the face of Senator Servo which made him inwardly smile but which he pointedly ignored. He saw that he had the Emperor's attention and began speaking again.

"Sire, not all Christians are Jews. A significant number are Romans."

Before he could continue, Servo virtually exploded with a loud interjection. "And all are in the lower classes or slaves."

Acquinas stopped speaking, directed a stern look at Servo, before continuing with an evident note of exasperation in his voice. "Not so, my friend, some are nobles of Rome and many are from the Legions, including Tribunes and Centurions." Here he directed a sharp look at Servo, adding his next words with a sharp emphasis.

"As you very well know, Senator Servo, the Tribune Cornelius is a Christian, and has been for some time." Looking now at the Emperor, he added in a respectful tone of voice, "Sire, if you will recall, Tribune Cornelius was a Centurion of the Roman Legion in Caesarea who was an early convert to the creed of Jesus. He was baptized by the Christian leader Peter shortly after we executed Jesus unjustly. Cornelius became one of your Tribunes, Sire, in defeating the Jews in Judea. He is now living in Rome in retirement."

Servo appeared flustered at the mention of Cornelius. His face reddened with suppressed anger as he realized he had made a major error in his argument. He almost interrupted, but decided to remain silent.

Acquinas paused, and looking again at Servo, continued. "We are not facing a Jewish problem, but rather

23

uncertainty about the Christians. Nero accused the Christians of wanting to burn Rome to mask his own error in attempting to clear the slums with fire. Nero was mad as we all know. He sought to remain in power by using the execution of Christians as a diversion."

Turning and looking directly at Servo, he virtually spat out his next words. "Senator Servo, the Christians are not necessarily a problem. In my experience they are peaceful and law abiding people. To repeat, Nero used them as a scapegoat when his plan to clear the slums of Rome failed."

Turning to the Emperor, he added in a strong and respectful voice.

"Sire, your goal is to establish order in Rome and in the Empire." Pausing for effect he added quietly and earnestly, "Sire, the Jews and the Christians are scapegoats for those who seek to create turmoil in Rome, and use that as a pretext to attempt to seize power. I suggest we thwart their endeavor. I recommend a thorough investigation of these Christians. If they are a threat, then quash them throughout the Empire." And here Acquinas snapped his fingers for emphasis. Then he continued, "But if they are not any threat to Rome, Sire, then let them live in peace, and aim to secure their support."

Acquinas stopped speaking, remaining silent for a moment. Then for dramatic effect, he added in a soft voice, almost a whisper, "Who knows, Sire! The Christians could very well be the stabilizing influence we need in restoring order in Rome."

Sensing the impact of his words, Acquinas stopped, his gaze resting directly on the Emperor. Servo seemed to explode with indignation. His voice rose in wrath as he almost screamed, "Nonsense!"

Vespasian silenced Servo with a stern look, and then remained silent, moving his eyes to look appraisingly at each Senator in turn. Then he looked down, quietly stroking his chin. Before looking up, and then looking at each in turn, he said, "Thank you both for your recommendations." He stopped, seemed to draw a deep breath that lifted his shoulders before adding. "My objective is to restore order in Rome, and to thwart those who would seek disorder as the road to power. Banishment and execution are an easy solution, but it might lead to even greater disruption. Extermination is never easy. I agree we must find out more about these Christians. Why do they follow the teachings of an executed criminal? Are they criminals themselves? Was this Jesus the Christ a charlatan, a trickster, and a fraud? What are his teachings? How can they attract such noble Romans as Cornelius? How many are they? How widespread is their influence? And finally, are they a future threat to Rome, or a major asset for Pax Romana?" He paused. Looking directly at Acquinas, he asked, "Who do you recommend I appoint to lead this criminal investigation?"

Without any hesitation at all, Acquinas answered immediately. "Sire, the best man would be Senator Quintus Gaius Caesar." The Emperor nodded. Servo gasped and frowned. Acquinas went on, well noting the smile and look of acceptance that seemed building on the face of the Emperor.

"Yes, Sire, our good friend Quintus is the best person I know to undertake this task for us. I believe he served you well in Judea as Deputy to your son Titus who commanded your Legions in the conquest of the revolt. If you will recall, Sire, some years ago, he served Emperor Tiberius with distinction in traveling to Judea to investigate the mysterious disappearance of the body of the executed Jesus."

Vespasian stroked his chin for a moment, a thoughtful gleam coming into his eyes. He seemed to nod imperceptibly. "Yes, of course. I know him well. He led the final assault that defeated the Jews in Judea. A brilliant general and now a Senator." A thoughtful look came into his face. Vespasian pondered quietly for a moment. He remembered that Quintus had also served with distinction as Deputy Prefect of the Praetorian Guard. That connection could prove useful for the Emperor, especially now that his son Titus was the Prefect of the Guard. Vespasian smiled inwardly at his coup in protecting his flank with that appointment.

The Emperor looked directly at Acquinas as he stated, "An interesting and excellent proposal, Senator." Vespasian paused again, apparently in deep thought. Then he added quietly. "The rumor is that he is the illegitimate son of Emperor Tiberius." The Emperor stopped. His next words came slowly. "How fitting to have someone who might very well have been the Emperor recommend what is best for Rome with these Christians."

He nodded and remained silent obviously in deep thought. Abruptly, and with decision, looking at each Senator in turn, Vespasian commanded. "Ask Quintus to join us here tomorrow at the sixth hour to settle this question about the Christians and the Jews."

Then he arose and strode from the Council Chamber leaving the Senators to their task.

******

Promptly at the sixth hour the three Senators entered the Council Chamber, walked to the dais, stopped,

26

and stood waiting for the Emperor. They remained silent. A moment later, Vespasian strode into the Chamber, walked to the chair on the dais, nodded to each senator in turn, and then sat facing them. After again staring silently at each Senator, he fixed his gaze on Quintus. With a deep smile, he began.

"Welcome, Quintus. I see you have recovered from your wounds and are now an esteemed Senator, continuing to serve Rome as you always have. I am sure you have been told of our discussion on the problem of the Jews and the Christians." Quintus nodded but remained silent. The Emperor raised his right arm pointing to Servo as he added, "Senator Servo would have me banish," and with a firm smile added, "if not exterminate, the Jews and Christians." Turning his raised arm towards Acquinas, the Emperor added, "And our esteemed colleague Senator Acquinas would have us investigate thoroughly before deciding whether to eliminate them, or learn how to live with them as supporters of the Peace of Rome." Vespasian dropped his arm, and looking directly at Quintus, added, "You have been recommended as the one to lead this investigation. Will you do this, or do you have another suggestion, either concerning the leadership of such a criminal investigation, or some alternative plan of action?" The Emperor stopped and looked directly at Quintus.

Quintus seemed to stand even more erect. The years had been kind to him. He stood ramrod straight, lean and strong. His face was furrowed and his hair was whitened by his age, but he still looked like a soldier about to enter the field of battle. His eyes were clear and alert. His voice rang out strongly as he saluted with his right arm and said, "Sire, I am yours to command!"

The Emperor was pleased. He decided to be certain there was complete agreement on the scope of the investigation. As he spoke he looked at each Senator in turn seeking confirmation of his words, even though he had no intention of letting any of them dictate to him. While he sought their opinion, he would make all the decisions.

"Quintus, let me be very clear on this issue. I seek your recommendation on how to dispose of any threat to Rome from the Christians and the Jews. Your investigation must consider their beliefs, their motives, and their plans, especially as they may affect Rome." The Emperor paused and a steel glint came into his eyes and voice. "Let me be very clear. I seek harmony in the Empire. I will extol or exterminate" and here he smashed his right fist in his left hand, adding, "Either way!" He paused again, and looked pointedly at Senator Servo, without singling him out specifically. He continued. "If the Christians are not a threat to Rome, I will leave them in peace. If they are a threat now or in the future, I will execute them or banish them." Then looking directly at Quintus, he continued. "What Claudius or Nero did will be no factor in my decision. I will rely completely on the results of your investigation. I expect you to be thorough in your findings, and specific in your recommendations."

He stopped, pausing for his words to take effect. They were directed mainly at Senator Servo. Turning his gaze on Quintus, he smiled fondly as he added, "Is there anything you need from me to complete this assignment?"

Looking directly at the emperor, Quintus replied in a clear, strong yet respectful voice. "Senator Acquinas has told me of your questions and concerns, Sire." Pausing for emphasis, Quintus added: "I will formulate my plan, execute it, and report to you with my findings and recommendation." Quintus paused for a moment, before continuing. "Sire, I will need two or three Centurions and perhaps as many as a hundred Legionaries to help me. May

I use members of the Praetorian Guard, and their headquarters, during this investigation?"

The Emperor was pleased. Nothing could be more favorable to his thinking. Almost beaming, the Emperor added, "Of course, Quintus. When do you expect to report your recommendations to me?"

Quintus was silent for a moment before responding. "Sire, I will investigate as quickly as possible, and report to you on the last day of each week. I would hope to complete my investigation in less than a month, unless it becomes necessary to travel to Judea or elsewhere to determine all the facts. Naturally I will only make such a decision with your approval." After a short pause, he continued: "If that is agreeable to you, Sire?"

Vespasian was pleased. He smiled warmly as he replied. "Thank you, Senator. I expected no less from you." Then looking at the other two Senators, and keeping an imperial neutral appearance and tone of voice, he dismissed the Senators with "Thank you all for coming here today to discuss this important issue before us." Then he paused and added in an imperial tone of voice. "We will meet at the sixth hour on the last day of each week." With that he rose and strode from the Council Chamber.

Senator Servo nodded brusquely to Acquinas and Quintus, and abruptly turned and left without saying a word.

Quintus turned to Acquinas. "Maxim, my friend, I thank you for suggesting that I undertake this task for the Emperor. Do you have any specific suggestions for me?"

Senator Maxim Valerius Acquinas remained silent and apparently deep in thought for a moment. Then he turned, grasped Quintus by the arm, and slowly walked with him from the chamber. "Quintus, my friend, it is unnecessary for me to suggest that you be thorough. You

29

said you would, and I know you will." Acquinas stopped, turned to Quintus and added in a worrisome tone of voice. "My only concern lies with our esteemed friend Senator Servo. I am deeply disturbed by the strong feelings on the part of Senator Servo. He is a thoroughly evil man, but he is also a very astute man, careful that his position is strongly supported. I fear there are many who would agree with him to exterminate the Christians and Jews one way or another." He shook his head somewhat before adding. "He will be a formidable opponent of your investigation. He will do everything possible to have you agree with him, or to have you fail if you do not." Then with a grin he added, "Getting his hands in the wealth of the Jews and Christians, or of securing more young slaves for his appetites, must not be discounted as a motive."

Quintus laughed. He stopped, turned to Maxim, and added in a dry manner, "There is an old proverb in our family that suggests counting the chicken eggs is done best after the eggs are laid."

"By the way", my friend, why did the Emperor ever invite that old fox to the meeting?" asked Quintus. "I know he invited you because you are probably his closest supporter, and he trusts your opinions. By why Sarto? Why not a number of Senators?"

This time Maxim laughed. "Quintus, you must have guessed the Emperor likes to keep his enemies close to himself. He would rather have Servo sounding off in a meeting with him than with conspirators in some dark room." Maxim laughed again as they walked along.

After a short time, Maxim proceeded to ask Quintus how he planned to conduct his investigation.

Quintus did not answer immediately. He walked a short distance with Maxim in silence as they left the Emperor's Palace and walked towards the Castra Praetoria, headquarters of the Praetorian Guard. Then he abruptly began to speak in a thoughtful tone of voice. "The first thing is to meet with the Prefect, Titus, and gain his support and assistance in this investigation." Then, with a broad grin, he added, "I am sure he will be most supportive!" With a shrug of his shoulders, Quintus added, "Then it is dig, dig, dig. Separate facts from rumors and lies, and only then to use the truth to come to logical conclusions. Only then will I formulate recommendations for the Emperor."

After a slight pause, Quintus continued. "The Emperor's mandate is clear. He is concerned with four basic points." As they walked, Quintus enumerated them.

First, establish that Christianity was truly a religion and not merely a subterfuge for sedition, possibly leading to a potential revolt, or any other form of threat to Pax Romana.

Secondly, if Christianity in truth was a religious movement, then was it something that would prevail in time, or was it merely a temporary attraction that would soon die of its own volition? If it was more than a temporary movement, what was the set of beliefs or dogma to be embraced by the members? What practices supported and enhanced these beliefs?

Third, was there a structure and leadership to the movement? In particular, was there a line of succession to the leadership to ensure perpetuation of Christianity beyond the current leadership? Was that leadership effective? In fact, was the leadership truly sincere to the beliefs of Christians, or was it in reality despotic, cloaking hypocrisy with a mystique?

Finally, with regard to the membership, why did individuals become followers of the sect? What was their motivation to become members? What did they do as

31

members of the sect? Why were they willing to die rather than recant and deny membership in the sect?

Quintus kept expanding on all these points as they walked. He would certainly have to interview many Christians, and also to command any Legionaries at his disposal to interview extensively. All of these findings would then be correlated in an attempt to establish the truth. It was unfortunate that the initial great leaders of the Christians in Rome, Peter and Paul, had been executed on orders of the Emperor Nero. Because of that, he would not be able to interview them, but he would certainly be able to establish what they did, what they believed, and why. He would also seek out the successors and interview them.

The more he pondered, the more he remembered the interviews in Judea during his investigation of the mysterious disappearance of the body of the crucified Jesus. A smile came across his face as he remembered is meeting an interview with Maryam, the mother of Jesus. If she were still alive, he would have to seek her location, and interview her again. If she was not alive, then perhaps he could find someone who might be able to tell him of her views of the movement created by her son Jesus – the movement now referred to as Christianity. He mused further. Hopefully this would not take him away from Rome. He knew the Emperor was impatient for an answer.

Before undertaking any such travel, he would have to evaluate the delay impact on his final presentation to the Emperor

"Well, Maxim" concluded Quintus, "have I omitted anything in my plan?"

Maxim turned deadly serious. He stopped to give emphasis to his words. Surprised, Quintus too stopped and turned towards his friend.

"You might have an unforeseen problem in your investigation" said Maxim.

Quintus was startled. "What do you mean, Maxim? Who or what are you referring to?" asked Quintus.

Maxim took a deep breath, and began. "Senator Sarto is determined to scuttle the investigation, and to destroy Vespasian as Emperor. He is a thoroughly evil and unscrupulous person. His goal is to become the Emperor. He truly believes he should be the Emperor now. He will oppose any project initiated by Vespasian, and will do everything he can to discredit any action Vespasian espouses or supports." In a strong and stern voice, Maxim added. "Sarto fears your report. He seeks turmoil in Rome as the road to power for himself. If it does not exist, he will create it. He will seek to make the Christians appear to be fomenting revolt. He knows you will be painstaking and fair in collecting evidence and arriving at your recommendations. The only recommendation he wants is to have the Christians destroyed. That will create more unrest and turmoil. Sarto is certainly capable of creating false evidence to support his cause and destroy your report. He might even attempt your assassination if he feels your report will go against him."

Quintus remained silent, pondering what he had just heard. His mind raced, considering all the possibilities. He looked at his friend and bleakly smiled. "Thank you, my friend, I am forewarned." Quintus paused, and seemed to brace himself as he added "Be assured, Maxim, my friend." Adding sarcasm to his voice, he added. "The esteemed Senator Sarto has never been in battles as I have." His face hardened, and his voice took on a deep command tone. Through teeth almost clenched, the old warrior added. "He will never know what is happening until the battle is over and he is defeated. I know how to handle situations like this." Abruptly his face softened, as he looked directly at Maxim. He placed his right hand on his friend's shoulder, as he added with a deep smile, "Thank you, Maxim. I truly appreciate the warning." Then he turned and resumed walking to his destination. Maxim too resumed walking with Quintus.

Quintus broadened his stride as his words played over in his mind. The battle was joined. Quintus, the battle-hardened Tribune was in command.

Chapter Two

Cornelius

Quintus and Maxim parted at the Castra Praetorian, headquarters and barracks of the Praetorian Guard in Rome. Quintus presented himself to the guard on duty, identified himself, and asked to see the Prefect, Titus. By chance, Titus was in the barracks at the time.

Quintus was ushered into the Council Chamber of the Guard. It was a barren room, devoid of ornament of any kind. A large circular table filled the center of the room with twelve chairs around the table. The sides of the room had chairs along each wall, with chairs on both sides of the large double door entrance to the room. A high vaulted ceiling gave the room a commanding presence. Tapers and torches along the walls and a large candelabra over the table illuminated the room.

Quintus felt at home. For years he had sat in this room as the Deputy Prefect, together with the Prefect, and the nine Tribunes of the Legions making up the Guard. The last chair was for a scribe if needed, to record minutes of meetings.

Quintus walked to the chair reserved for the Deputy Prefect and stood behind it, waiting for the Prefect, who entered with rapid steps almost immediately. He strode over to Quintus, and with a deep smile on his face, offered his arm in welcome. His words mirrored his pleasure. "Quintus, my friend, I am pleased to greet you here. Welcome to your second home." Then sweeping his arm to the chair of the Deputy, he added, as he sat in the Prefect's Chair which he turned to face Quintus, "To what do we owe this pleasure?"

Quintus turned his chair to face Titus before sitting down. Titus seemed a little older and more settled than he had been in Judea overcoming the revolt. Now, as Prefect of the Praetorian Guard, and heir apparent to become Emperor, he was already sensing and using power. It suited him. The thought quickly passed in Quintus' mind of how fortunate he was to be free of that burden.

Returning to the matter at hand, Quintus related the Emperor's mandate and command to investigate all aspects of the activities of the Christians in Rome and in the Empire. He was to be especially concerned with any current or potential threat to the security of Rome. Titus nodded thoughtfully as Quintus outlined his mandate from the Emperor. With a slight grin, Titus began. "My father has always been thorough. This Christian problem is connected to our troubles in Judea. We can't have a repeat of that revolt, especially here in our homeland." Titus paused. He gazed into space for a moment in deep thought. Then he continued, with a quiet sigh, "So, Quintus. You are at it again with these followers of that man Jesus. Refresh my memory of your investigation many years ago."

Quintus proceeded to relate his memories of the investigation of the mysterious disappearance of the body of the executed criminal, Jesus of Nazareth. He had been commanded by Emperor Tiberius to determine the truth of what happened to the body of Jesus. He had conducted a thorough investigation with a hundred Legionaries and three Centurions. The entire country had been scoured for evidence or rumors concerning the missing body, as to whether or not it had been stolen. No evidence of any kind could be found that the body had been stolen. Furthermore, the Roman Procurator, Pontius Pilate, had posted Roman guards at the tomb site. These guards, even when tortured, claimed that the body had walked out of the tomb. Even when executed they did not change their testimony. The Centurion Longinus, who had officiated at the execution of Jesus, had verified that Jesus had truly died on the cross, and supervised the burial of the body in the tomb. Hence, the body placed in the tomb was that of a dead man. Quintus himself had examined the tomb and had found no exit of any kind other than the sole opening at the front of the tomb. It had been sealed with a large stone.

Taking all the evidence into account - the dead body placed in the tomb, the single entrance with a large stone covering it, and the testimony of the sixteen Roman guards on duty - Quintus had concluded that Jesus had truly risen from the dead.

As part of his investigation he interviewed many of the followers of Jesus and had been impressed by their courage and willingness to die rather than deny their beliefs. Such courage had not always been evident, especially on the part of their leader, Peter. When interviewed, Peter had shown remarkable courage even daring Quintus, 'Are you going to execute me or free me'!

In his investigation, he was impressed with the miracles of Jesus, even to raising individuals back to life from death. His interview with the mother of Jesus had been especially impressive, solidifying his impression that Jesus was a truly remarkable person, and in fact Quintus was quite prepared, following his detailed and thorough investigation, to conclude that Jesus was some form of deity and he so reported to the Emperor Tiberius.

He also reported to Tiberius the unrest and controversy surrounding Jesus that existed with the religious leaders of the Jews. The high priest, Caiaphas, had been concerned about the threat Jesus posed to his power and his financial stability and had engineered Jesus' execution by convincing the Procurator, Pontius Pilate, that Jesus was a threat to the public order. In reality this was not true. Quintus had found no evidence that Jesus or his followers were, or would be, a threat to Pax Romana – the peace of Rome.

Hence, the current investigation launched on command by Emperor Vespasian would concentrate on the current philosophy, mode of operation, and scope of ambition of the current followers of Jesus.

Titus had been silent and alert during the entire recitation of the history of his initial investigation and his approach to the current one. Vespasian was not only the Emperor, but his father. Titus would become Emperor on the death of Vespasian. Turmoil would play into the hands of the enemies of Vespasian. Hence this investigation was important to him as well as to Vespasian. When Quintus mentioned the warning of Senator Acquinas, Titus scowled. "Quintus, Sarto is evil. He will do all in his power to control your report. If it is contrary to what he wishes, he will try to stop you, even attempt an assassination. Beware of false testimony as you proceed in your investigation." After a short pause, he continued. "I will assign a contingent of guards to be with you until you report to the Emperor. I will also have your quarters here readied for you if you wish. Now what else can I do to help you? You have only to ask."

38

Quintus was not surprised. It was as he expected. "Thank you, Titus. I now realize the guards may be needed. Thank you also for the offer to reside here, but I think it best to stay at my own villa. The guards will protect me as I travel. In addition, I will need three Centurions, a hundred Legionaries, and the use of meeting space here at Castra Praetorian."

"Granted" committed Titus. "Any Centurions in particular? You know most of them from your years here as Deputy Prefect."

"Yes", answered Quintus. "I would select Centurions Antinus, Julius, and Paulucci. All three of them worked under my command not only here but in Judea. They speak Aramaic and that could be helpful in our questioning of the Christians here in Rome. We may have to go outside Rome, but that is to be determined. I also understand that Antinus was in charge of the execution of the leader of the Christians, Peter; and that Julius was in command at the execution of Paul, the co-leader of the Christians. Paulucci was one of the major pursuers of the Christians who were arrested, with many of them executed, upon the order of the Emperor Nero. With their background, I will let them select the Legionaries for this investigation."

"Granted, of course. I will have them report here the instant we are done. Anything further?"

"Yes", said Quintus, "It would be better to have them report in the morning with the Legionaries."

"Of course, Quintus. So be it. What else can I command to help you?"

"I am seeking three men," said Quintus. "The first you know quite well, he is a Tribune, Cornelius." Titus immediately smiled and nodded.

"Yes of course, I was with him earlier this week. He is well known as a man liberal with the giving of alms. His home is a shelter at any time to those seeking his help in any manner. His reputation is that of a kind man and yet a renowned soldier. I am not surprised that you would want to meet with him. Rumor has it that he is a Christian but in no way does that interfere with him being a great Roman. His Villa is a short distance from here and as soon as we finish our meeting I will have you escorted to his home."

Titus had smiled all through this. He was obviously quite fond of Cornelius and admired him.

"And who are the other two men you seek?"

Quintus answered, "The first was a Centurion in Judea, Longinus, who was of major help to me years ago in Judea when I investigated the mysterious disappearance of the body of Jesus, the Founder of the Christians."

"By the way, Longinus is here in Rome, Quintus" the Prefect stated. Then he added, "He is a Christian now. Nero had him arrested and he was scheduled for execution. Emperor Vespasian pardoned him." He paused, before adding. "I can have Longinus summoned to meet with you." On seeing Quintus nod in agreement, Titus continued. "And the second person?"

"A former slave, a freed man now, a scribe named Marcus whom I left in Judea with Peter, the leader of the Christians. Peter was executed by Nero, but I understand Marcus is here somewhere in Rome."

The Prefect was quick to answer. "He too is a Christian, scheduled for execution by Nero, but now freed. He too can be summoned to come here."

"Please do so. Thank you for the information."

Titus pushed back his chair and stood up. So did Quintus. "I will take my leave, now Quintus. I will issue the orders to have these men report to you. You can use the

40

assembly hall tomorrow morning to address them. You can come to me at any time that you need help, or someone to discuss your findings. Use me as a testing ground. This study is very important to me and the Emperor." As he said this he smiled, as if to say I will inherit the problem anyway. With that he left.

A moment later eight guards entered to escort Quintus to the home of Cornelius.

******

Just as Titus had indicated, Cornelius' Villa was a very short walk from the headquarters of the Praetorian Guard. By chance, Cornelius was home. Quintus was immediately ushered into his meeting room. A moment later, Cornelius entered. Cornelius was the same fit soldier Quintus remembered, shorter than most, he exuded great strength and confidence. He had the aura of command. Cornelius had always been a person of solid thinking with attention to logical reasoning. Quintus was looking forward to his encounter and discussion with his old friend Cornelius.

After greeting one another as two old friends do, they sat at a small table. Cornelius had his steward bring wine to sip as they sat and talked. For a few more minutes they reminisced over some of their exploits in Rome and Judea.

Quintus abruptly came to the point of his meeting. "Cornelius, my friend, we have served in battle together and I know you to be a brave and valiant soldier, dedicated to maintaining the peace of Rome. I have learned that you have become a Christians, a follower of this man Jesus the Christ of the Jews. You served with distinction as a Centurion in the Roman Legion in Caesarea and Judea for many years. Unlike most of our Legions that contain significant numbers of conscripts from our occupied territories, the Roman legion was composed entirely of Romans."

"I am here today on command from the Emperor to investigate the followers of Jesus - Christians so called. This sect began with the Jews. You are not a Jew. You are a Gentile and a Christian. Why did you become a Christian? What is the attraction of the Christians? How do you reconcile being a Christian with being a soldier of Rome? How do you justify killing in battle when the Christian faith is one of peace, love and a turning of the other cheek?"

Cornelius was taken aback. He did not seem surprised by the questions as much as the scope. Looking directly at Quintus, Cornelius began, "I understand why you want the answers to those questions, and I will certainly do my best to provide that information. But perhaps I should tell you of some of the history of how I came to know Jesus and some of the specifics of how I became baptized a Christian. Then I will be able to answer all of your questions once you fully understand those two points."

With a grin, Quintus answered "Cornelius, it doesn't matter so much how you go about answering all of these so long as I can formulate an evaluation as to what is the attraction to lead a brave and noble soldier of Rome to become a Christian. Perhaps as you say, the best thing is to begin by asking how you first learned about Jesus of Nazareth."

Cornelius put down his wine goblet, sat back, and spread his hands with fingers touching, and seemed to look into space. His words came slowly as he seemed to be reliving the scene he was describing. "As you know, we were stationed in Caesarea. We had heard many rumors about an itinerant preacher who was traveling around Judea curing the sick and performing what people were calling miracles. There was even a rumor that he had raised someone from the dead who had been in his tomb for four days. Lazarus I think he was called." Cornelius paused, searching his memory before continuing.

"You will recall I was a Centurion at the time. In another incident at that time, a fellow Centurion came back to the barracks one day saying that he had witnessed a raising of the dead of a boy in Naim during his funeral cortege. "

"There were more and more reports of curing the sick and disabled. Paralytics walked, the blind saw, and the deaf could hear. These events were all confirmed as real."

"We also received detailed reports of the teachings of this Jesus, especially of his continued use of the rule of the separation of religious belief from political action. As reported on more than one occasion, he was reputed to have said 'Render unto Caesar that which is Caesar's, and unto God that which is God's.' That particular statement struck me forcibly. I was and am a soldier. My duty is to follow orders and maintain the peace of Rome. This may involve killing those who violate the peace of Rome. That is my duty. As a Roman I always found a conflict between my feelings as a person and my duty as a soldier. So the reports I heard about Jesus intrigued me, especially his comment about separating matters of religious belief from matters of political structures."

"I did see Jesus once. My troop was on patrol when I saw a huge crowd gathered in a field. I wondered what it was all about. I sent some Legionaries to examine what was going on and I found that there was one man who was addressing thousands of people. Apparently they could all hear him, which I found extremely remarkable. Then he fed them, though I saw no wagons of food, I saw only a single boy with two baskets and yet thousands were fed. I learned afterwards that the boy had two fish and five loaves of bread. It was further reported to me that twelve baskets of crumbs had been collected after everyone had eaten their fill. My first reaction was that that is impossible. And yet, I saw it with my own eyes."

"As you know, as a Centurion of the Roman Legion in Caesarea, we were considered the headquarters of the occupation forces. We were privileged to hear all the rumors of any potential problem anywhere in Judea. Jesus had stayed away from Jerusalem, touring the countryside and visiting town after town until finally he entered Jerusalem in triumph just before Passover. Five days later he was executed by crucifixion by the Roman troops. The rumors were that the high priest had engineered the unjust murder of this man and then his body disappeared." Cornelius paused and remained in deep thought momentarily. Then he began again. "I continued to think about Jesus but did nothing about it."

Once more, Cornelius paused and seemed to drift into a deep reverie. Slowly the words came.

"One particular day a few years later, I had been quite busy, distributing alms to the needy, when suddenly about the ninth hour of the day, I clearly saw a vision of an angel coming to me and saying 'Your prayers and your alms have ascended as a memorial before God. And now send men to Joppa, and bring one Simon which is called Peter: he is lodging with Simon, a tanner, whose house is by the seaside.'"

Cornelius remained silent, reliving the entire vision, before he continued. "I called two of my servants and sent them and a troop of soldiers to Joppa to escort Peter to me."

Once again Cornelius stopped in a deep reverie. From the depths of his memory and with deep feeling he continued, "I did not know then but learned later that Peter had a similar vision. As he told me after we met, he was told three times in a vision to come and see me even though it would mean days that he would be eating common or unclean food. But the voice in his vision told him that 'What God has cleansed, you must not call common.'"

"Peter came. He told me more about Jesus and his followers, who are now called Christians. Sensing the importance of what Peter was going to say, I invited all of the members of my family, all of my household, and all of my circle of friends to come and hear Peter. A very strange event occurred. Peter and I had spoken in Aramaic, a language which I had learned to speak. Peter did not speak Latin or Greek. Yet, when he began to address our group, everyone understood him in their own tongue – Latin, Greek, or Aramaic – all at the same time. This did not immediately come to our consciousness but gradually we began to wonder how it was that we all understood what he was saying when he normally did not speak our language. We discussed the matter for days until finally we all decided to become followers of Jesus and to become baptized. That is how I, my family, my household and my friends became Christians. Then   I   freed   my household."

Quintus had listened quietly but interjected, "What was the attraction of this man Jesus? Was it what he did? What he said? Or the reaction of the people he was with? Or all of that?"

Cornelius remained silent in deep thought for a moment before his answer. "Jesus was a remarkable man. In fact he was God. He preached love. He died asking that those who were executing him to be forgiven. There was nothing devious or untruthful in anything he did or said. He cured the sick, and raised the dead back to life. He continually preached the gospel of peace and repentance promising that the true kingdom was not of this world, but of the next. He castigated his own followers whenever they gave evidence of following him because of ambition, the hope of position, or the hope of gain."

Cornelius remained in deep, silent thought before continuing. "That was the attraction! It was an attraction to good, to nobility of spirit, to self-denial, and more importantly, to being a person for others. Jesus was the ultimate example of his preaching. He was willing to be executed, unjustly as you know, without condemning in any way those who were committing this crime against him. This was love, love of the deepest kind." Cornelius moved his gaze around the room, staring into space as he spoke, obviously in deep thought, and then looked directly at Quintus.

"Christianity provided a personal relationship with God through Jesus. Christianity was a religion of love, love of God and love of each other. It gave me hope for the future, hope that all would be well, hope that everything I did was worthwhile. And if I sinned, and was remorseful, then I could be forgiven and everything would go back to what it was before I sinned."

Making direct eye contact with Quintus, Cornelius added, "That is why I became a Christian!"

Quintus was agreeably surprised. Cornelius was not only articulate, but profound in his thinking and reasoning for a man of his position. It was remarkable for a man of his stature as a Centurion of the Roman Legion to become a Christian so soon following the execution of Jesus. Quintus decided to certainly use this experience in probing the motivation of others to become Christians. He found the motivation of Cornelius to become Christian to be purposeful and noble. It was certainly stripped of any blind ambition. In fact, by becoming a follower of Jesus, Cornelius would be putting in jeopardy any chance at promotion within the Roman Legion and in fact even his position as a Centurion. At the very least he would be considered 'different' which would lead to suspicion and rejection. And yet, Cornelius had overcome this because of his bravery and effectiveness as a soldier. He had truly separated his religious belief from exercising his duty as a soldier.

Quintus nodded quietly to himself as he evaluated what Cornelius had told him in the context of his mandate from the Emperor. Certainly Cornelius was no threat to Rome but rather an outstanding asset. But what about Nero?

"Cornelius", Quintus began, "what happened during the persecution of Christians by Nero? Were you arrested?"

A sad look came over the face of Cornelius. "No, Quintus. I was not arrested, but many of my Christian friends were. Some were executed in horrible ways, often as spectacle for the amusement of the masses." Looking directly at Quintus, Cornelius asked "Did you not know all of this? Did not Nero use the Praetorian Guard to execute his commands?"

Quintus was slow to reply. "I knew nothing of this until I returned to Rome with Vespasian. I was in Judea fighting with the Legions to put down the revolt of the Jews." Again Quintus slowed his speech, he recalled his service in Judea. He served directly under Titus. His assignment from Tutus was to destroy the final remnants of the revolt against Roman rule in Judea. He personally directed the assault on Jerusalem which led to its destruction, and that of the Temple. As a soldier he obeyed orders. As a person, he had moments when the slaughter appalled him. The price in human life for principle seemed excessive. He reconciled this in his mind with the need for order and the rule of law. However, that was different than Nero's indiscriminate execution even of women and children for his own amusement or political gain. Quintus recalled his own role in forcing Nero to abdicate by suicide, and of leading the small group of the Praetorian Guard that assassinated Caligula. He could understand the dilemma of Cornelius, especially when the factor of his religion was added to the mix of emotions.

Sensing the depth of feeling on the part of Cornelius, Quintus abruptly changed the subject. He decided to examine other aspects of the followers of Jesus, especially the linkage to the Jewish people and the Jewish religion. In that vein he asked Cornelius "Were you concerned that Jesus was a Jew? Do you know anything about the Jewish religious law – the 613 rules of behavior in their code called the Mitzvot?

"No. I do not. That was not an issue for me. I was not interested in the Jewish religion. I knew nothing about it. I was interested only in the teachings of Jesus. I am not circumcised nor did I wish to be." And here Cornelius laughed before continuing, "I don't know how I would have reacted if circumcision was vital. I was following the dictates of my vision to have Peter come and tell us more about the teachings of Jesus. I just wanted to follow Jesus. Peter made no restrictions on becoming a Christian that I also had to become a Jew, There is no connection except that Jesus was a Jew, Peter was a Jew, and the fundamental beliefs of those who follow Jesus are based upon the traditions and beliefs of the Jews. But we, as Christians, are not Jews, we are Christians. Many Jews are Christians.

Many Jews are not. We both believe in the same God. We are like cousins who have the same grandfather, but yet we are different families. We can be very friendly and work together so long as we both concentrate on our similarities. If we concentrate on the differences, then we may come to disagree significantly and even drift apart. But if we concentrate on the same grandfather and concentrate on family matters of mutual interest, then of course we will come closer together. So while Christianity began in Judaism, and while they share the same God, there are differences just as there are differences between Latin and Greek. We can say the same thing in Latin and in Greek, but they will appear different because they are in the Latin or Greek language. We as believers in God will seek to understand the sincerity of others who believe in the same God even if they speak in a different language. The difficulty would come when men like the High Priest Caiaphas would seek to advance their position or power by either falsifying or twisting the truth for their own purposes, and by so doing influence others to follow a false path. That is how Caiaphas manipulated Pontius Pilate to crucify Jesus as a threat to Rome when in reality he was not a threat but rather an asset to maintain the peace of Rome."

"You are right, Cornelius," interjected Quintus. "But the Jewish question still becomes important in terms of how did Jews, and especially Jews who are Christians, look upon Gentiles who became Christians. Jews cannot associate with Gentiles. In particular they cannot have a meal with them because part of the meal will be considered unclean. And yet, you asked Peter to your home and actually dine with you. How do you think Peter felt about that?"

"Peter and I discussed that very point," replied Cornelius. "He told me that in his vision God told him that what he had cleansed was made clean. Peter then continued, 'With the command to visit you I took that to mean that I was to dine with you and to consider that God who commanded our meeting had also given blessing to my breaking bread with you.' I knew that Peter was a deeply religious man as a Christian and a Jew. He was also a very sensitive man, very concerned not to be offensive to his friends and fellow believers – followers of the teachings of Jesus. He knew they would be very concerned about his association with a Gentile and would become especially concerned about the reasoning allowing the baptism of a Gentile to become a Christian without requiring adherence to the Jewish law. While circumcision and the dietary laws were the obvious point of discussion it was in reality the entire Jewish laws, the 613 rules of the Mitzvot that was a fundamental point to be decided. Peter accepted the mandate of Jesus to 'Go and teach all nations' to include Gentiles. He knew that his great friend Paul, also known by his Hebrew name of Saul, was equally and strongly in favor of the baptism of Gentiles. But Peter also knew that there were many baptized Jews who would be opposed and had to be convinced. He was prepared to undertake that task."

Quintus remained deep in thought. The Peter he had met during his investigation was a man of deep courage and conviction. He also knew that Peter had denied knowing Jesus during the day of crucifixion out of fear, denials which he afterwards remembered with deep sorrow to the point of tears that almost created furrows in his cheeks. Peter had gone from being a fearful man during the crucifixion to being a fearless tiger of courage afterwards. He attributed this change to the Holy Spirit who came at Pentecost, some ten days after Jesus had ascended into heaven.

Quintus decided he would have to look into that particular matter quite thoroughly in his investigation to ensure that this would not be a factor for potential disruption of the Roman Peace. Were the Christians organized? Did they have a leadership that would continue beyond the death of each new leader? Could they act as a unified force?

He decided to question Cornelius about two very important aspects of this aspect of his investigation. The first would be the impact on Cornelius if the Christians were outlawed and persecuted more vigorously than they had been under Nero. And the more difficult questions would be what opinion Cornelius had if the Christians would ever be the center of a revolt against Rome.

Quintus asked, "Cornelius, what would you do if Christians were outlawed? In fact what if you were in command of a troop ordered to round up Christians and move them to prison   prior   to their execution?   To be more specific, what if you had been in Rome during the reign of Nero, and had been ordered to arrest Christians? "

Cornelius laughed. "Quintus, you always were a stickler for asking tough questions. Now you want to bring me back into my old job. I can duck the issue by saying I am retired. But that would be cowardly."

Cornelius stopped and his face took on a very serious look. "I said it was a tough question. It would put me in a position of having to choose between my duty as a soldier and my beliefs as a Christian. Being a Christian I am more apt to think of my duty as a matter of conscience. I would feel a moral responsibility to carry out my duties to the best of my ability and beyond. In other words, my sense of moral justice would lead me to try and excel in the duties I had agreed to undertake, but it would need to be in the context of my Christian beliefs. This will not always be easy. In my usual methodical fashion I will examine all the pros and cons, weighing each element in order to be absolutely fair in my assessments. To be rigidly doctrinaire never solves anything. Balance and judgment are required based on sound criteria for evaluation of alternatives. I will always let my conscience be the final arbiter of my actions."

Here Cornelius became very pensive before continuing. "The crux of the issue would be whether or not my orders were just. If I were commanded to kill a child for no reason whatsoever, I could not do it. And yet such an order, as you know, was given by Herod at the time of the birth of Jesus when he sought to execute all those who might be a threat to him. It is a matter of conscience. Conscience dictates that we do what we believe is right. If we have undertaken to become soldiers then we execute our duties as soldiers; and if we have been baptized as Christians, then we perform acts in accordance with what we believe to be right. When the two are in conflict, it is our conscience that must be our guide. That is the belief of Christians and that is the creed under which Christians live. We Christians believe that we are capable of making a distinction between what is right and what is wrong. To kill indiscriminately is wrong. To kill in defense of others is not wrong."

Here Cornelius seemed to grow in stature before Quintus' eyes. His next words came with deep conviction. "Now with regard to Nero, I would refuse to carry out my orders. I would admit I was a Christian. I would stand firm and even allow myself to be arrested. As a soldier, I would refuse to carry out a duty in conflict with my conscience, no matter what the consequences."

"You are a brave man, and a just man, Cornelius" said Quintus quietly. "It was certainly a difficult question and you answered it as I might have as a Christian. I am not a Christian but I would give you the same answer. As a member of the Praetorian Guard you witnessed the excesses of Caligula when he was Emperor." Cornelius nodded and Quintus kept relating some of the problems the Praetorian Guard encountered with Caligula. Quintus continued. "The Praetorian Guard was charged with the responsibility of guarding the Emperor in his role of Chief of State, but in reality it was charged with ensuring the continuity of power within the office of Chief of State. Caligula was a monster. We suspected that he had murdered Tiberius in order to become Emperor. His conduct as Emperor was reprehensible. He created a brothel in the Emperor's palace. He committed public incest with his own sister at a state banquet. He had rivals executed and was reputed to have murdered for greed. When his excesses became a threat to the stability of the state, then we in the Praetorian Guard executed him. It was I who searched for Claudius and found him, hiding and fearing for his life, to tell him he was the new Emperor." Quintus became silent for a moment as if he was reliving the past. Then he continued. "History repeated itself with Emperor Nero. He murdered his mother and his wife. He murdered untold numbers of Roman citizens who were Christians in order to mask his own corruption, and he burned most of Rome to make room for his palace. He squandered the national treasury in his pursuit of personal comfort and glory. We forced him to commit suicide as the alternative to execution."

"After the death of Nero we too succumbed to the lure of power as we sided with one or other of the four emperors during that terrible year. Finally, we came to our senses and returned to the basic principles on which the Praetorian Guard was founded and once again became guardians of the state and cooperated with the Senate. Vespasian seized power backed by his Germanic Legions, and then was confirmed by the Senate to become Emperor. Then he wisely appointed his own son, Titus, as head of the Praetorian Guard."

"I can see why you would support my answer, Quintus. You just told me that the Praetorian Guard has a conscience. Are you sure you're not a Christian?" Cornelius added with a wry smile.

Quintus grinned. "You almost make me feel hesitant to ask the final questions. Cornelius, my friend, do you see any possibility that Christians would ever be a threat to the Peace of Rome? Would Christians ever revolt against Rome?

Cornelius laughed uproariously. "In fact, Quintus, I think Christians are becoming the bulwark of Rome, the support to perpetuate the power of Rome. I see Christianity in alliance with Rome, and not the other way around." Noting the somewhat quizzical look on Quintus' face, Cornelius continued, "Christians stand for what is right. Christians have a sense of moral obligation of doing what is right, and hence would carry out their assigned duties to the best of their ability. As citizens they would obey the law, unless the law was evil as I have already considered. Contrast that with what is going on now. Many of our officials are thieves seeking their own advancement, either power or wealth or both. They have no moral responsibility and are concerned only with punishment if and when they are caught or made to pay for their behavior. Corruption is rampant. Sexual aberrations are accepted. Pedophilia is widespread and ignored. Those who ignore illicit behavior in my opinion are equally guilty. There should be no room and no place under the guise of Pax Romana for behavior and excesses outside the realm of civility, common decency and respect for others. Laws are enacted by government bodies as a means of maintaining order and protecting the rights, property and personages of the members of society. Law should never be arbitrary nor should it be used as a mask to protect or enhance greed, the desire for power over others and behavior that is reprehensible. This of course applies to all levels of authority. No one should be immune from justice."

Cornelius paused momentarily for emphasis. Then he continued.

"By your own admission, Quintus, the Praetorian Guard moved to execute one Emperor and force another to suicide. Much of Rome is rotten at the core. What is needed is a return to honor, respect, and performance for the common good. These statements are synonymous with the creative behavior of Christians. We have two commandments as enunciated by Jesus. They are to love God above all else and to love our neighbor as ourselves. We do for others because of love for God, who we believe loves us as well. We dedicate our lives to the principle that we are loved and we in turn must love. We can forgive and move on; but we move on to do what is right and to encourage and bolster others to do right. We could not ferment a revolt against law and order so long as the law and order are just. Just as the Praetorian Guard executed an evil emperor, we as citizens and as Christians, would move to bring to justice an evil Emperor. So in answer to your question, we, as Christians, are good citizens just as the Praetorian Guard are good citizens. We uphold the state unless the state is evil. But we will do everything we can to ensure that the state never becomes evil, seeking justice at all times through the structure of the state. So, you see Quintus, we will support Rome as a state and oppose any evil person attempting to usurp any power belonging to the state."

"Well said, Cornelius" said Quintus. "You have provided admirable replies to my questions. Now I wonder to what extent your opinions represent those of the majority of Christians," mused Quintus.

"I can assure you, Quintus, I stand as an example of all Christians. I would hope that you would question many and come to the same conclusion." With that Cornelius took a sip from his wine and changed the subject topic, once again reminiscing about former times. The two friends continued for a short period of time, reminiscing and sipping wine, then Quintus took his leave and left. As he walked to his Villa, he played over in his mind the discussions of the day. Cornelius had been forthright and refreshing in his honesty. There was much information that Quintus had to verify and compare with other findings. He must find Marcus soon to dictate his findings of this meeting while it was still fresh in his mind. He smiled as the further thought came to him. Marcus would provide a true account of all these interviews and facts; and make it all available for the future. As he strolled rapidly he felt somewhat relieved in beginning to see the positive direction for his investigation.

Chapter Three

The Beliefs of Christians

The next day Quintus proceeded to the Castra Praetoria, headquarters and barracks of the Praetorian Guard. He was immediately ushered by the guards into the assembly hall. The three Centurions he had selected together with the one hundred Legionaries were all present. He spent a few moments greeting the three Centurions before asking them to be seated in the three chairs that had been placed to the right side of the chair placed on a small dais reserved for him. He did not sit in his chair, but strode purposefully to the front of the room. As he stood for a moment the conversation in the room came to a halt and the Legionaries before him came to attention. The three Centurions stood at attention off to the side. Quintus stood quietly for a moment, casting his glance about the room. Titus had chosen well. This group looked seasoned and fit. Quintus was pleased but not surprised. This was his home. In a tone of command he began.

"Centurions and Legionaries of the Praetorian Guard, good morning." After a short pause he continued. "You have been selected to assist in an investigation of

Christians in Rome, and perhaps beyond Rome itself. That will depend upon what you discover."

"This investigation has been commanded by the Emperor. I will direct all of your efforts through the Centurions present this morning. Your task is to peacefully seek and question Christians throughout Rome whether they are citizens of Rome or not, whether they are citizens or foreigners, whether they are slaves or freed. The objective is to gather as much information as possible about their beliefs and motive in what they do. The most important element in this study is to discover whether or not they are a threat to Rome in any way, whether in fomenting disquiet, disrespect for the law of Rome, or disrespect for the Emperor. It is important for us to know whether they are currently or potentially enemies of Rome, sowing seeds of sedition and revolt, or in any way a threat to Pax Romana. Specifically, are they a unified force under a single command?"

Quintus stopped, pausing to ensure that his words were completely understood. He glanced about the room, making eye contact with as many of the Legionaries as possible as his gaze swept the room. As he did so, he recognized many who had served with him in the past. Then he continued. "Christians are in every segment of our society, from slaves to Senators. Many are soldiers and some are Centurions and Tribunes. As part of your investigation I would be interested in reports as to why they became Christians and what they personally expect will be the ultimate result for them and for Rome from their baptism as Christians."

Quintus paused, again glanced about the room, and then continued in a stern tone of voice. "Beware of false testimony. There are those who may attempt to pose as Christians and provided you with false information. In other cases, those posing as good citizens may accuse others as Christians plotting against Rome. In cases of doubt, or in cases of accusations against others, detain such persons for interrogation by the Centurions present today." Quintus paused and turned to look at the three centurions to his right. Raising his right arm in their direction he added "Centurions, Antinus, Julius, and Paulucci will direct your specific activities and receive your daily reports. You will be divided into squads by them. They will also personally interrogate anyone accusing others of sedition or troublemaking, or anyone you believe to be suspicious." Again he paused. Then turning to the Legionaries, he added. "We will meet each morning at this hour when they will present a summary of the findings of the day before." Again he paused. Quintus then asked, "Are there any questions?"

As Quintus had expected from the elite soldiers before him, there was complete silence. After a moment he turned once more to the Centurions and looking directly at Julius said, "Julius, please accompany me. Antinus and Paulucci please carry on with your assignments." With that, Quintus left the room followed by the Centurion Julius. They strode rapidly to a small meeting room that Titus had assigned for use by Quintus. On entering the room, Quintus had Julius sit to his right. Taking his chair, Quintus leaned forward and turning to Julius said, "I understand that you were in command of the unit that executed the Christian leader Paul. Is that correct?"

"Yes Tribune." began Julius, using the military title for Quintus. "I was commanded to that duty after Paul had been prisoner here for two years. That was his second imprisonment. The first time he was in house arrest for two years following his arrival from Caesarea. He was freed after a hearing and travelled extensively for some time before returning to Rome. He was arrested again on orders from Nero and became a prisoner of the Praetorian Guard. When Nero gave the order for his execution, it was we who carried it out. It was not a duty we looked forward to. In the two years that Paul was here we became very impressed with his gentleness and goodness, although he was very zealous and forthright when it came to his belief as a Christian. He would spend hours dictating his letters." Julius paused and looking directly at Quintus, asked, "Is there anything further you wish, sir?"

"Yes, I wish to learn more about Paul. And anything you tell me, anything you know will be of great interest to me. But for now, I am more interested in the whereabouts of a centurion named Longinus who may also have been imprisoned here by Nero. I am also interested in the whereabouts of a scribe named Marcus, a freed slave who may also have been imprisoned here."

"Yes, Tribune, both were imprisoned here on the command of Nero but both were released on the command of Emperor Vespasian. Prefect Titus told me that he had commanded both to be brought here this morning. I will check with the guard to see if they have arrived."

With that Julius rose and left the room. A short time later he returned followed by a man who had the appearance of having been a soldier. Quintus immediately arose and grasped both his arms in friendship. "Longinus, it has been many years. Please come in and be seated. There is much that I wish to learn from you."

Quintus led Longinus to the chairs on the left recently used by the Centurion. He motioned to him to be seated as he too sat, turning his chair to face Longinus. Quintus began, "Longinus, I have learned that you have become a Christian, were imprisoned, and scheduled for execution by the Emperor Nero. I am interested in why you became a Christian, and why you were imprisoned?"

Longinus looked directly at Quintus and began after a small sigh seemed to escape his lips.

"I was imprisoned because I was a Christian. As you know, I was the Centurion on duty at the execution of the carpenter Jesus of Nazareth. It was I who pierced his side with a lance to ensure his death. It was the words of Jesus praying from the cross for the forgiveness of his tormentors and executioners that led me to look further into the teachings and beliefs of Jesus. I was certain then that he was the son of God, the Messiah the Jews believed would come to lead them. They believed he would lead them to throw off the yoke of Rome. Instead he came to lead them to a different kingdom, what we Christians call heaven."

In a questioning tone of voice, Quintus asked, "So, what did you do about this belief of yours?"

"I decided to find out more", said Longinus. "I became very friendly with Peter, whom you also met during your investigation in Judea. I was continually impressed by what Peter told me. After a period of time, I was very attracted to becoming a Christian but I was hesitant because of the need in Jerusalem to accept the Jewish laws." With a rueful smile and soft chuckle Longinus added "Quite frankly, Tribune, I did not want to be circumcised at my age."

"Then how did you become a Christian?" asked Quintus.

"It was some time before Peter returned from his travels around Judea. I understand that he performed some miracles, including raising a woman from the dead, and I will tell you about those miracles in a moment. For now, let me continue with how I became a Christian. You may already know some of the facts associated with that."

Quintus was puzzled. "What facts?" He listened attentively as Longinus continued.

"Peter had been living in Joppa with the tanner Simon when he was summoned to Caesarea by the Tribune Cornelius, at that time a Centurion in the Roman Cohort stationed in Caesarea. After spending some time in the household with Cornelius explaining the teachings of Jesus, Peter baptized Cornelius, his family, his household and many in his circle of friends. He did not impose upon them any requirement to follow the Judaic law, which includes circumcision."

Longinus paused for a moment in deep thought, apparently recalling the time. "Peter came to Jerusalem to meet with the elders of the group comprising the followers of Jesus, all of whom were orthodox Jews as well as baptized Christians. As a matter of fact, Peter was also an Orthodox Jew, worshipping in the temple. After I met him, he told me of his conversion of Cornelius. I asked if I too could become a Christian without the need for circumcision. Peter said in his opinion I could, but he was currently in discussion on that matter with James, the brother of Jesus, and the head of that local group who were the followers of Jesus in Jerusalem. Later they became known as the Church of Jerusalem and the followers became known as Christians. At that time, however, they were all followers of the Judaic law."

"As you knew when you were in Judea, Tribune, Paul had been converted from being a zealous persecutor of the followers of Jesus to being one of the great supporters of Jesus and soon became a major leader in the movement. He was strongly in favor of Gentiles being baptized as Christians without the need to follow the Judaic law, the

Mitzvot. Peter had agreed with this when he baptized Cornelius, and when he dined with Cornelius. Upon his return to Jerusalem, however, he had sought to mitigate the turmoil of his actions with his orthodox brothers. Some assumed he had changed his mind and Paul even attacked him on that point. But Peter had not changed his mind but was only following a gentler approach to securing support for this acceptance of Gentiles to be baptized. A meeting was called in Jerusalem by James. Peter, Paul and the followers of Jesus in Jerusalem attended under the direction of James. This became known as the Council of Jerusalem. It was Peter, supported by Paul, who led the discussion to allow Gentiles to be baptized without any requirements that they follow the Judaic law. James concurred. The council issued a letter to all of the followers of Jesus that Gentiles were to be admitted to baptism."

Longinus stopped. He seemed to be staring into space as he added very slowly, "In my opinion that opened the floodgates of all those who wanted to become Christians but hesitated. In my own case the way was immediately open for me to be baptized. And I was!"

"If you will recall, Tribune, you brought with you from Rome a slave, Marcus, who was a scribe and left him in Judea to follow Peter and to write of his exploits. Marcus and I remained friends over the years, and he too was baptized as a Christian. I met with him last night after I was summoned to be here this morning by Prefect Titus. Marcus has been summoned to be here to meet with you at the sixth hour."

Longinus remained silent, as did Quintus, as he digested what he had been told. He was beginning to understand the dramatic shift made by the followers of Jesus in opening membership to the Gentiles. Christianity, then, while born as a sect of the Jewish religion was now

63

something distinct from it. While connected by having belief in the same god, they were different. Hence so far as Rome was concerned, consideration of Christianity was totally separate from consideration of Jews. In fact, as evidenced by Cornelius, Longinus, and Paul, it was conceivable that Christians who were Jews were probably in the minority. That had to be determined. For now, Quintus wanted to pursue a reason for the imprisonment of Longinus.

"Your explanation of how you came to be a Christian is very interesting, Longinus. I want to know specifically what teachings of Jesus led you, a brave and noble soldier, to become a Christian; and I also want to know why you, so dedicated to Rome, came to be imprisoned and scheduled for execution. Did you foment a revolt? Were you a threat to Rome? Are you a traitor? Basically, why were you to be executed?"

Longinus looked quizzically at Quintus for a moment. Then he began. "'Tribune, you always wanted to know everything all at once. Let me take this one step at a time."

After a short pause he began. "Being a Christian is to be a whole person. Even a slave can be a whole person. Everyone is equal in the eyes of God. We are the creatures of a God who loves us. The only requirement placed upon us is to love God above all else and love each other as we love ourselves. But even as creatures we are free, free to do what we choose. Our choice is always governed by our own personal conscience to distinguish between what is right from what is wrong. On that basis, we judge ourselves at all times."

A small smile lit up his face as he added, "Tribune, we are all human. With humanity comes imperfection, error, and the commission of error. When we falter or fail, we call that a sin, an evil act, or something that is judged wrong by our own conscience. We sin when and if we knowingly do something our conscience says is wrong. Then if we repent of our own free will, we can seek forgiveness. We must repent of our sins, and make restitution if our sin is grievous. Without repentance, there can be no forgiveness."

Here Longinus paused for some moments. Quintus had listened raptly, beginning to understand the attraction of the Christian belief to so many people, and especially to such noble persons as Cornelius and Longinus.

He interjected, "Longinus, this is a very straightforward explanation of Christian belief. I can well understand the attraction it can have for so many. But don't you find it difficult to be at the same level as a slave in the eyes of your god? You worked hard to be a soldier, to become a Centurion, to strive for higher rank. Don't you feel that you have lost something in becoming equal to a servant or slave who has no responsibility and seeks none? Is there truly no ambition among Christians?"

Longinus laughed heartily. "Of course Christians are ambitious. But our ambition has a different goal. Our ultimate goal is in the next world, 'Heaven' as we call it, where we will be rewarded for our goodness." After a short pause, he added, "As for inequality, it works both ways. As Christians, we are all equal in the eyes of God. We all have a personal relationship with God. He is our Father, a loving and indulgent parent who will excuse our sins so long as we are penitent."

Quintus remained skeptical. What Longinus was telling him sounded idyllic, but totally impractical. He doubted that highly disciplined soldiers could follow such a regimen of behavior more suited to young children. He decided to ask about this.

"Longinus, I do not question your sincerity nor do I question the strength of your belief, but I do wonder how practical your Christian belief can be in the real world, especially your world as a soldier? In your world, a mistake often leads to death. There is no repentance from death. Even success in the form of victory can lead to death, either as a price for achieving that victory; or from the vengeance of the vanquished seeking to place a price upon their loss with renewed fighting vigor."

"What you are saying, Tribune, is true in portraying outcomes in battle and in life. But we Christians are concerned not only with outcomes but with motivation and purpose. What is in our hearts and minds is more important to us. For example, as a soldier, it may be necessary for me to kill. If I kill in order to defend myself and others, I am doing no wrong. But if I kill in vengeance for a wrong done upon me by the person I am killing, then I am doing wrong."

"I can accept that" said Quintus. "But I still question whether or not your god is never guilty of vengeance? Don't you Christians fear your god?"

Longinus paused for a moment in deep thought before replying. "Yes and no! I do not fear my God as my Creator. I feel the love of God in my everyday life and in everything I do."

"I believe that God is my bulwark, and my strength. I believe I will never be tempted to evil beyond my capability to resist. But I also believe in the justice of God if I become evil, if I commit terrible acts against the will of God or against my fellow human beings, and if I refuse to repent for these acts of evil. No matter what I do, so long as I repent, and make restitution I need not fear punishment from a just and loving God." Before Quintus could interrupt, Longinus continued, his face lit with a rueful smile. "And what, you may ask, Tribune, is that punishment?" Looking quizzically at Quintus, now with an even broader smile, Longinus added, "The punishment is the denial of the vision of God. In other words, the punishment is the denial of heaven. We believe that is the ultimate punishment, and we seek to avoid it."

Quintus stroked his chin in deep thought. What Longinus had told him was very profound, yet quite simple. It was also very disturbing. He would have to verify that this was the opinion of others who had become Christians and not necessarily the unique belief of one military man, Longinus, or of all military men. Quintus decided he would have to revisit Cornelius and ask him the same questions. He would also, of course, have to ask the same questions of many Christians in order to arrive at a consensus of opinion.

A sudden thought came to him. Perhaps there was a way to identify false testimony. "Longinus," he asked, "can you separate a true Christian from one who is not?"

When Longinus asked the point of his question, Quintus explained his concern about false testimony, adding that there might very well be those who wished to discredit and harm the Christians.

Longinus became pensive for a moment. With a deep frown he answered, "That is very difficult. Normally the false witness could be asked some basic questions about Christianity. But that might not be enough. The false witness might be a fallen away Christian, fully capable of answering your questions about the basic beliefs of Christians." Again Longinus became very pensive. "Tribune, you must become very familiar with Christianity, and look for inconsistencies in what you are told. In addition, you should perform the interrogation with a Christian in attendance with you." Longinus pursed his lips before adding, "This is not an easy thing to uncover."

Still somewhat skeptical, Quintus changed the direction of the questions. In a very pensive voice he asked, "As the man who ultimately killed Jesus, how do you feel about your relationship with your god? Do you feel you will be punished for this?"

"Yes, I did kill Jesus. But, Quintus, if you will recall, Jesus asked his father, Our God, to forgive us as He was dying on the cross." Longinus stopped, remaining in deep thought for a few seconds, before beginning again. "That is a major element of Christianity, Tribune - the ability to repent and to be forgiven. Our religion is one of hope - of hope and salvation - hope and forgiveness, hope and love, and hope of attaining eternal rest in heaven."

After a long pause, Longinus went on, with a radiant smile on his lips. His words were strong and powerful. His voice was vibrant, full of meaning. Quintus knew he was speaking from the heart. "In fact, Tribune, that is probably the most relevant aspects of Christianity. We have hope. We have love. We can forgive and be forgiven. We have free will to do as our conscience directs us. And most important of all, we can feel that we have the Holy Spirit with us at all times. We are not alone! That is what being a Christian means."

Quintus looked puzzled. "What do you mean by the term 'Holy Spirit'?"

Longinus gazed thoughtfully at Quintus for a moment and then began. "We think of God as a single being or entity with three distinct natures. These are the Father, the Son, and the Holy Spirit. The Holy Spirit we believe is the essence of God's presence among us at any given time. It was the Holy Spirit that Jesus sent on the Pentecost after His Resurrection to infuse the Apostles with the strength of their faith, to proclaim the teachings of Jesus, and witness the fact of His resurrection. In that sense, then, we think of the Holy Spirit as a fountain of grace providing direction and security in our daily life. We can look upon the Holy Spirit to provide the courage to withstand assaults upon our faith. It was the grace of the Holy Spirit which converted the fear of the Apostles into the aggressive evangelizing that marked the rest of their lives. It was the grace of the Holy Spirit that gave them the courage to endure terrible forms of death without wavering from their faith in Jesus and His teachings.

The sincerity of the Centurion's words was very impressive to Quintus. He was impressed, although still skeptical. He still could not see the practical aspects of being a Christian in the current Roman world. It all seemed too altruistic and unreal to him. And yet he was hearing this from a hardened soldier who served in heavy and major combat. This was also a soldier who had officiated at many executions, including that of Jesus. He decided to try and rattle Longinus with a remark that would be a challenge.

With a cynical tone to his voice, Quintus stated, "Longinus, this seems totally impractical to me. You and I live in a brutal world. It is hard for me to understand how a seasoned soldier such as yourself can be attracted to a set of religious beliefs more tuned to the tender sensibilities of women and children than to men." Sensing that Longinus was about to explode in anger, Quintus held up his hand in order to add his final remark. "What you have told me about the belief of Christians just doesn't seem to fit the needs of the world today."

As Quintus stopped, Longinus almost exploded. His words tumbled in rapid succession. His face took on a stern appearance, and his entire body became rigid as it prepared for battle. "Tribune" he snapped, "you are terribly wrong! I am afraid that my words have misled you and for that I beg your pardon. But Christianity is not for cowards. It is for brave men and women to lead a life directed towards the will of God. Doing what is right is often very difficult. Submitting to every impulse and temptation is easy compared to rejecting them on behalf of doing what is right." As he spoke, his anger left him, and a smile came upon his lips. A look of understanding came across his face and into his words. His smile broadened as he added, "Tribune, I can see your strategy. You deliberately provoked me to gauge the depth of my feeling and understanding." Longinus nodded his head and the smile on his face broadened into a grin. "Christianity is for the tough and the brave. Dying on the cross with no complaint calls for the ultimate in moral strength and bravery. Being willing to die for your principles is also the ultimate in moral strength and bravery." Longinus became very serious, and spoke his next words with deep feeling. "Christians always have their eye on reality. We know the stakes. There is nothing weak in our actions. We are motivated by a greater love of God and of our fellow humans. We are also strengthened at all times with the grace of God." Longinus stopped, and looking directly at Quintus, concluded with, "No, Tribune, you are wrong. We are not weak, but rather strong in the eyes of God and in the eyes of the world. We are persecuted because we are strong. If we were perceived as weak, we would be ignored. And because of our great strength, our ranks grow even in the face of adversity and persecution."

Despite his skepticism, Quintus was even more impressed. Impressed but not convinced. He would have to verify the accuracy of what he had just heard by questioning a number of Christians on the same topic. In particular, it was vital that he return to Cornelius for his opinions. He would also want to question Longinus again after he had talked to others as well. He had one final topic to cover with Longinus.

"Longinus", he began, "why were you arrested on orders of the Emperor Nero? Were you plotting against him? Were you plotting against Rome? Were you leading any kind of sedition or revolt with the Christians against Rome?"

"My answer to all of that is a loud and resounding 'NO!' Tribune!" Longinus virtually shouted. "I don't know why we were persecuted or arrested. We had heard rumors of the instability of the Emperor, rumors of murder and greed. We were not surprised since so many of us remembered the excesses of Caligula. We minded our own business, and went our own way. There was no persecution of Christians. Even Caligula had left us alone. When Claudius expelled the Jews, it was significant that he did not expel the Gentile Christians or persecute them at the same time. Life proceeded even though we lived in turbulent times under the Emperor."

Longinus stopped and seemed to swallow as if to collect himself for what was to follow. "Then the fire broke out. Many of the homes of the Christian brethren were destroyed. The rumor was that Nero had created the fire in order to level sections of Rome for his new palace. But the fire got out of control. About half of Rome was destroyed. The people began to murmur against the Emperor. There were loud complaints that he had gone too far, that he had created the fire to make room for his palace and that he played his violin while Rome burned, thinking that was a great entertainment. Many of us had expected that the Praetorian Guard would take matters into their own hand, just as they had in executing Caligula. But it was not to be. Suddenly the Christians were being arrested and charged with treason in having created the fire. No reason was given for this ridiculous charge. Everywhere Christians were being denounced and arrested. We learned that it was Nero himself who was accusing the Christians of setting fire to Rome. The charge was ridiculous. But the people who were angered by their losses in the fire were ready to believe anything. Nero succeeded in diverting the attention from himself to the Christians." Longinus looked meaningfully at Quintus as he added, "Tribune, diversion is the main element of strategy in military actions. The enemy must never know the true location of your attack, or be allowed time to regroup to counter your attack. The objective is to divert, strike quickly, and overcome the enemy before he has an opportunity to counterattack. So it was with Nero. He wanted space to build a new palace. He set fire to the area he wanted cleared for his palace. When the fire raged out of control, he immediately sought to divert attention from his error. The Christians were a convenient scapegoat. He not only denounced them but had them arrested and executed. This provided not only a diversion, but an entertainment. Needless to say it also instilled a major element of fear on the part of citizens of Rome. Even if they saw through his stratagem, they were afraid to speak up lest they be accused as well. If Christians could be arrested and executed for no reason whatsoever, perhaps they would be next. Fear kept them silent. Nero not only used the tactic of diversion, but also the tactic of divide and conquer." Longinus paused before continuing. "Nero was certainly an evil man, but he was also a brilliant strategist."

Looking directly at Quintus, Longinus challenged him. "Why was the Praetorian Guard silent? Surely, as Tribune, you knew the truth? Why did you not intervene?"

"Yes," said Quintus. "I remember. There were many of us in the Praetorian who saw through the subterfuge. We knew of Nero's madness. But many of us were involved in the revolt in Judea. I personally, as you know, was in Judea with Vespasian and Titus. Rumors that reached us were months after the fact." Quintus stopped. He pondered deeply over his role in terminating the reign of Nero. Even at a distance, he had been intimately involved in the decision to force Nero to abdicate with his own suicide. The Praetorian Guard had been the instigator of this strategy. It had been thoroughly disgusted with the excesses of Nero. It had been particularly incensed at being forced to participate in many of the executions. That of Paul was particularly disturbing. He thought it best to make Longinus aware somewhat of these secret facts.

"Longinus, despite the distance, I was involved in the deposing Nero as Emperor."

Longinus gave Quintus a startled look, which rapidly turned into one of deep appreciation. Before he could say anything, Quintus in a very quiet voice asked him to continue.

Longinus nodded slightly, and continued, "Many of the Christians were executed. Some were beheaded and some were forced to combat wild animals for the entertainment of the spectators. It was tragic to see whole families slaughtered, with young children hugging their parents in fear." Longinus became very sad as the memory of those times almost overcame him emotionally. Very slowly he added, once again recalling the difficult times of the persecution under Nero, "Tribune, we hid in the catacombs, among the graves of our ancestors. We hid anywhere we thought we would be safe. We were pursued everywhere. The Roman soldiers searched for us everywhere. They specially looked for locations where we held the prayer meetings of the breaking of the bread. To fool the soldiers, and still show the way for our followers, we used the symbol of the fish, with the head pointing in the proper direction. We referred to this by its Greek name, 'Ichtus'. They were easy to draw, using a sharp stone on the walls, and just as easily erased. But even with this subterfuge, ultimately many of us were found and thrown into prison. Executions for public entertainment occurred every day. It was during this time that Peter and Paul were both executed. I am sure that Antinus can tell you about Peter and Julius can tell you about the execution of Paul.

Quintus nodded, "Yes I intend on questioning them in detail on those executions; but for now I am interested in your recollections."

"There isn't much more, Tribune. We were arrested, and thought we would be executed and imprisoned. We knew that many of the Christians were being killed and we kept our own record about who was martyred. But there was no news and no hope that we would be freed. We faced martyrdom, calmly, willing to die for our faith. And yet, we lived in the hope either of release or paradise. Our religion and our beliefs made all of us face the reality of an unfair execution calmly." The last words of Longinus were said calmly and with conviction.

Quintus was subdued. The recitation of the terror inflicted by Nero and the injustice, while not a surprise, still was devastating to his spirit. Quintus had killed in battle. But that was battle with belligerents. The thought of killing defenseless women and children sickened him. As one who had lived his life at all times close to the imperial crown, Quintus was well aware both of the power of the office of Emperor and of the possibility that that power would corrupt the spirit of whoever would occupy that office. He felt some sense of accomplishment in his role of ridding Rome of the monsters Caligula and Nero. Yet he was subdued as he looked directly at Longinus and added "My words could never convey the depth of my dismay at the misuse of power by Nero. What he did was totally unjust and it is extremely unfortunate that so many people suffered needlessly, until his own madness was terminated with his enforced suicide. As a matter of fact, he was weak to the very end and it was his valet who actually killed him, even though on orders from Nero to stab him." Both men remained silent, rapt in their own thoughts. Quintus would have to gather much more evidence to verify that there was no plan for revolt, and that the Christians were unjustly accused and executed by Nero. For now, he would accept the word of Longinus, but verification was needed since he knew it would be mandatory to create validity in his report to the Emperor.

As Longinus was about to resume speaking, a guard entered and told them that Marcus had arrived. Quintus dismissed the guard and turned to Longinus. "Longinus, thank you for this testimony concerning the belief of Christians and the tragedy of the persecution by Nero. As you have just heard, Marcus is here and I wish to learn what happened to him after I left him in Judea so many years ago, and also to receive his firsthand report of his knowledge of events, and especially those associated with Peter. You are welcome to stay during my discussion with him. But first I would appreciate if you could take a few minutes to try and summarize for me the way of life for Christians. In other words, Longinus, what is the daily approach of Christians to each other and how do they react to the events that occur every day?"

"I think I can do that. As a matter of fact, I will give you a summary as presented by Jesus himself. He enunciated these eight rules of behavior. They are not commandments, but beatitudes. He first stated these beatitudes when he addressed the thousands in the field while he fed them, with two fishes and seven loaves of bread." These latter words he said with a deep grin. And then he proceeded to enunciate the eight beatitudes as stated by Jesus in that field in Galilee.

"Blessed are the poor in spirit,
for theirs is the kingdom of heaven.

Blessed are they who mourn,
for they shall be comforted.

Blessed are the meek,
for they shall inherit the earth.

Blessed are they who hunger and thirst for righteousness,
or they shall be satisfied.

Blessed are the merciful,
for they shall obtain mercy.

Blessed are the pure of heart,
for they shall see God.

Blessed are the peacemakers,
for they shall be called children of God.

Blessed are they who are persecuted for the sake of righteousness,
for theirs is the kingdom of heaven."

Longinus then added. "Perhaps these are the questions you can ask those claiming to be Christians or pointing accusation of seditious planning at others. Ask them to quote these beatitudes. Ask them to tell you the two basis commandments of Christians which, as you know are to love God above all else, and your neighbor as yourself. That should do it." Longinus paused and then went on. "Tribune, one final point. Christians are an asset to Rome, not a detriment or threat. Rome is decaying from within. The lure of power and wealth has turned brother against brother. Families are no longer important. Murder, incest, and pedophilia are commonplace. Christians, on the other hand, believe in family, civility, and morality. They are an asset to Rome, and might very well be the bulwark to prop up Rome and stop the decay from within. Christianity, then, is not a threat, but a potential support. The beatitudes of Jesus are the steel in the spine of Christians."

Longinus paused and looked thoughtfully at Quintus before continuing. "We all recognize, Tribune, that Rome is corrupt. We also fear this corruption will destroy Rome. Militarily Rome is impregnable. Our legions have, can and will conquer all before them. But the rot of decay from within can destroy what no enemy can ever hope to accomplish. This is the cycle of the past and may spell the future for Rome. The one great hope for Rome may very well lie with the civility, morality, and respect for law by the Christians. It is the Christian character and influence which I believe can overcome the rot from within. Christianity, including the beatitudes of Jesus can become the steel of Rome"

Quintus was impressed. He had heard of this presentation by Jesus in his lifetime. The words of Jesus served now as the capstone of the presentation by Longinus of the belief of Christians, and especially their potential role as an asset for Rome.

He concluded his meeting with Longinus with, "Thank you, Longinus. What you have told me this morning is of great interest and will serve as an important element in my study for the Emperor. Now let us continue our discussion by asking Marcus to join us." Quintus clapped his hands loudly. When the guard appeared Quintus asked him to escort Marcus into the room.

Chapter Four

Peter the Leader

Marcus entered the room with his usual bag of slates and rolls of papyrus over one shoulder. As Quintus stood to greet him, the years rolled away. It was almost yesterday that they had parted at the dockside in Caesarea, Quintus on his way to report to Tiberius, leaving Marcus in Judea to be with Peter. Quintus could not suppress a deep sense of elation at seeing Marcus again. With a broad smile, he said, "Marcus, you haven't changed. You still carry your slates ready to make notes and to prepare detailed summaries of what you have heard and seen." He grasped Marcus by the arm in welcome. "I hope you will do that again in this investigation."

A quiet smile crossed the face of the usual taciturn Marcus. "Tribune, of course I will be your scribe. It will please me greatly to be of service to you at any time. I too am happy to see you after all these years. It gives me an opportunity to personally say thank you for granting me freedom. That word reached me shortly after you left for Rome. I learned also of the acceptance of your report by Emperor Tiberius. I well remember working with you in establishing the truth that the carpenter Jesus had truly risen from the dead."

Quintus was pleased. The study of the missing body had been difficult. Fortunately, he had been able to establish complete and verifiable proof that the body had not been stolen, and that in reality Jesus had truly risen from the dead. After a brief smile and nod, Quintus began "Thank you, Marcus. I think you remember Centurion Longinus who has worked with us during that investigation," said Quintus as he turned toward Longinus who had risen from his chair, and had approached. Grasping Marcus by the arm, Longinus said looking at Quintus, "I know Marcus well, Tribune. As you know, we are both Christians and often break bread together."

Quintus looked puzzled at the statement. Longinus and Marcus spent a moment talking. After giving the two friends sufficient opportunity to greet each other, Quintus asked, "What do you mean 'break bread together?"

It was Longinus who turned and explained to Quintus, "In our meetings, we pray in thanks and in supplication. We pray for those who live and those who have died; those who are well and those who are sick. Those who are traveling, and those who are with us. We pray for forgiveness of our sins, and for the strength to forgive those who harm us in any way. Then we pray for our leaders and finally for ourselves. The highlight of our entire meeting is the breaking of bread and drinking of wine as directed to us by Jesus. He promised that the bread would become his body, and the wine would become his blood. He promised that he would be with us at all times and that we had to eat His body and drink His blood. This we do at our meetings as the leader or priest prays and converts bread to the body of Christ and wine to His blood."

Quintus remained puzzled. To give himself a moment to reflect, he asked both men to be seated while he pondered what he had just heard.

"This seems rather bizarre," said Quintus. "How can bread be turned into the body of your founder, Jesus?"

It was Marcus who laughed, but quietly. "Tribune, maybe I can answer your question by asking another."

Quintus looked directly at Marcus, once again with a look of puzzlement. Marcus continued. "How can someone who is dead bring himself back to life?"

Marcus looked directly at Quintus and continued, "Tribune you verified to your own satisfaction that Jesus had risen from the dead. You also were willing to accept that Jesus was some form of deity. With power like that, how can you question Jesus saying that he could convert bread into his body?"

Quintus remained skeptical. He was not convinced. Casting his glance back and forth between Marcus and Longinus, gauging the reaction of his words, he added, "I know you believe that. I do not question your belief. I simply cannot believe it. To me it seems absolutely impossible."

Both Longinus and Marcus smiled. A long silence ensued. It was Marcus who broke the silence. His words were calm and quiet. "Tribune, we do not understand the rising and setting of the sun and of the moon day after day. We know it happens. We have learned men who measure the cycle and can predict its variation. They can even conjecture at the different appearance of the moon, as it too goes through its cycle, from nothing to full blossom and back to nothing. This we can all see, but this we cannot understand as to how it all came to be. And so it is with the resurrection of our Lord Jesus, the Christ. He truly died. He truly was buried. And yet on the third day he walked from

81

his tomb, exploding out of the tomb and walking through the guards posted to ensure that no one could steal the body. In this case the body rose from the dead. It was seen by the guards, it was seen by many afterwards. His follower Thomas placed his hands in the wounds. And yet, we don't know how it happened. We do not know how a body can rise from the dead. We don't know how, in life, Jesus could cure disease, restore sight, restore hearing and make the lame to walk, and also raise the dead back to life. That is a mystery. But that, Tribune, is the power of God. We can see the power of God, we do not understand where that power comes from, but we know it comes from outside the natural world we live in. We address it as being super natural, or above nature, which it certainly is. Once we accept Jesus as the Son of that God, and actually an integral part of that God, then of course we can accept that He has the power to change bread into His body and wine into His blood. As Christians we accept that. It is the cornerstone of our meeting where our leader or presbyter, our priest, has received the power to perform that miracle."

Quintus remained deep in thought. What he had heard affected him deeply in one sense and disturbed him as well. It brought into question many of the things that he had pondered all his life. What was life? Why was there life? What was consciousness? What allowed him to see and hear and think? All his life, he had been a soldier living under discipline, heavily self-imposed but also coming from those in command. When orders were issued to him, he accepted and obeyed. When orders were not issued, he would observe, evaluate and decide upon his own personal course of action. He knew right from wrong and would make his decisions seeking at all times the maximum advantage or 'good'. Pax Romana was 'good'. He had spent his life time supporting this principle. On and on the thoughts circled in his mind. For some time he continued to ponder good from evil, right from wrong. These Christians were brave. They were willing to die for their beliefs. This religion was not for cowards. While he could not accept as true what he had just heard, he could accept as true the sincerity of the two Christians before him; and accept, because of that, the need for Christians to truly live the teachings of their founder, Jesus the Christ.

This was something he would have to consider in greater depth over time in order to arrive at his own personal acceptance or rejection of the belief of Christians. For now, that was not an issue in completing his mandate from the Emperor. Were the Christians a potential threat to Rome or not?

Quintus rose from his chair and began to pace back and forth, stroking his chin as he did, obviously in deep thought. Longinus and Marcus remained seated, well sensing the turmoil in the mind of the man they admired so greatly. Abruptly, Quintus stopped. Standing before the two, he exclaimed, "You have given me much to analyze! For now I will accept that you believe what you have told me and that this represents a major aspect of your Christian belief. That is important in my study, but to be complete, it is important for me to learn whatever you can tell me about the growth of Christianity here in Rome, and especially how it all came to be. I know it started with Jesus, but what happened after I left Judea? What happened to Peter and his fellow apostles?"

Looking at Marcus directly he added, "When I left Judea I asked you to stay particularly close to Peter. Did you do so? Did you make a record of what he said and did?"

"Yes, I did," said Marcus.

"Can you give me a quick summary of Peter's activities up until the time he came to Rome, and why he came to Rome? When this is complete, we can examine what he did in Rome, and the matter and manner of his execution. Are you ready to proceed?"

"Yes Tribune, I will attempt to do so."

Taking a deep breath, Marcus began his recitation. He described how Peter had continued preaching the teachings of Jesus which he now characterized as the word of God in the temple, in the marketplace, and wherever he had an audience of at least one. He also began to cure the sick. One day, accompanied by John, at the hour of prayer, the ninth hour, Peter was in the temple and walked by a man who had been lame from birth. The cripple asked Peter for alms. Peter told him he had no alms but would cure him, and he did. The man was elated and began to dance, suddenly freed of his affliction. This caused quite a commotion and Peter and John were detained. The next day they appeared before the Chief Priest and the council of seventy elders, the Sanhedrin. The council members were vehement in their denunciation of Peter and threatened him with punishment. Peter vigorously defended himself, reminding them he had done no wrong. Curing a man crippled from birth was no crime. He further reminded them of the miracles of Jesus, and of his Resurrection from the dead after his unjust crucifixion. The Chief Priest Annas, and the former Chief Priest, Caiaphas, once more threatened to punish them. The discussion went on for some time. The members of the council could not understand how these uneducated common men could challenge knowledgeable scholars. The curing of the man with limbs paralyzed from birth could not be disputed. Nor was it a crime. After a heated discussion, it was the great teacher Gamaliel who convinced the other elders that there was no wrong in curing someone of illness. The temple guards were ordered to keep a watch on Peter and detain him only if he continued to preach about Jesus but not if was curing the sick.

On that basis, finally Peter and John were freed but warned to be silent or they would be arrested again and punished severely.

Peter, of course, ignored the attempt to have him stopped. He continued to preach as did a very ardent disciple called Stephen. Stephen was very outspoken in his advancement of the teachings of Jesus and of the need for repentance. He advanced the teachings of Peter and was especially strong in describing the miracles whereby Jesus and now Peter had cured the sick. The high priest Caiaphas became alarmed at the resurgence of what he considered to be a potential threat to the civil order and to his own personal power. Just as he had manipulated innocent statements into the appearance of sedition and blasphemy in the case of Jesus, he now applied the same technique to the case of Stephen. Stephen was condemned. He was stoned. During this murderous execution, a zealot, Saul of Tarsus, minded the garments of those who were stoning Stephen. He secured letters from Caiaphas empowering him to seek out followers of Jesus and to arrest them and set out for Damascus. On the way he was thrown to the ground and received a vision which totally converted him. From being a zealot against the followers of Jesus he now became one of His   strongest advocates.

As Marcus recited this history, Quintus nodded. He had met Saul in Tarsus and well-remembered him as a zealot. He had heard of the conversion and had not been surprised, since, in his interview in Tarsus, he had detected a certain questioning within Saul as to the validity of Saul's vehement opposition to the teachings of Jesus. He had also heard that Saul was using his Roman name Paul. He interjected, "I certainly wish to learn more of Paul, but for now I really want to learn what happened to Peter. We can return to Paul at a later time. Please continue concerning Peter."

Marcus continued with his recitation concerning Peter. Peter continued his preaching and continued in exercising miraculous power in curing the sick. He was arrested once more, and scheduled to be examined with a view to being punished the next day. When the guards went to bring him to the council, the jail cell was empty. Peter had disappeared. The Council was enraged but could find no explanation as to why or how he had escaped.

Peter went about the country side preaching and curing the sick. In Lydda he cured a paralyzed man named Aeneas. In Joppa, close to Lydda, he raised a woman, Tabitha, also known as Dorcas, from the dead. This continued to give Peter visibility.

Herod of Judea was determined to stamp out the followers of Jesus. He had James, who headed the church in Jerusalem, arrested and executed by being thrown to his death from a cliff top. Herod had learned Peter was in Judea. He had him arrested, scheduled for execution the following morning. Knowing of his miraculous disappearance when jailed by the temple guards, Herod had Peter placed under a guard of sixteen men organized into four troops of four men each. He was chained with guards on each side. There was no way he could escape. He was to be executed the next day.

That night, an angel of the Lord appeared and told Peter to walk out of the jail. The guards on each side of him were asleep. His chains dropped from his body; and the door opened. Peter walked out past the guards who were all asleep. He proceeded to the home of his friends. They could not believe that he was free. Peter had brought with him his chains, which he left with them. After much consultation it was decided that he should leave Judea.

Peter travelled to Antioch. After preaching there for some time, he travelled extensively throughout much of Asia Minor, converting many fellow Jews to become followers of Jesus. He taught once again in the synagogue and in the streets. Upon the death of Herod, he returned to Judea and took up residence in Joppa with the tanner Simon. It was there that he received a vision commanding him to visit the Gentile Cornelius, at that time a Centurion in the Roman Legion in Caesarea.

"Do you know of that visit, Tribune?"

"Yes. I spoke to Cornelius who told me of the visit of Peter and his conversion."

"Did Cornelius also tell you of the controversy surrounding the baptism of Gentiles without the need for them to adhere to Mitzvot, the 613 rules of Judaism and quoting circumcision?"

"Yes, he told me all of that."

"It was a very difficult time for Peter. Peter and Paul had become quite close as friends and believers in the teachings of Jesus."

Marcus looked directly at Quintus and continued, "You may not know, Tribune, that Paul had spent three years after his conversion virtually in isolation is Tarsus pondering and thinking over the vision that converted him. Then he went to Jerusalem and stayed with Peter for fifteen days. It was Peter who told Paul of many sayings of Jesus. Then Paul returned to Tarsus for eight years before Barnabas was sent to him by James in Jerusalem. That is when Paul began his travels and his teachings in such places as Corinth, Ephesus, Antioch and Damascus. Of course these travels will most likely be detailed in your later discussions concerning Paul. During that time he wrote letters to many of the groups that he had converted."

"Letters?" interjected Quintus. "What are these letters that you are speaking of?"

Marcus was surprised. Knowledge of the letters, of course, was common with the Christians. He was surprised that no one had told Quintus about them. "Yes," said Marcus, "Paul, Peter, James, John and others, wrote letters which we call Epistles, to various congregations in different locations. I have copies of most and can bring them to you."

"I would be pleased if you would do that when we have completed our discussion today. I wish to study these letters and then meet with you a few days from now to go over them in detail. Can you bring these letters to me today?"

"Of course, Tribune, I would be pleased to do so. What can I tell you now about these letters?"

"Tell me more about the letters of Peter."

"We have only one letter from Peter. What can I tell you about it?"

"Did Peter discuss in his letter anything concerning the relationship of Christians to authority? In other words, how did he address the fact that Christians have a divided loyalty between their god and their rulers?"

"Tribune, that is no problem whatsoever for Christians. We know that Jesus often remarked, 'Render unto Caesar that which is Caesar's and unto God that which is God's.' Peter always stressed that point and in his letter made it very explicit. He wrote:

> Be subject for the Lord's sake to every human institution, whether it be to the emperor as supreme, or to governors as sent by him to punish those who

88

do wrong and to praise those who do right. For it is God's will that by doing right you should put to silence the ignorance of foolish men. Live as free men, yet without using your freedom as a pretext for evil; but live as servants of God. Honor all men. Love the brotherhood. Fear God. Honor the emperor. [1Peter3:13-17]

"He went on to give the same admonition to servants, wives and husbands, essentially writing to tell us all to be submissive and to follow what we are told by those who have some authority to speak, so long as what we are told is not contrary to our conscience.

Servants, be submissive to your masters with all respect, not only to the kind and gentle but also to the overbearing. For one is approved if, mindful of God, he endured pain while suffering unjustly. For what credit is it, if when you do wrong and are beaten for it you take it patiently? But if when you do right and suffer for it you take it patiently, you have God's approval.

For to this cause you have been called, because Christ also suffered for you, leaving you an example that you should follow in his steps. He committed no sin; no guile was found on his lips. When he was reviled he did not revile in return; when he suffered, he did not threaten; but he trusted to him who judges justly. He himself bore our sins in his body on the tree, that we might die to sin and live to righteousness. By his wounds you have been healed. For you were straying like sheep, but have now returned to the Shepherd and Guardian of your souls. [1 Peter 3:13-25]

"Finally, Peter concluded his letter with his advice on the proper conduct of a Christian "

Finally, all of you, be like-minded, be sympathetic, love one another, be compassionate and humble. Do not repay evil with evil or insult with insult. On the contrary, repay evil with blessing, because to this you were called so that you may inherit a blessing. For, whoever would love life and see good days must keep their tongue from evil and their lips from deceitful speech. They must turn from evil and do good; they must seek peace and pursue it. For the eyes of the Lord are on the righteous and his ears are attentive to their prayer, but the face of the Lord is against those who do evil. [1 Peter 3:8-12]

Quintus was impressed. Peter had been very clear in what he wrote. He looked at Marcus and asked, "You will remember to bring the letters around for my examination?"

"Of course. I will go to retrieve them as soon as we are completed here today. I will leave them with the guard for your attention. I am at your disposal at any time to provide any additional information about them, or about anything I know, and even to give you some of my personal observations on the letters."

"Thank you Marcus, I am looking forward to that. Be assured I will contact you after I have had the opportunity to examine the letters in detail." Quintus paused, reflecting on what he had heard about the letters. Then he asked, "Will these include the letters of Paul?"

"Of course. There are many of them and you will find his writings to be consistent with those of Peter and with what I am sure you will find in your discussions with other Christians."

Marcus looked directly at Quintus and added, "Tribune, you must meet with the gentile physician Luke who also created reports and documents of what he has been told about Jesus by Peter and others who knew Jesus. Maryam, the mother of Jesus, also told Luke of the birth and childhood of Jesus."

Quintus looked up, startled somewhat, but pleased. Having records would be important in his investigation. He decided to learn more from Marcus about Luke. "Who is this man Luke, Marcus? Can he tell me more about the Christians in Rome as well?" he asked.

"Yes he can, Tribune." replied Marcus. "Luke is a Physician. He heard about Jesus and decided to seek him out to learn more. He came to know the Apostles and the major disciples of Jesus. He became very friendly with Maryam, the mother of Jesus. As a learned man, he was almost a scribe. He used his talent to make notes of what he knew or was told. Luke knows a great deal about Jesus and all his disciples, especially much about Peter, Paul, and the actions of the Apostles and the other disciples. He travelled with Paul extensively."

"Where is he now?" asked Quintus.

"Here in Rome." answered Marcus.

"When can you bring him to me?" asked Quintus.

"I will try for tomorrow "said Marcus.

"I am looking forward to that meeting" said Quintus.

Quintus remained silent for a moment, deep in thought. He was gratified at the mounting evidence in the form of letters and documents from many different sources.

91

If these documents were consistent, then his investigation would be significantly helped in determining the nature of the belief of Christians, and of their purpose in life. Essentially that was the most important element of his investigation and would be a critical part of his report and recommendations to the Emperor. So far everything he had heard was consistent. And what he had heard came from two persons whom he judged to be completely trustworthy. He could not foresee the result of meeting with Luke, his continuing discussion with Marcus and others, and his detailed examination of the scrolls he would be receiving from Marcus containing the letters of Peter and Paul. But he was confident that he was well on his way to understanding what Christianity concerned.

Quintus looked at Longinus. "Longinus, now I begin to understand some of the belief items we discussed. Can I assume that there is a uniformity in the belief structure and dogma of all Christians? And is that belief to a large extent based upon the letters of Peter and Paul?"

"Only to a limited extent, Tribune. The belief structure of Christians is based upon the teachings of Jesus. These teachings have come to us in many ways. Some have been fortunate to have heard Jesus speak. Most have not. Most Christians have come to know and accept the dogma of Christianity from the reflections, experiences, and words of other Christians. This is augmented by the writings of some, either expounding on the principles enunciated by Jesus, or relating their own personal experiences, reflections or commentary." Looking at Marcus for confirmation Longinus went on. "I would expect, and I hope Marcus agrees with me, that this accumulation of knowledge and experience will increase dramatically with time, especially as more and more people of the world become Christians.

When Longinus paused, Marcus added "The number of Christians increases each day as more hear about the teachings of Jesus and the reinforcement of what they hear, with knowledge of the miracles he performed and the miracles performed since then, our numbers swell. This became especially true during the persecution under Nero. Peter wrote eloquently about that and I can even remember his words, which I am sure you will see when you examine the documents he will bring you. Peter wrote:

> Dear friends, do not be surprised at the fiery ordeal that has come on you to test you, as though something strange were happening to you. But rejoice inasmuch as you participate in the sufferings of Christ, so that you may be overjoyed when his glory is revealed. If you are insulted because of the name of Christ, you are blessed, for the Spirit of glory and of God rests on you. If you suffer, it should not be as a murderer or thief or any other kind of criminal, or even as a meddler. However, if you suffer as a Christian, do not be ashamed, but praise God that you bear that name. For it is time for judgment to begin with God's house-hold; and if it begins with us, what will the outcome be for those who do not obey the gospel of God? And, "If it is hard for the righteous to be saved, what will become of the ungodly and the sinner?" So then, those who suffer according to God's will should commit themselves to their faithful Creator and continue to do good. [1 Peter 4:12-19]

"Peter was a great leader," said Quintus. "I remember in my discussions with him how impressive he was. I understand that at one time he was fearful, hesitant

93

and uncertain. When I met him, however, I found him to be decisive, direct, and fearless. I know he underwent a complete reversal at the feast of Pentecost, following the resurrection of Jesus. But if I am any judge of character, Peter's ability as a leader was always present. He was an outstanding individual and Christians are fortunate to have him as their first leader. I am sure that Jesus discerned those qualities of leadership in Peter and was very patient in bringing them forth so that Peter could truly be the rock upon which he could found his church."

Both Longinus and Marcus nodded in agreement. It was Marcus who added, "I saw Peter in many situations which called for great patience and bravery at the same time. I am sure that when you learn the details of how he died, your impressions will be enhanced."

"Yes, I wish to know more about how he died," said Quintus, "and I wish to know more of his activities in Rome. For now I would prefer to complete the examination of what he did before he went to Rome, and why he went to Rome."

Both Marcus and Longinus remained silent. They appeared somewhat puzzled. It was Marcus who broke the silence. "We are not sure why Peter went to Rome. We know he travelled extensively in many cities, advancing the words of Jesus and baptizing thousands. He was very effective in his presentations because he was factual and kept his words to the main issue at all times. For him the basic truth was that Jesus was the Son of God and had come to earth to lead the people of the earth to salvation; and that the key issue was to repent. Jesus did not condemn those who sinned, but exhorted them to repent and sin no more. Jesus offered hope in redemption and offered reward for virtue, and he exhorted all of us to take care of each other, most especially those who could not take care of themselves. It was that vision and mandate of life here on earth that Peter always managed to establish as a goal for those who heard him."

"Peter was a man full of love," said Longinus. "He cloaked his kindness and warm heart with an outward bluster, which always melted away when he encountered suffering that he could not alleviate. From my perspective as a military man," added Longinus, "the bravest are those who can function under adversity, those who can lead even as they feel the suffering of those they lead, and those who never falter no matter what the obstacle. That was Peter!"

"How do you reconcile that view of Peter," asked Quintus, "in the light of two things? First, his denial of Jesus prior to the crucifixion; and second, his vacillation with regard to the Gentiles, even after he baptized Cornelius?"

"He was frightened," said Longinus. "He had spent many months with Jesus and had heard him under many different sets of circumstances. He saw Jesus cure the sick and raise the dead. He had been with James and John when Jesus was transformed before his eyes into a figure of immense power. He believed that Jesus was truly the Son of God. And then he saw him chained and beaten. Peter wondered why Jesus allowed himself to be so treated. Why? Peter believed that with one blink of an eye, Jesus had the power to destroy everyone tormenting Him. So, for a moment Peter was confused. During that confusion he denied knowledge of Jesus three times. And then with one glance from Jesus, he realized how wrong his momentary weakness had been. He wept bitterly and never forgot his denials. That gave him the strength and resolution never to deny Jesus again. He never did!"

Quintus was silent for a lengthy period of time. He began to see into the character of Peter. Peter was a true leader, a man of immense and deep commitment to a cause giving him the strength of purpose to convince others of the rightness of that cause. And yet Peter was a man of deep feeling, one who could take upon himself the suffering of others, if only to relieve their distress; one who had the sensitivity to understand the basis of disagreement, and hope to overcome it without confrontation. It was that characteristic which led Peter to baptize Cornelius and embrace him as a Christian without insisting that he embrace all elements of the Jewish law. It was that same trait of character that led Peter to downplay this act knowing that time would help him overcome resistance to this apparent radical change in philosophy. He knew that Paul was strongly supportive of baptizing Gentiles. He also knew that many of the church of Jerusalem were opposed. He was certain that he would be able to change their opinion once he had an opportunity to discuss the matter in detail. Hence, Peter's strategy was to delay confrontation as long as possible until all of the leaders of the church at that time, essentially the leaders in Jerusalem, could meet together. That appeared to be Peter's strategy. It was simple. Delay confrontation until it would be possible for a factual presentation with the support of Paul. Now Quintus began to understand what Longinus and Cornelius had previously told him.

"I think I begin to see," said Quintus. "Peter baptized Cornelius after a vision virtually commanding him to meet and dine with Gentiles, following a vision by Cornelius commanding him to summon Peter. Taking both events into account, I must assume that the baptism of Cornelius or the conversion of a Gentile was mandated by God. Peter understood this, as anyone must when apprised of both visions and the ensuing baptism of Cornelius. Gentiles were to be admitted as Christians. That was a mandate. This mandate had to be understood, in order not to disrupt Christians who were not Gentiles. Peter's strategy was to accomplish this as soon as possible, with a minimum of disruption." Looking at Longinus, Quintus added, "Now I understand the importance of the Council of Jerusalem."

With a wry smile, Longinus continued, "Ever the zealot, and an impatient one at that, Paul could not understand what Peter was doing. He attacked Peter for his apparent vacillation. Peter must have chuckled. At the Council of Jerusalem I understand they spoke as one, and soon convinced James and the other elders of the rightness of baptizing Gentiles."

Then looking directly at Marcus, Quintus asked "Did James ever write a letter about this?"

"Yes and no," said Marcus. "James was a man of great virtue and piety. He was a very holy man. He wrote extolling the power of virtue in overcoming temptation to sin, and was strong in his exhortation about the power of prayer." Here Marcus paused. "But his support of the baptizing of Gentiles was in the form of private communications to disciples and to missionaries. There was no vacillation on his part in supporting the baptism of Gentiles and their non-adherence to the Judaic rule of circumcision."

"I see", said Quintus. "Please make sure the letter of James is included in the documents you leave with the guards for me."

After a brief pause, he continued.

"Jesus was right to appoint Peter as the head of his church. He was a very capable man. You should be appreciative not only of his ability to explain great truths in simple words, but more importantly his ability to strategize and overcome obstacles without the need for significant controversy."

Marcus added: "You will see the same characteristics in Paul, although different in context. Paul spoke more as a teacher than as a leader. But he certainly led in his teaching. I look forward to our discussion about Paul, Tribune."

"So why did Peter go to Rome?" Quintus asked again. Longinus and Marcus both laughed. "You certainly know how to persevere, Tribune," said Longinus. "Speaking for myself, I can only conjecture that he went to Rome because of the challenge. Christianity was moving forward, despite setbacks such as the murder of James when Herod had him thrown from a parapet to his death. Paul was doing well in his preaching and baptisms in many different cities. Many of the other apostles had gone to other lands. Andrew preached in Asia Minor and in Greece, where he is said to have been crucified. Thomas was most active in the area east of Syria. Tradition has him preaching as far east as India, where Marthoma Christians called him their founder. They claim that he died there when pierced through with the spears of four soldiers. Philip was said to have a powerful ministry in Carthage in North Africa and then in Asia Minor, where he converted the wife of a Roman proconsul. In retaliation the proconsul had Philip arrested and cruelly put to death."

Matthew preached in Persia and Ethiopia. It is possible that he was stabbed to death in Ethiopia. Bartholomew travelled extensively: to India with Thomas, to Armenia, and also to Ethiopia and Southern Arabia. There are various accounts of how he met his death as a martyr for following Jesus. James the son of Alpheus went to Syria and reports say that he was stoned and then clubbed to death."

Longinus added: "Simon the Zealot ministered in Persia where he was killed. Matthias was the apostle chosen to replace Judas. He was reported to have been in Syria with Andrew and condemned to death by burning.

John is still alive, living in Ephasus where he is taking care of Maryam, the mother of Jesus. He has built a home for her. He spends considerable time on a nearby island of Patmos."

"I can only assume that Peter became restless. Rome was the capital of the Roman Empire and could be looked upon as the capital of the world. His followers in Antioch and elsewhere were certainly able to continue without him. So Peter went to Rome!"

"Was there a church in Rome at the time?" asked Quintus.

"Yes, there was, Tribune," said Marcus. "The church in Rome was well founded with disciples that came from Jerusalem during the lifetime of Jesus. The Jewish population of Rome was greater than that of Jerusalem. There were many Jews in Rome who learned of the teachings of Jesus who learned from relatives or from direct contact since it is safe to assume that some Jews who heard Jesus in Judea subsequently moved to Rome. In any event, Christianity was quite prevalent and had many adherents in Rome amongst those who were Jews and those who were not. Many Gentiles flocked to baptism once the necessity of being a Jew was removed as a requirement prior to baptism as a Christian. While many were in the lower economic levels, including slaves, this was not necessarily true of all Christians. Neither Longinus nor I were slaves, although I was prior to being freed by you in Judea. Many former Legionaries and officers also became

Christians. One of the more interesting groups was the gladiators, who saw in Christianity some hope to emerge from their miserable lives. And so the Christian population grew, and grew, and grew."

They were interrupted by a guard who came to the door with an announcement for Quintus. "Tribune, Senator Antonio Caesar Servo has presented himself in the hope of being able to see you. When will you be available?"

Quintus was somewhat surprised but actually pleased. He had every intention in spending significant time with Servo. He well knew from the standard military maxim that 'there is no better time than the present.'

Turning to Longinus and Marcus, Quintus said "I wish to thank both of you for your time to day, and I expect that we will spend more time together shortly. I wish to examine in detail what you both know concerning Peter in Rome and the manner of his execution. "Turning to Marcus he said "I look forward to reviewing the documents which you will leave for me shortly. After examining them, I wish to discover more about Peter and his activities prior to his execution on orders from Emperor Nero. Then we will examine in detail the activities and writings of Paul."

"Tribune, may I make a suggestion?" asked Marcus.

"Of course. What is it?"

"May Luke join us for that meeting?"

"An excellent idea," concurred Quintus. Then he added. "Marcus, please remember to deliver the letter scrolls for me as soon as possible."

"I will go and retrieve them now and return with them" said Marcus.

Quintus smiled appreciatively and then added, his smile broadening. "Now I wish to thank you both for a very informative meeting. I bid you good day as I greet Senator Servo."

As Marcus and Longinus left, Quintus turned to the guard and said "Please return and escort Senator Servo to me."

As Longinus and Marcus left, Quintus continued to smile. He waited with expectation, for what he expected be to be an exhilarating confrontation with Senator Servo.

Chapter Five

The Political View

The guards escorted Senator Servo into the meeting room. He was all smiles, as he strode purposefully over to Quintus. He stopped before him and saluted. In his most unctuous manner he stated, "Tribune, or should I say Senator, thank you for meeting me here today. I know how busy you must be in this investigation you have been commanded to complete by the Emperor. While my visit may appear superfluous, I believe it will be important in your investigation. I hope to discuss with you matters of state. I felt it incumbent upon me to discuss these directly with you."

Quintus could almost hear the trumpets blaring in the background as he listened to Senator Servo pontificate. Exercising strong self-control and restraint, Quintus too smiled as he greeted Senator Servo.

"You are always most welcome to express your opinions or to bring me information touching on my investigation," said Quintus. Extending his hand in the direction of the chair beside him, Quintus said, "Please be seated, Senator." Quintus clapped his hands for the guard. When he appeared, Quintus commanded him to bring wine and fruit. As the steward left, Quintus turned, and sat facing Senator Sarto.

"Specifically Senator, what matters did you wish to discuss with me today?" asked Quintus.

Senator Sarto pursed his lips, and then very carefully, measuring each word, began.

"I wish to discuss with you the policy of the Emperor Nero to exterminate the Christians. As you may know, Tribune, I supported that effort. But my reasons were different from those of the Emperor." Here Senator Sarto paused for dramatic effect. He had expected that his words would come as a surprise to Quintus. He detected no reaction. Quintus remained passive, apparently dispassionate, although with a look only of rapt attention on his face. Senator Servo seemed annoyed at this passive response from Quintus. He paused, seemed to swallow, then his look hardened as he abruptly said, "My good friend, Senator Quintus, you are wasting your time on this study." Quintus looked up in surprise as Servo continued. "You should know in advance these Christians have to be exterminated from Rome by banishment or by execution. They are a monolithic force that the Emperor cannot continue to allow to exist. The Christians, as the Jews before them, do not assimilate with the rest of the population. As a matter of fact, their very philosophy is to choose between good and evil. As a result, they think for themselves."

Drawing himself up with a deep breath, he stood up, standing very erect, exuding an overbearing posture of command and arrogance, Senator Servo continued. "No group can be allowed to exist that would think for itself. Such a group poses a danger. They would challenge the power of the state, and especially that of the Senate and of the Emperor. They cannot be allowed to continue to exist!"

He stamped his foot to give emphasis to his words, gazed grimly to all about, then just as suddenly sat down.

Quintus was somewhat surprised. The direct frontal attack on his study, and upon the Christians, came as no surprise since he knew that Senator Servo was opposed to tolerance for the Christians.

Quintus mused, what could be his motive? Was it fear, envy, vengeance, or greed for any wealth that might accrue from confiscation? Perhaps all of these. Servo was an evil man, and very dangerous! And ruthless! He had been one of the strongest supporters of Emperor Nero to exterminate the Christians.

Yet Quintus was surprised at the openness of the attack. He decided to be equally frank, albeit courteous.

"My good Senator, your views are somewhat extreme. While my study is incomplete," said Quintus, "I have discovered enough to realize that the Christians are a people who live in peace and seek only to be allowed to live in peace. They are not a pressure group demanding anything from the state in the way of special privileges or special consideration. They go about their daily work and they go about their religious observances without being any problem whatsoever to the civil authority. I cannot understand why you would fear such people."

"Quintus you are a fool." The abruptness momentarily startled Quintus. He considered it to be a blunder on the part of Servo. He decided to let Servo continue venting. He remained passive as Servo continued.

"I am surprised that you have such an attitude, taking into account your success as a Tribune in the field and your position at the highest level in the Praetorian Guard. Surely you must realize that to maintain authority it is necessary to have the support of the citizenry at all levels. Certainly at the command level such as the Senate, such support is gathered either by favors which perpetuate the power of the Senate, by bribery or by fawning, flattery and the issuing of awards or honors. At the middle levels, the worker class, support is ensured by rigid enforcement of the law though force, or once again by a form of bribery through favors and reduced taxation. As for the slaves, their support is gathered through grain and games. What cannot be tolerated is a citizenry that would think for itself; that cannot be fooled; that will see through subterfuge and any diversion. As you know, it is common practice when there is corruption to divert attention by some foreign intrusion so that the corruption will not be discovered or, if discovered, will not be taken as a major element for concern because of other graver situations confronting the citizenry."

Senator Servo paused for breath, as he noticed that Quintus was shaking his head side to side, in strong disagreement to what he was saying. But Quintus allowed this evil man to continue, knowing that the best approach was to let him vent totally before he replied to any of the statements that were made. Quintus kept his own counsel and his temper.

Servo continued, "So you see, Senator, a continuation of power depends upon preventing any group of citizens either in power or not in power from coalescing to become a powerful force thinking for itself to operate contrary to what one wishes. That is why Nero sought to destroy and extinguish or eradicate all of the Christians. They were a power that could see through his manipulation, his corruption, his greed. The Christians were ones who understood how wrong Nero was in everything he did. Nero could fool those to whom he gave grain and for whom he held games, and he could fool all of those on whom he gave awards and fawned his benevolence in order to secure

105

their support for his continuing corruption and power. But Nero could not fool the Christians. They saw through him and understood totally how evil he was. He had to get rid of them. He had to exterminate them totally. And that is why he set about the arrest and execution of as many Christians as he could find. He was particularly strong in the arrest and execution of the leaders of the Christians. That is why he had their leader Peter and their most eloquent spokesman Paul executed for no reason other than his own whim."

Quintus winced. He could not continue to remain silent. He spoke up, his voice strong and resolute. "Senator Sarto, you are wrong if you have those views. You are condoning murder as a valid procedure to continue in power. Would you have me murdered if I disagreed with you and were a threat to your own power?"

Senator Sarto laughed. "Quintus you are being dramatic. Of course I wouldn't have you murdered. You are no threat. You understand what I'm trying to do and if you oppose me, I will oppose in return. Whichever one of us is the more powerful and the one with the greatest support will become the victor. That is how the game is played, as you know."

Quintus was close to absolute and uncontrollable anger. His voice took on great strength as he virtually shouted, "Senator Sarto this is not a game. This is a matter of life and death for many people, and a matter of life and death for the Empire as well. You know very well the Empire has become corrupt." Getting control of himself he continued. "What we have just experienced in the war of the Four Emperors is a perfect example. Various power groups were attempting to seize the office of the Emperor for their own purposes and not with regard to the continuation of the power of Rome, nor for the grandeur of

Rome, nor for the benefit of the majority of the people of Rome. It was for their own private gain, whether it be greed - a greed for wealth or a greed for power. This greed often results in the infliction of grievous harm upon many people who stand in the way of the onslaught towards grasping such power or wealth. And so it was with Nero. And so it was with Claudius who feared the power of the Jews as a monolithic group and banned them even though they had performed a noble service in advancing the commercial wealth of Rome."

"You will recall, Quintus," retorted Sarto, "that the history of Rome is replete with cases where murder was used as a vehicle for the enforcement of power within the state."

Quintus looked up in surprise. He wondered where Senator Sarto was going with the discussion. He began looking for the real agenda. Sarto continued.

"Quintus, if you will recall, Julius Caesar was murdered when he was about to be proclaimed Emperor by the Senate. He was succeeded, after a brutal series of conflicts, by Augustus who ruled justly and peacefully for many years. He in turn was succeeded by the Emperor Tiberius who in turn ruled with a firm hand and avoided many of the pitfalls of seeking support from different constituencies. He ruled by dividing and conquering. No force was strong enough to oppose him. It was only in his later years that he allowed himself to be murdered by Caligula. He feared assassination, as you know, and moved his palace to Capri in order to be free of the threat of assassination in Rome. How ironic that he was suffocated in his own bed by his anointed successor." Sarto paused for dramatic effect, and then continued.

"Caligula was a tyrant. He alienated so many that it was difficult for anyone to support him. His vanity, coupled with a brazen disregard for consequences, led him to demand that a life-size statue of himself be placed in the Temple of the Jews in Jerusalem. That act alone did much to initiate the ultimate revolt of the Jews. In Rome, his atrocious lifestyle alienated much of the Roman populace, most especially the power brokers. Finally, it was the Praetorian Guard that murdered him, or executed him as you may wish to say. The Praetorian Guard then selected his uncle, Claudius, to rule as Emperor. Claudius, supported by the Praetorian Guard, was careful not to alienate them in any way, using them as his power base. Upon the advice of many senators, including myself, he expelled the Jews, because he feared them as a solid power base which might rise in opposition to him. In addition, of course, he looked upon their wealth as a source of benefit to the treasury of Rome and to himself." Sarto beamed as he spoke of this confiscated wealth.

"It was upon the murder of Claudius by his wife, Agropina, assisted by Nero, which led to the ascension of Nero to the position of Emperor. Nero's behavior was reprehensible. He murdered many people for greed, sex, or whim, including his own mother, Agropina. The Praetorian Guard had enough. Once again it rose as the major force in opposition to the behavior of the Emperor. Nero was commanded to seek honor by committing suicide by his own hand, or he would be in turn executed just as Caligula had been. He weakened at the last moment, and ordered his own valet to stab him, which he did."

"The war of the four Emperors, as you refer to it, was unfortunate. This was a time when the Praetorian Guard itself was divided in terms of which of the Emperors it was to support. If you recall, Tribune, the Praetorian Guard even reorganized itself from nine legions to thirteen to give itself more power. When it was defeated, the

Praetorian Guard was reduced to the normal nine legions that we have today. Civil war reigned for a year after the death of Nero. A succession of short-lived Emperors reigned during the year of civil wars. Galba was murdered by Otho, who was defeated by Vitellius. Otho's supporters, looking for another candidate to support, settled on Vespasian. Vespasian seized power with the support of his Germanic legions. He then forced the Senate to confirm him as the Emperor. Vespasian was then wise enough to appoint his own son, Titus, as the Prefect of the Praetorian Guard. In that fashion he was assured of support from the single most powerful group within the Empire."

"And so, Tribune, you cannot deny that the office of Emperor has always been associated with a struggle for power, and with a division of any power that might rise up against it. I would vouchsafe to say that while Titus would support the Emperor, his younger brother Domitian might not. Perhaps it would be worthwhile for you to interview and investigate both Titus and his brother Domitian. You must realize, of course, that Domitian might very well become the Emperor if Titus is assassinated or killed in battle."

Throughout this diatribe, Quintus had remained silent. He carefully weighed his words. Looking directly at Senator Sarto he replied, has voice stern and strong."Senator, you know that I do not share your view. I am well aware of many of the political maneuvers that are necessary for the Emperor to exercise. The Praetorian Guard is charged with protecting the Emperor at all times. The Emperor represents the empire. The Praetorian Guard is charged with the responsibility of protecting the empire. When the Emperor goes mad, as in the cases of Caligula and Nero, it is the duty of the Praetorian Guard to intervene and to take action to protect the interests of the empire, the state, and the office of Emperor. That was done in the past, as you have referred to, and could conceivably be done in the future. Control of the Praetorian Guard would seem to be a major requirement for the Emperor to remain in power."

Quintus paused, well remembering the situation where Tiberius had executed the Prefect of the Praetorian Guard, Sejanus, who had been guilty of treason in his attempt to depose the emperor, and even to the point of murdering the heir apparent, the son of the Tiberius, Drosus.

Very carefully and calmly Quintus continued, "Senator Sarto, I know we disagree. Maybe you should take your argument to the Emperor and to the Senate. I would be interested in learning what the majority opinion of the Senate is on this point of the ability of the Emperor to rise above the law, and to be independent of the law, or whether even the Emperor is subject to the law of the land." Quintus smiled as he concluded this jab at Sarto's arguments.

Senator Sarto was taken aback. Collecting his thoughts and himself, he very carefully agreed to a meeting of the Senate and to the presentation of both their views.

The two Senators then proceeded to exchange courteous views on other matters of no consequence to the discussion until an appropriate time came for Senator Sarto to take his leave. As he did, looking directly at Quintus, he said, "I will speak to other senators and convene a meeting at which you will be asked to address them in opposition to the points that I will make. Until then, I bid you good day." With that Senator Sarto departed.

Quintus mused in deep thought. Affairs of state were very important since they affected not only the present but also the future. The Christians and the Jews were not the issue here, but rather the perpetuation and the power of Rome. Pax Romana was at stake. The Christians were merely pawns in the hands of evil power brokers like Senator Sarto. Vespasian had been wise in commissioning and mandating this investigation by Quintus. The study was becoming even more important, not with regard to the future of the Christians so much as with regard to the future of the Roman Empire. Pax Romana was certainly the issue here. Sarto sought power. He aimed to gain it but any means possible. The Christian issue was only a pawn in this endeavor. Quintus would have to be very careful preparing his presentation to the Emperor, and, by his direction, to the Senate. All the more reason to proceed expeditiously with his study, so that he would be in a better position to be very factual in his presentation. Tomorrow he would recall Marcus, and hopefully Luke would be able to attend, to go into detail with Peter's activities in Rome.

At that moment the guard entered with news that Marcus had returned. Quintus told the guard to escort him in.

In a moment Marcus entered carrying a satchel. Quintus brightened. The scrolls. He asked Marcus, "Are these the scrolls with the letters?"

"Yes, Tribune," said Marcus as he extended his satchel to Quintus. "They are all here for your examination and study. They are in Greek and Aramaic. "

As he accepted the satchel from Marcus, Quintus smiled and said, "Thank you, Marcus. If I have any difficulty with the texts, I will certainly ask for your help."

Looking quizzically at Marcus, Quintus added, "Marcus, you have participated in many of these events beginning with our study in Judea of the facts many years ago of the death and resurrection of Jesus. You also have met many of the apostles, and spent considerable time with

111

Peter in particular. You also have copious notes from our meeting in Judea, and I am sure for other encounters since, including our present investigations." As Quintus spoke, he noticed Marcus nodding in agreement with every point that he made.

After pausing for a moment, Quintus smiled and quietly issued his challenge to Marcus. "Why don't you write the history of these events? From everything that you have been told, from everything you have witnessed, why don't you write a history of Jesus, his teachings, and his resurrection? This document could serve Christian generations to come as a guide to the teachings of Jesus and the impact on the people of his time. Needless to say, the story of his miracles would be vital for the belief of Christians." Quintus gazed directly into Marcus's eyes. He noticed they were full with the understanding of the challenge Quintus was posing.

Without blinking, Marcus said, "Thank you, Quintus, for your faith in my ability to do this. I have thought about it for some time. I will do as you suggest. You are right, by the way. I have been making notes. I have even discussed this with Luke. I have encouraged him to create notes of matters that he knows about, especially with regard to Paul. In addition, I know that Luke has spent considerable time with Maryam discussing the birth and childhood of Jesus. These historic facts known to Luke will amplify and extend the scope, veracity, and ultimate acceptance of these memories as true history. The entire story of Jesus is fascinating beyond any words I can use. I am sure that he will go down in history as the most remarkable person who ever lived, even among those who did not believe he was divine."

Quintus was pleased. While he did not have the belief of a Christian, he had the greatest respect and admiration for Jesus and was personally convinced, as he had reported to the Emperor Tiberius, that Jesus was a deity.

Looking again directly at Marcus he said, "Good. I think the collaboration and independent work by Luke will certainly add significantly to the completeness of what you individually create. Most certainly the memories of both of you will complement what each of you writes. Please let me see your history as soon as you have it completed." After a short pause he added, "I bid you good day, Marcus."

When Marcus left, Quintus resumed his musing on how to handle Sarto. Various stratagems came immediately to mind. For now, however, Quintus decided to consult his good friend Maxim, Senator Acquinas, concerning his opinion of this startling challenge from Senator Servo. He knew that Maxim was in the city. He summoned the guard and commanded him to proceed with a small contingent of a Legionaries to the villa of Senator Acquinas. There he was to invite the Senator to accompany the guard back to the Castra Praetorian to meet with Quintus. If this was not possible, then he was to ask the Senator when this could be done. In any event, he was to report back to Quintus.

The guard departed as commanded. Quintus sat quietly and pondered very carefully the challenge presented to his investigation by Senator Sarto. Quintus was not personally concerned with this challenge to himself, but rather to the acceptance of the conclusions he expected to develop from his investigation. He had always expected that his conclusions had to be totally verifiable in order to satisfy the Emperor, but now he knew his conclusions had to be immune from false accusations and distortions. The issue now was power. He would have to thwart Servo. His report on the Christians would allow him to expose Servo

113

as the corrupt and evil power monger he was. He was sure the Emperor had already diagnosed the real issues here when he established the study and appointed Quintus to complete it. Quintus smiled to himself. The Emperor was certainly a wily fox.

Quintus remained deep in thought for some time. Once again he went over in his mind all the steps in his plan and how it was being followed. His own interviews were only part of the investigation. The findings of one hundred Legionnaires scouring Rome would certainly provide much factual evidence to support whatever conclusions and recommendations he developed.

He was in the midst of weighing what he had discovered up to now when the guard returned. Senator Acquinas was with him.

Quintus immediately arose, strode over to the Senator, and grasping him by the right arm, said, "Thank you for coming on such short notice, my good friend Maxim. We have an important development to discuss or I would not have been so abrupt in asking you to come and meet with me." Gesturing towards the chair, Quintus added, "Please be seated while I have the steward bring us some wine and fruit." With that, Quintus clapped for the Steward. When he appeared, Quintus commanded him to bring refreshments. Then he sat beside his good friend Senator Maxim Acquinas.

Quintus proceeded to inform Maxim of his meeting with Senator Sarto. Maxim was surprised, but not concerned. He was about to explain, when stewards appeared with the wine and fruit. As soon as they left, Maxim began to explain. With a twinkle in his eye, he began "The old reprobate hasn't learned his lesson yet. He is so proud of his opinion, that he telegraphs his punch well before he has fully developed his reasoning and support for his opinions. In this case, Quintus, he is vulnerable if he continues to bluntly espouse his opinions before the Emperor and the Senate."

Then he proceeded, in detail, to develop a full counterattack that Quintus could use before the Senate. As he outlined the full measure of the logic and facts, Quintus nodded in approval. The more Maxim talked the more Quintus smiled until it became a very broad grin.

Maxim had been quick to respond to the charge made by Sarto. "Quintus, as I told you, Sarto is evil. He always has a hidden agenda. He is taking this pose to suit his own purposes. We must show that he is wrong! When Christians think for themselves to establish the difference between right and wrong, they are concerned with the spiritual nature of an act. In other words, it was something good or bad that they were doing, and not whether it was good or bad for the governance of Rome, or how to achieve the office of Emperor. You must recall that many of the Emperors were murdered. This is certainly an act that is wrong. It does not require a Christian with a conscience to establish that such an act is a willful wrong. So Sarto is not really telling the truth when he says that Nero feared the Christians because they could think for themselves. Everybody can think for themselves. The difference is that Christians balance acts in terms of the nature of the act being good or bad; and whether or not this is something that would advance or retard their ability to achieve salvation for their souls."

"Maxim, you are sounding like a Christian," said Quintus.

"No," said Maxim. "I am not a Christian, but I do understand what Christianity is all about. I am not a Christian because I do not have the conviction or the faith. I can understand them, it is merely a case of not, perhaps at this time, accepting it. In any event, I do not agree with our good friend Sarto that the fact that Christians can judge between right and wrong makes them dangerous. On the other hand, I would think that the fact that they can judge right from wrong would make them better citizens and less dangerous than those who have no conscience, and commit wrong merely from the point of view of their own greed, or their own desire for power." With a twinkle in his eye, Acquinas added. "Stifle the challenge in his teeth and that will so embarrass him that he will lose his aplomb and openly expose himself for the evil person he is." Acquinas chuckled. "Hang him with his own rope!"

Quintus nodded. After a moment of deep thought he replied, "Maxim, my good friend, I think you have presented me with the answer to Sarto." Quintus raised his goblet and toasted his friend. "Well done, my friend, I totally agree with you and if you will allow me, I will use your approach as the cornerstone of my presentation to the Emperor."

"Of course, Quintus" that Maxim as he chuckled. "My, but won't Sarto be surprised!"

The two friends continued to discuss various matters, tasting wine, and eating fruit, as they reminisced. Finally Senator Maxim Acquinas rose to take his leave. Upon this, Quintus clapped his hands for the guard. When he appeared, Quintus commanded him to accompany Senator Acquinas, with a contingent of Legionaries, to his villa. Then he bade his good friend a pleasant evening, adding that he was looking forward to their next meeting together. With a bright smile, and a spritely step, Senator Acquinas left with the guard.

After a moment's hesitation, Quintus decided to seek a meeting as quickly as possible with the Physician, Luke. He summoned a guard and made his request known.

Then he paced the room in deep thought. He went over in his mind what he had heard from Senator Sarto and from Senator Acquinas. As he paced, he thought about his presentation to the Emperor and perhaps afterwards to the Senate if the Emperor so commanded. His recommendations and conclusions would terminate with a request to make his opinion known to the Senate, on the basis of his most recent discussion with Senator Sarto. That had been the major point made by Senator Acquinas, who had also laid out a strategy for his presentation to the Senate. Basically that strategy was to recall the history of Rome, and in particular, the presentations by the great orator Cicero in denouncing the Cataline conspiracy to overthrow the government of Rome. The point to be made was that threats to Rome always seem to come from power brokers and not from the people. Christians were not the threat; but Senator Sarto was!

Deep in thought, he suddenly became aware of the presence of a guard who stood waiting for Quintus to acknowledge him. Quintus stopped his pacing, and asked the guard to speak up.

The guard told him that the three Centurions had returned from their daily investigation in various parts of Rome, and as a group wished to speak with him. They had already interrogated the Legionaries and had the reports of the findings for the day.

Quintus nodded in agreement and asked the guard to bring in the three Centurions. Very shortly they appeared.

Each of them in turn greeted Quintus. Quintus then motioned for them to be seated while he seated himself, adjusting his chair so that he faced the three. Then he asked them to report in turn their findings.

It was Antinus who spoke first. Quintus immediately sensed that the other two Centurions looked upon him as the senior of them all. This was significant.

"Tribune, the Legionaries have continued their investigation in all parts of Rome. They have sought to establish the motivation of those who call themselves Christians, and whether or not this sect is a religious one, or a political movement. All the valid evidence secured up to now indicates that the Christians do follow a religious faith, and that it is based upon a single god who sent his son to earth in a form of a man, and that this man was Jesus of Nazareth, a carpenter. As you know, we executed him by crucifixion and legend as promulgated by the Christians is that he rose from the dead on the third day after his execution. That is the cornerstone of their belief. Without this resurrection of Jesus, the basis of Christianity is in doubt."

Quintus nodded. He was well aware of the mystique of the resurrection, having verified that, in his opinion with all of the evidence he had been able to secure, was a valid concept. He decided it best to tell the Centurions of his own opinion, which he was quite certain they were aware of. "You must know that I was commanded by the Emperor Tiberius to proceed to Judea to investigate all elements of that mystery, the mystery being the disappearance of the executed criminal's body from his tomb. I investigated all elements and found, by testimony and by observation, that Jesus was executed and did indeed die, that he was buried, and that even with guards at the tomb, he rose and walked out of his own burial place. I concluded that he had risen from the dead, and that he was some form of deity. I so reported to the Emperor Tiberius. So far as my investigation was concerned, the resurrection of the carpenter Jesus was a provable fact and not a mystery, and not an element to be believed as a matter of faith, but as a matter of fact."

After a short pause, Quintus recalled what Antinus had said about the acceptable evidence in their investigation of Christians. He abruptly asked Antinus, "What do you mean when you say 'valid evidence' with respect to the Christians following a religious faith?"

Antinus was quick to answer. "There have been some who came forth to denounce others as being Christians and fomenting a revolt. When we questioned such persons thoroughly, we discovered many inconsistencies. At other times, we noticed groups of roughly dressed and unkempt men threatening others whom we later discovered were Christians. When we appeared these groups disappeared. Statements made in such circumstances we took to be questionable."

With a smile, Antinus then added, "I then took a small contingent of Legionaries dressed in normal clothing of a poor quality. We visited inns and places frequented by brigands and other criminal elements. There we were often approached and asked if we would denounce Christians. We were offered gold to do so. At other places we heard others approached, and even agree. As a result, Tribune, we can tell you that there is a conspiracy to denounce the Christians as troublemakers. However, from our own direct observation and interviews, we could find no corroboration of these accusations. Hence we have categorized them as doubtful if not totally false."

"Well done, Antinus," said Quintus.

Antinus smiled in appreciation and then looked directly at Quintus as he asked, deferentially of course because of military rank, but also because of the respect the three Centurions had for Quintus. "Tribune, are you a Christian?"

Quintus very calmly, and firmly stated, "I am not a Christian. I respect their opinions, but I do not share them. My concern at this time is not to examine the belief of the Christians so much as to place that belief within the context of whether or not they are a potential disruptive force within the empire. I am concerned with Pax Romana and not with regard to any personal feelings I may have toward the belief of Christians."

"Thank you, Tribune," said Antinus. "That is exactly what we believed. We knew that you would never undertake this assignment if in any way you would be influenced by your subjective feelings. Your reputation is that of being a very cautious and deliberate pursuer of the truth. We are proud to be part of your investigation."

Quintus smiled in appreciation. Then he asked, "So what did you and your men find?"

"We found the Christians to be a religious sect, as was important in your investigation," said Antinus. "We also found that they were motivated towards helping each other and helping others, even if they were not Christians. This help was given without any reservation as to return. We have been informed and have actually seen, instances where Christians were feeding the poor, even curing them of their illness, aiding them, and asking how they could be of help. We have found that they also help each other in many different ways, rendering assistance even in the smallest detail, such as caring for children, caring for the aged, and their own sick. They share their food, and often meet for a ritual that they call the breaking of the bread. They pray very intently, and then one of them proceeds to break bread distributing it amongst them, telling them that it is the body of Jesus. He also distributes wine, telling them that it is the blood of Jesus. They proceed from this ritual seemingly strengthened in their faith and perseverance in their activities with their fellow Christians and with those who need their help, even, as we indicated, if they are not Christians."

"And are their numbers growing or falling?" asked Quintus.

"Their numbers are increasing from what we can determine," said Paulucci. "Quite often those who are cured of an illness, or those who are helped, ask to learn more about the people who are helping them. The Christians are not reticent or shy about proclaiming their belief. They are quite vocal in telling anyone who will listen, even a party of one, of the teachings of Jesus, of his life, his unjust execution, and his resurrection from the dead. They also comment extensively upon his ascension into heaven, and of the descent of the holy spirit upon them."

"And how did they become Christians?" asked Quintus.

"There is a small ritual by which they are baptized by one of their priests," said Paulucci.

"Who are the priests?" asked Quintus.

"They are selected from the Christians as devout men and instructed thoroughly in all elements of their belief. This includes writings that have come to them from Peter and from Paul and these are quoted extensively. They have among them now one called Clement who is also very eloquent in his description of Christianity and of the teachings of Jesus and of the interpretations of Peter and Paul and the other apostles, most notably James and John. These holy men who were selected then undergo a longer ritual and become priests. The leaders are called presbyters or bishops. It is these men who lay their hands upon those selected to become priests. They anoint them with oil on their forehead and pray over them. In that fashion, the bishops perpetuate the rituals that Christians follow through a line of succession by creating priests. Through a process of selection, certain priests are in turn anointed to become bishops. This cycle of selection and anointing then provides the continuity of a priesthood for the Christians."

"So the Christians do have a structure?" said Quintus.

"Yes they do. And so it has been established in all of our investigations in Rome," said Antinus.

"Antinus, you were present at the execution of Peter. Did you gather from anything that he said as he died concerning the Christians?" asked Quintus.

"Peter died calmly, accepting his execution, and as I told you, asking only that he be crucified upside down, since he was not worthy to die in the same fashion as Jesus. He did, in his writings, give some indication of the perpetuation of the structure of Christianity. We know the letter exists, and hopefully you will have an opportunity to read and study it in detail. The quotation that is often stated to us as attributed to Peter, was as follows, so far as I can remember it: 'But grow in grace and in the knowledge of our Lord and Savior Jesus Christ.'"

"Thank you Antinus. I will be studying all the letters in detail. The scribe Marcus, whom I believe you have come to know, has brought these to me and I am in the process of studying them. I have already come to some element of conclusion about these documents, but I would reserve that until some later time. It is my intention, when I have virtually completed my investigation, and come to some conclusion, to verify some of these facts with all of you before I present it to the Emperor."

"We look forward to that, "said Antinus. " In the meantime, Tribune, is there anything else that you wish to ask of us at this time?"

Turning to Julius, Quintus asked, "Centurion, you are the one who was with Paul when he was executed. Is there anything you wish to add now concerning his death that would be of substance to our investigation that you have not already told me?"

"You are correct. We have not previously had an opportunity to discuss in detail Paul's life and his execution under my direction," said Julius.

"I still remember his words to the extent 'I have competed well; I have finished the race; I have kept the faith.' [2 Timothy 4:7] Paul went to his death quietly, in acceptance of his martyrdom, well knowing that his death was a witness to his faith."

Quintus was silent for a moment. Having been reminded once more of the bravery of Peter, whom he had met, and who had made a tremendous impression upon him and the quiet acceptance of the brilliant Pharisee, philosopher and scribe Paul, who was the spokesman to a large extent of the belief of Christians. He was impressed by Paul, recalling their encounter in Tarsus. Peter and Paul were very brave men. They died for their faith, as witnesses and as examples of the strength of their belief. "Peter and Paul were brave men," said Quintus. "They were strong in their belief and true witnesses to the validity of what they espoused and what is now recognized as Christianity. They certainly started a major movement." Quintus paused for a moment and asked, "Have successors been appointed to Peter and Paul?"

It was Antinus, once again, who took the lead in answering. "It is commonly said among the Christians interviewed by us and by the Legionaries that the leader here in Rome at this time is a man called Linus. He is a Roman. It would appear that he has two major aides, one called Anacletus, and often Cletus, and the other is called

Clementus. Cletus is a Greek, and Clementus is a Jew. Clementus is also a scribe and seems to have assumed some of the writing skills of Paul. But in all of the interviews, it seems that no one at this time appears to be a successor to Paul in terms of his writing about the faith in ways that everyone understands, and which has rapidly become the cornerstone of the written documents of Christianity. On the other hand, Peter's mantle of leadership has certainly been assumed by Linus from everything that we have been able to establish."

Quintus mused for a short period of time over what he had heard. He had already decided that he wanted to speak to the successor leaders of Peter and Paul, but this information made it more specific. When he met with Marcus and hopefully with the physician Luke to detail the work of Paul, he would ask them to arrange a meeting with Linus. For now, he was satisfied this meeting with the three Centurions had been very informative. Standing up, as the three Centurions also stood, he said, "Thank you very much for meeting with me. Is there anything further that you wish to discuss or have we concluded this meeting?"

"Thank you, Tribune. We have told you everything that we feel is significant to be relayed at this time. We thank you for seeing us."

With that the three Centurions saluted and left.

As they did so, the guard entered the room and informed Quintus that Luke would present himself with Marcus the next morning. Quintus acknowledged the information, and then summoned his guard contingent to accompany him to his villa for the night.

Chapter Six

Peter in Rome

The morning was bright and sunny. Quintus felt elated. The study was well underway, and he had been briefed on many reports from the Legionaries concerning the Christians. All of the reports indicated that the Christians were all law-abiding citizens, were not interested in any revolt against the Emperor or against Rome. They were concerned with their daily affairs, whatever they might be, and were true to their religion. All of the Legionaries who scoured all of Rome, and the environs outside of Rome, came back with similar reports. The Christians would periodically meet and pray. They would break bread and drink wine together; and then they go their separate ways and continue with their daily lives. The frequency of the meetings depended upon the fervor of the particular Christian or group of Christians. Meetings were at least on the first day of each week, a day they termed 'the Lord's day.' The meetings were all in individual homes and were presided over by a presbyter, a man whom they refer to as their priest.

Despite the strenuous examination of each Legionary, and of the three Centurions in command,

Quintus was unable to discern any underlying threat to the Pax Romana.

With that he was pleased since it simplified dramatically the scope of his investigation.

There was still the question of why there existed in some quarters so much animosity towards the Christians. It is a normal trait of human nature to fear what one does not understand. This is especially true in the case of Christians whose behavior is still moral and upright. Such behavior is a challenge to the corruption and immorality so rampant in Rome today. In addition, there could be other motivation, leading to the animosity of persons such as Senator Sarto. He well understood the animosity of people such as Senator Sarto. Such men would use the Christians as scapegoats or as a lever toward satisfying their own ambitions by giving them the ability to seize power if the Emperor should falter in any way.

As Quintus came into the meeting room, he saw that Marcus was already there, attended by a stranger, a man he assumed to be Luke. He had the bearing of a learned man, standing upright and yet there was a certain quizzical expression on his face, almost a smile as if he saw the world through an optimistic view. If this was indeed Luke, then he was a man with a sense of humor and a balanced perspective. In any event, Quintus was looking forward to meeting with him, whoever he might be.

He approached Marcus and asked to be introduced to the other gentleman. Marcus introduced him as Luke, the Physician. Quintus was pleased.

"Thank you for coming to meet with me," said Quintus. "I am very interested in hearing your comments about your memories of Peter and I understand you travelled extensively as well with Paul."

126

"Yes," said Luke. "I was privileged to know both of these outstanding leaders. They are Saints now, reposing in the bosom of the Lord in heaven. Both were martyred on orders of the Emperor Nero."

"So I understand," said Quintus. "Before you tell me about Paul and the death of Peter, please tell me more about Peter's activities that you are aware of."

Turning to Marcus, Quintus added, "I am assuming that you have told Luke everything that you told me so that there will be no repetition in any of the areas that we have already examined. Is that so?"

"Yes," said Marcus. "I so informed Luke this morning. I further told him we would concentrate our discussion on the activities of Peter in Rome. Luke may well be aware of additional incidents concerning Peter."

Marcus paused and looking at Luke, then at Quintus, he added, "Is that satisfactory?"

"Yes," said Quintus. "Let us begin."

Looking at Luke, Quintus said, "I am very interested in your recollections and your conclusions concerning the growth of faith on the part of Peter. As I have been told, Peter was a very humble fisherman, gruff, but full of heart and love for his fellow man. He was a good family man, a good provider, and a good fisherman. It was Jesus who came along and challenged him to become a 'fisher of men' rather than a normal fisherman. But Peter wasn't solid in his faith as evidenced by his vacillation and outright denial of Jesus three times during the last night of his life prior to the crucifixion. This denial weighed heavily upon Peter throughout most of his life. I understand, leading not only to significant sorrow and remorse, but also strengthening of his faith in terms of never denying Jesus again." Quintus paused and looking at both men in turn added, "Is that true in your opinion?"

127

After both Marcus and Luke agreed that this was so, Quintus continued. "I have heard of two incidents concerning Peter that I would like you to verify. One concerned a fishing expedition when they were all in a boat and a vicious storm arose. Jesus was asleep. They were all afraid that the boat would be destroyed by the storm so they woke Jesus. Apparently he chided them as being men 'of little faith' and immediately subdued the storm. He told them to 'be not afraid' as he totally dispersed the storm and calm came back. This must have had a tremendous impact upon all of the Apostles, and especially upon Peter."

Quintus once again looked at both men, both of whom nodded. It was Luke who added, "Yes, that is the incident exactly as it was told to me by Peter, one of the Apostles of Jesus.

Quintus continued. "The second incident that I learned about concerned a day that they were fishing, when Jesus came to the shore and walked on the water towards the boat. Peter seeing this jumped out of the boat and started to walk across the water until he suddenly realized what he was doing, lost confidence and began to sink, when he cried out to Jesus to save him. Jesus reached out his hand and pulled Peter out of the water, and they both remained standing on the water." Quintus looked toward the two men once again. It was Marcus this time who spoke up "Yes, that too was told to us by Peter. Is that not right Luke?"

"Yes," said Luke. "Those two incidents also stand out in my mind, but they were reported directly by Peter who was there at the time." Looking appraisingly at Quintus, Luke continued. "Why is this important Tribune?"

"Because it indicates the growth in the faith of Peter. If you will recall my words, and your own recollections, Peter was a humble fisherman. He was not a

128

learned man. Suddenly he was plucked out of his environment and became not only a follower of Jesus, not only a 'fisher of men', but also the leader of the movement created by Jesus. Jesus appointed Peter the head of his church. Peter grew into that position over the months and years that he followed Jesus and learned from him. He also grew from the incidents in which he was personally deeply involved. His faith grew until it became as solid as the strongest iron and steel imaginable with the coming of the Holy Spirit at the Jewish feast of Pentecost after Jesus had ascended into heaven. I learned of this from all of our discussions. Do you agree with this?"

Both Luke and Marcus nodded as Quintus spoke. It was Luke who spoke up and said, "Yes, Tribune. I agree with you." Marcus then spoke up and added his agreement.

Quintus stopped and thought of his encounters with Peter so many years ago. He was impressed at that time with Peter's forthrightness, and his courage. To this day he still remembered Peter's words when he was detained, if not under arrest, by Quintus during his investigation of the missing body of Jesus. Peter at that time said "Are you going to free me or kill me?" Quintus had evaluated Peter as a great leader. Quintus had not known Peter in the early days of his becoming a disciple of Jesus, but he knew him after Jesus had been crucified and after the descent of the Holy Spirit, as Peter had told him. The Peter he knew was a man of great strength, great courage, and profound and extensive qualities of leadership. He had pondered for some time the growth of this faith, and the growth in Peter and he now began to appreciate more and more, as he considered all of the factors, how great a leader Peter was with the Christians in Rome.

"Leadership calls into account many different aspects. One of these is to mete justice to those who err. Do you know of any incident where Peter became stern with regard to his post as leader?"

It was Luke, who suddenly appeared very sad, and who then relayed an incident where it was Peter's task to enforce the rules of the organization. Apparently there was a couple, Ananias and Sapphira, who were Christians and members of a Christian group. They had pledged to give to the group for common use the proceeds of a property that they owned upon its sale. When indeed it was sold, they conspired secretly to retain a portion for themselves, giving to the commune only a portion of the proceeds. When Peter asked Ananias about it, Ananias claimed that he had turned over all of the proceeds. In that he lied. He immediately fell dead before Peter."

Luke paused, once again with a deepening sense of sadness on his face and in his voice added, "When Sapphira came in, she too relayed that they had contributed all of the proceeds, even though she knew that they had retained a portion. She was not aware that Ananias had died before Peter. At that moment she too died immediately."

Quintus was appalled. It seemed to him to be a matter not justifying execution. And yet as he thought more and more on the matter he began to realize that Ananias and Sapphira had probably executed themselves knowing their transgression, and fearing the wrath of the Lord and their refusal to continue with their promise. Quintus doubted that it was Peter who actually had called the wrath of the Lord upon the couple. He was certain that Peter was deeply saddened by his knowledge that they had done such an act. It seems strange that a couple would pledge and then only remit part of their pledge. He had to ponder this, he decided to ask Luke.

"Luke, do you think the punishment was justified in this case?"

130

Luke and Marcus looked at each other. It was certainly difficult to imagine that a man full of kindness and love like Peter would merit such dire punishment. The same was true even more so with Jesus. Jesus continually showed his love of everyone by curing the sick, and by forgiving their sins. How could Jesus, or Peter, condemn Ananias and Sapphira to death in this particular instance? But yet, justice is necessary. It must be assumed that this couple actually telegraphed what they had done in the manner in which they responded to Peter's questioning. Fear must have gripped their hearts. The fact that they were baptized Christians indicated they had a conscience. We can give them the benefit of the doubt by saying that they felt such deep sorrow at their sin that they died of fright on the spot."

The three remained silent. There was a great deal of emotion evident, even though little was said. There was certainly a question as to how this couple came to die. From his knowledge of the Christians, and his evaluation of Peter's character, he was leaning more and more to the belief that the couple in their fear and in their guilt brought death upon themselves. Hopefully they repented in their minds and hearts before they drew their last breath.

After a few moments of silence as they all considered this sad case of this couple who had the sincerity to become Christians and then rejected the basic tenets of that faith by conspiring to withhold part of their gift for their own personal use. How can one be a part-time Christian? Was this symptomatic of other Christians? Did people become Christians not because of belief but because of ambition, greed, or the quest for power? Quintus decided to pursue this point with both Luke and Marcus.

"Are there other instances that indicate there is blind ambition in the Christian community?"

Luke and Marcus remained silent until Luke spoke up. "The church is composed of people. All Christians are people. People have consciences which allow them to distinguish between what is right and what is wrong. But people have free will. They can choose to do wrong, even knowing that it is wrong. On the other hand, they may select a course of action which they believe is proper but it is still wrong. They can stifle their conscience in one way or another, but their conscience ultimately will speak up to indicate that what they are doing is wrong. "

"Can you give me an example of this?" asked Quintus.

Once again it was Luke who spoke up. "There were times in the discussions between Jesus and the Apostles that some of the Apostles would mention and ask about their position in heaven when Jesus would lead them into Paradise. At that time Jesus would always chide them, telling them to put away their ambition and to obey the word of God. He told them that all would be amply rewarded. As one who often used parables for his teachings, Jesus would then relay the parable of workers in the field who had been hired throughout the day, some even at the closing hour of the day. Yet all would receive the same payment for the labor. Some of the disciples may have considered that this was unfair, that those who had worked the entire day only to receive the same as those who had worked part of the day. But it was Jesus who said all would be rewarded equally."

Quintus was impressed. The more he heard of Jesus and the more he learned of his teachings, the more he began to understand the motivation of people to become Christians. When he coupled this with his knowledge that the resurrection of Jesus was real, that he had risen from the dead, there was the added realization that Jesus was a deity.

This must have some great impact upon people to realize that the teachings of Jesus came from the same source that created the universe and created everything all about us. That was the belief of Christians. Quintus was not ready to accept that belief, but he was beginning to understand it. From a completely logical point of view, what had to be considered was whether or not Jesus was a deity. The fact that he raised himself from the dead was a great indication that he was indeed a deity. The question was did he or did he not rise from the dead, or was his body stolen and a story circulated that he had risen from the dead. All of the evidence denied that story. All of the evidence that Quintus could find, and that all of the others who had searched could find, indicated the contrary. All of the evidence pointed to the fact that Jesus had died, that his body was placed in the tomb, that soldiers guarded the tomb, which soldiers claimed that the body had walked out of the tomb, and the tomb was found to be empty afterwards, with the burial cloths neatly folded. There was no question in the mind of Quintus that Jesus had risen from the dead.

That was the fundamental tenet of the belief of Christians. Quintus began to wonder if he were becoming a Christian. He unconsciously began to shake his head. He was not becoming a Christian, he was just understanding why both learned men and slaves were attracted to this set of beliefs. For him knowledge was not conviction or acceptance as it was for others. The basic message of Christianity concerned hope, hope in the future, hope in justice, hope in being recognized for what a person did. This would be a great asset to a slave under great duress, for a criminal about to be executed, for a rich man fearing what lay in the future after death. In all walks of life, no matter how affluent, no matter how powerful, no matter how poor or downtrodden it was vital for everyone to have hope. Christianity provided that hope.

Quintus decided to question Luke about this concept of hope. "Luke, I am beginning to appreciate the importance of hope as part of the nature of Christianity. Can you comment on this as to how it affects the behavior of Christians? In particular can you comment upon how this gives them courage to withstand adversity, and even death, perhaps even a very painful death?"

Luke pursed his lips, looked inquiringly at Marcus, looked down at the ground for a moment in deep thought, and then looked up, looking Quintus directly in the eye. He began, "Let me tell you the story of Peter when he became concerned about the persecution of Christians in Rome by Nero. He decided to leave Rome and return to Asia Minor to continue his pilgrimage and his missionary activity. He met Jesus on the Apian Way. He was startled. Jesus said only two words to him. They were 'quo vadis?' – 'where are you going?'" Luke paused. Then he continued, "Peter turned around and went back to Rome where he was executed."

"That was very brave of Peter and it certainly indicates hope in the future, but also faith in Jesus, and a love of his fellow man."

Quintus continued with his probe of ambition within the church. "How have you Christians established a succession within your leadership?"

It was Luke who answered, with Marcus looking on and nodding slightly as Luke proceeded to explain the succession principle followed by Christians.

"We recognize that we are all mortal. Hence our leadership will age and ultimately leave this earth for their eternal reward. What we have done is to establish leaders or presbyters, priests as we call them, who officiate at the breaking of bread. We have established those who are the creators or the anointers of priests, or bishops. Amongst all of these bishops we have established that one should be the first amongst equals. Peter was the first of these. Upon his death we elected Linus to be his successor."

"I would like to meet with Linus but for now tell me more how this arrangement of election began?" asked Quintus.

Luke continued. "The apostles initiated the principle of election when it became necessary upon the treachery and death of Judas to find a replacement to keep the original number up to twelve. While there were many more disciples than just the twelve, they were grouped into the original twelve, then an additional one hundred and twenty, then others. It was decided to hold an election and two candidates were put forward to replace Judas. One of these was Matthias, and the other was Joseph Barsabbas, with the Roman name Justus. Matthias was elected by drawing lots and took his place as one of the twelve. Thus began the concept of election to various levels of leadership within the community, which rapidly became known as the Christian community and then the Christian church."

"I see," said Quintus. "But surely, being human, there must be some jockeying for position. Granted that all are imbued with the concept and the faith and the belief in Christianity, and granted that all wish to follow in the footsteps of Jesus, would it not be natural that some would seek position more from a sense of pride or desire to have power over others?"

"Yes," said Marcus and Luke almost simultaneously. Marcus continued. "It is natural to assume that men being men, there will be some jockeying for position based upon ambition or other motivation. But you must remember, Tribune, which these men are still all

Christians. Hence, their jockeying would not be as vicious as you would assume in other pursuits."

"I disagree, Marcus," said Quintus. "While the initial motivation might be as Christians, I am certain that there are some who would harbor other reasons and other motivation and even use Christianity as an excuse and a lever in their attempt to seek power, position, wealth, or all of these. Surely you have seen examples of that motivation."

Both Luke and Marcus remained silent for a moment and then Luke spoke up. "Yes, I can think of a very good example. Let me tell you about Simon the Magician. He was called various things, Simon the Sorcerer, Simon the Magis, and on and on. He was a man well versed in the principles of magic and had for some period of time achieved notoriety and fame as a great conjurer and magician. He became acquainted with the teachings of Jesus and became a convert to Christianity and was baptized. Seeing the miracles that Peter was performing, and seeing the impact of this upon other Christians and upon the population at large, Simon approached Peter and asked if he could be given the power to heal and cure as Peter had. He offered money in return for information on how to acquire this power. Peter, of course, rejected this totally out of hand. Simon, on the other hand, was determined that he would acquire this power. He began to sense that he had acquired the power and went about conjuring his tricks and extended his reputation even more. He came to the extent of believing that he could fly. He called for a demonstration of this capability, and had a tower built. He climbed to the top of the tower and threw himself off, saying that he would fly to the ground. As you might imagine, he fell to the ground and was killed instantly. There were those then buried him expecting him to rise in again in three days since Simon said he would do that. He did not. There was great evidence that his body remained in its tomb well after the three days had expired. Hence this is an example of a man who became a Christian, said that he truly believed, when he had the ulterior motive or at least the motive of using the power of Christianity to advance his own reputation and his own wealth and influence."

Luke and Marcus both became very quiet as they considered over and over in their minds the motivations of others within the Christian community. Quintus too remained silent for a moment and then asked again, "Is that the only example? Can it not be said that there must be others who have the same motivation to use Christianity for their own ends, rather than for their strong belief in the principles of Christianity as enunciated by Jesus and as promulgated by Peter and understood by Paul? Can it be said that Christianity, like all associations, has those who are sincere in their belief, and those who would use this for their own purposes?"

It was Luke who spoke up. "That may be true in most associations but not totally so with regard to Christianity. It must be remembered that to become a Christian requires a dedication to the principles enunciated by Jesus of loving God above all else and loving our neighbor as ourselves. Our daily lives hopefully are motivated by the beatitudes. But those who become Christians are not forced into this belief. Becoming Christian is something that they do on their own. Unless they are born into the faith, it is something that they take on willingly by their own decision. Christians also believe that they have a conscience and can understand the difference between right and wrong. Hence Christians, by and large, can think for themselves to a very large extent making

137

decisions as to motivation and the actions of those around them. This would lead Christians to become more perceptive of some of the motivation factors, and it is unlikely that they would be fooled or hoodwinked for any length of time by those who become Christians merely as a means of securing power or wealth. That is not to say that is does not happen, but you can acquire power or wealth without becoming a Christian, so why incur the obligations of being a Christian if that is your only objective. I do not believe that there are any significant numbers of those within the population of those espousing Christian beliefs who really are not Christians in their hearts but only Christians in name."

"I see your point," said Quintus. "Perhaps that is the major reason that Christianity has prevailed in the midst of significant persecution. It takes a great deal of faith and perseverance to espouse and select death rather than to disavow belief in the principles enunciated by Jesus. In other words, only a Christian in fact and in heart would be willing to be executed for his belief. I can understand that. I will accept what you say, that Christians by and large are devout and sincere in their belief. I will also continue to believe that, here and there, there may be one who is not quite sincere. For example among the twelve, all selected by Jesus, there was one, Judas, who was treacherous and betrayed Jesus to the palace guards who arrested him."

Quintus then surprised Luke and Marcus. "I believe Peter was well aware of potential treachery and false prophets. I can find no letter writings from him on this. I found only one letter."

"That is because there is only one letter, Tribune," said Marcus. "I spent time with him on preparing an outline of a second letter, I brought this scroll with me and I believe there are sections in this representing the thoughts of Peter on the subject of treachery and false prophets. He removed a scroll from his satchel and handed it to Quintus.

Quintus took the scroll and started reading from it. He found pertinent sections. He read these aloud.

> But there were also false prophets among the people, just as there will be false teachers among you. They will secretly introduce destructive heresies, even denying the sovereign Lord who bought them—bringing swift destruction on themselves. Many will follow their depraved conduct and will bring the way of truth into disrepute. In their greed these teachers will exploit you with fabricated stories. Their condemnation has long been hanging over them, and their destruction has not been sleeping. [Marcus Scroll 2:1-3]

> These people are springs without water and mists driven by a storm. Blackest darkness is reserved for them. For they mouth empty, boastful words and, by appealing to the lustful desires of the flesh, they entice people who are just escaping from those who live in error. They promise them freedom, while they themselves are slaves of depravity—for "people are slaves to whatever has mastered them. [Marcus Scroll:17-19]

> It would have been better for them not to have known the way of righteousness, than to have known it and then to turn their backs on the sacred command that was passed on to them. Of them the proverbs are true: "A dog returns to its vomit, and, a sow that is washed returns to her wallowing in the mud.

139

[Marcus Scroll:21-22]

"Well chosen, Tribune." Luke said. "Peter certainly understood and was aware of false prophets."

"Amen" said Marcus.

After a short pause, with all three in deep thought, Quintus looked toward each in turn and asked, "What can you tell me about the execution of Peter?"

It was Luke who spoke up. "Peter was arrested on orders of Nero to arrest and execute all Christians. There was no trial. It was merely a case of if he was a Christian he was to be executed. Rather than being thrown to the lions, Peter was to be crucified. Many Christians were crucified and rows and rows of crucified Christians were seen in different parts of Rome at that time. When it came time for Peter to be crucified, he very calmly asked his executioners to crucify him upside down, since he was not worthy to be crucified in the same manner as Jesus. He was so crucified, with the cross upside down. "

"What happened afterwards?" asked Quintus.

"His body was placed in a tomb that became a site of deep reverence by the Christians. A church is planned over this site. This church is expected to be the central worship point for Christians."

Quintus nodded. "Thank you. Later today I would like one or both of you to take me to that site so that I can see for myself where Peter is buried and verify that he was indeed buried here in Rome." Both Luke and Marcus nodded and simultaneously agreed to this.

"Did Peter leave any final message?" asked Quintus.

Luke spoke up. "His whole life was a final message" he said. "But, Tribune, if you wish last statements, he is reputed to have stated when close to death his hope that we would 'grow in grace and in the knowledge of our Lord and savior Jesus Christ. To him be glory now and to the day of eternity. Amen.'"

Once again all three were silent. After a moment Quintus, looking at both in turn, asked of each, "How do you assess Peter as the leader?"

Each in turn spoke of the growth of Peter from being a humble illiterate and ignorant fisherman who stumbled and fumbled, but at all times showed his great heart and love not only of Jesus but of all men. They both spoke of his growth in faith to where he became a champion and a great leader. Yet it was Paul who became the catalyst of the growth of Christianity in various parts of the world with his letters and explanations of the teachings of Jesus. It was Peter and the other apostles who carried the message. It was Peter together with Paul and all of the apostles and followers who worked towards carrying the teachings of Jesus to others.

It was certainly Paul who created the structure of the philosophy and the theology of Christianity but it was Peter who became the leader and spokesman of Christianity as a force. It was Peter's leadership and his continuing fearlessness and courage in the face of opposition, persecution and even execution, that became the symbol of the strength and perseverance of Christianity. It was the example of Peter that strengthened the resolve of many who faced death rather than renounce their belief. Peter's eloquence and conviction converted thousands, but his leadership gave them the courage and the strength to persevere. Peter was a true human, stumbling at times, but always moving forward in sanctity and faith. It was Peter's faith that shone through repeatedly in all circumstances, clothing all of his actions with the aura of goodness and the aura of the teachings of Jesus. Peter was certainly a worthy successor to Jesus, and truly the appropriate selection to be the leader of the church after the departure of Jesus. It was Marcus who added that he had often been told by many that Jesus had looked upon Peter and said "Thou art Peter and upon this rock I will build my church." That vision of Jesus certainly was wise; and certainly was achieved by Peter in his actions prior to coming to Rome and most especially in Rome as he showed his leadership. The capstone of all of this is that he asked to be executed upside down deeming himself unworthy to be crucified in the same manner as Jesus.

"I agree with you, Marcus" said Quintus. "I met Peter over 30 years ago and was impressed then with the qualities of leadership he demonstrated. Everything that you have told me confirmed that my impression of him was correct. I wish he were still alive now so that I might be able to discuss with him the potential growth of Christianity and its relationship with Rome. In his absence, it is important that I recognize his legacy in evaluating that matter for myself from conversations with others. I must continue my study the scrolls of his writings and those of Paul and others that you left with me. "

Then he turned to Luke and said, "Please arrange for me to meet with Linus as soon as possible. In the meantime, I wish to reconvene this meeting at the sixth hour tomorrow when I wish to go into great detail on the contribution of Paul to Christianity."

With that, Quintus left the room.

Chapter Seven

Paul

When Quintus entered the council chamber of the Praetorian Guard, Luke and Marcus were already present. After the initial greeting, they all sat facing each other.

"I have read some of the letters of Paul which you gave me, Marcus" said Quintus. Looking at Luke, Quintus asked "Are you aware of these letters as well?"

Luke laughed. "I'm not just a chronicler. I was there when Paul wrote some of them." said Luke. "I even traveled with him."

"Then you would be an excellent person to tell me about Paul" said Quintus. "How would summarize his life?"

Again Luke laughed, a laugh of joy at the mere thought of telling Quintus about Paul. With a broad smile, Luke replied "Trying to tell you about Paul is like trying to empty the sea into a cup." Luke became very quiet as he pondered in his mind how to summarize Paul for Quintus. After a short period of quiet contemplation, Luke began.

"Paul was a very complex man. He was extremely clever, energetic beyond measure, absolutely clear in his logic, and determined in everything he set out to accomplish. He was a dedicated and ardent missionary, a brilliant teacher and one of the greatest scholars in history. I find it difficult to find words that adequately describe this complex yet single minded person. He was complex in terms of combining so many talents yet simple in the directness of his message and the example of his life. Perhaps it might be best for you to ask questions about Paul and then for me to answer. Is that satisfactory, Tribune?"

"Yes," said Quintus. With a broad smile he added, "With the knowledge you have, and with your ability as scribes, I would hope that both of you will produce your recollections of these events." Both men smiled, but remained silent. Quintus was now certain that this was certainly their intention. Turning to Luke, he continued. "Perhaps we can start by telling me who was Paul? I met him in Tarsus on my way to Judea on command by the Emperor of Tiberius to investigate the mysterious disappearances of the body of the crucified criminal Jesus of Nazareth. I found him, at that time, to be a zealous and dedicated foe of those who followed the teachings of Jesus. Tell me about him."

"Paul was born of a Jewish family," began Luke. "Paul was of the tribe of Benjamin, one of the twelve tribes of Israel, with King Saul one of his ancestors. His father was a Pharisee, one dedicated to the strict observance of the Jewish law, the Mitzvot, or the 613 Rules. At birth, Paul was given the Jewish name Saul. But since he was a Roman citizen, he was also given the Roman name Paulus. We now know him as Paul."

"At a very early age he showed great promise as a brilliant scholar. His first languages were Greek and Hebrew. His first education was in Greek literature and philosophy. Then he was sent to Jerusalem as a teenager to study under the great Rabbi Gamiliel. In Jerusalem he also learned Aramaic. He became a Rabbi and a Pharisee. Since his family was well versed in making mohair, the fabric used in tents, Paul learned the art of tent making. Upon completion of his studies, he returned to Tarsus where he had a leading role in the synagogue, and earned his living as a tent maker."

"It was there that I met him" said Quintus. "I was impressed by watching him in his role as a tent maker. He impressed me with his strength and dexterity. He also impressed me with his logic, which at that time, was directed towards destroying the sect of believers in the teachings of Jesus, whom he saw as a great threat to his Jewish faith. And yet," Quintus said, "I detected a certain sense of doubt when he spoke of Jesus. He found it difficult to condemn one who did so much good. Paul was well aware of all the good works and miracles of Jesus but he still saw the teachings of Jesus as a threat to the Judaic law. This puzzled him to some extent, but did not prevent him from attempting to root out and destroy this sect which was termed 'the Way'".

"Yes" said Luke. "Until his conversion on the road to Damascus, he was a dedicated and zealous persecutor of those who followed the teachings of Jesus. As a matter of fact, as you must be aware, Tribune, he was present at the stoning of Stephen. He did not take part in that stoning, but minded the cloaks of those who did. In his zealous pursuit and persecution of the followers of Jesus, he procured letters from the chief priests attesting to his role of rooting out these heretics. He was on his way to Damascus with these letters, intending to persecute the followers of Jesus in Damascus, when he was blinded by a vision, and heard the voice of Jesus calling him. Paul fell to the ground with the voice of Jesus chiding him for his persecution. He proceeded to Damascus, blinded, until miraculously cured of this affliction."

"What happened then?" asked Quintus.

Luke was very thoughtful momentarily before proceeding. "He went to Arabia for three years. From Arabia he returned to Damascus and began to preach in the street and synagogue. He so incensed his listener's, that he was about to be arrested when he was let down in a basket through a window in the wall and so escaped. Then he went to Jerusalem and spent fifteen days with Peter before returning to Tarsus, where he remained for some ten years, plying his trade as a tent maker."

"What was he doing in Arabia and in Tarsus during those years?" asked Quintus.

"Recall your reading of his letters, Tribune," said Luke, with Marcus nodding in agreement. Then Luke went on, "He was obviously preparing for his life of travel and missionary effort both in the sermons he presented and various cities, as well as his letters which you have read."

"Yes," said Quintus. "These cover the quiet years of contemplation before starting his missionary travels. I have found reference to this in his letter to the Galatians."

I want you to know, brothers and sisters, that the gospel I preached is not of human origin. I did not receive it from any man, nor was I taught it; rather, I received it by revelation from Jesus Christ.

For you have heard of my previous way of life in Judaism, how intensely I persecuted the church of God and tried to destroy it. I was advancing in Judaism beyond many of my own age among my people and was extremely zealous for the traditions of my fathers. But when God, who set me apart from my mother's womb and called me by his grace, was pleased to reveal his Son in me so that I might preach him among the Gentiles, my immediate response was not to consult any human being. I did not go up to Jerusalem to see those who were apostles before I was, but I went into Arabia. Later I returned to Damascus.

Then after three years, I went up to Jerusalem to get acquainted with Cephas (Peter) and stayed with him fifteen days. I saw none of the other apostles—only James, the Lord's brother. I assure you before God that what I am writing you is no lie.
Then I went to Syria and Cilicia. I was personally unknown to the churches of Judea that are in Christ. They only heard the report: "The man who formerly persecuted us is now preaching the faith he once tried to destroy." And they praised God because of me. [Gal 1:11-24]

"I also saw reference to his difficulty in Damascus in his second letter to the Corinthians."

In Damascus the governor under King Aretas had the city of the Damascenes guarded in order to arrest me. But I was lowered in a basket from a window in the wall and slipped through his hands. [2 Cor 11:32-33]

Both Luke and Marcus were agreeably surprised at the depth of understanding that Quintus appeared to have derived from his examination of the letters of Paul. These comments showed that he had gone far beyond a cursory examination of the letters.

"I would appreciate learning about Paul's travels and missionary activities. As I understand from his letters, he made numerous trips to various parts of the world, and established churches in various cities. He continued his teaching to the followers of Jesus in those cities with his letters." Quintus paused for a moment as if collecting his thoughts and then proceeded, "Paul seems to have been everywhere. His letters also comment upon everything - the love of husband for wife and wife for husband, behavior towards children, the relationship of a loving God with his creatures, the importance of the message of Jesus, the sacrifice of Jesus for the sins of mankind, and the fundamental foundation of the resurrection of Jesus in the belief of those we know as Christians."

Quintus paused. "I see all these matters addressed in his various letters." He sorted through the scrolls and continued. "Love is a recurrent theme in those letters. I found especially profound:

"If I speak in the tongues of men or of angels, but do not have love, I am only a resounding gong or a clanging cymbal. If I have the gift of prophecy and can fathom all mysteries and all knowledge, and if I have a faith that can move mountains, but do not have love, I am nothing. If I give all I possess to the poor and give over my body to hardship that I may boast, but do not have love, I gain nothing.

Love is patient, love is kind. It does not envy, it does not boast, it is not proud. It does not dishonor others, it is not self-seeking, it is not easily angered, it keeps no record of wrongs. Love does not delight in evil but rejoices with the truth. It always protects, always trusts, always hopes, always perseveres.

Love never fails. But where there are prophecies, they will cease; where there are tongues, they will be stilled; where there is knowledge, it will pass away. For we know in part and we prophesy in part, but when completeness comes, what is in part disappears. When I was a child, I talked like a child, I thought like a child, I reasoned like a child. When I became a man, I put the ways of childhood behind me. For now we see only a reflection as in a mirror; then we shall see face to face. Now I know in part; then I shall know fully, even as I am fully known.
And now these three remain: faith, hope and love. But the greatest of these is love. [1 Cor 13:1-13]

Furrowing his brow in thought, Quintus added. "Paul continued his treatment of love in other letters to the Romans, Ephesians, and Colossians."

Let no debt remain outstanding, except the continuing debt to love one another, for whoever loves others has fulfilled the law. The commandments, "You shall not commit adultery," "You shall not murder," "You shall not steal," "You shall not covet," and whatever other command there may be, are summed up in this one command: "Love your neighbor as yourself." Love does no harm to a neighbor. Therefore love is the fulfillment of the law. [Rom 13:8-10]

Therefore, since we have been justified through faith, we have peace with God through our Lord Jesus Christ, through whom we have gained access by faith into this grace in which we now stand. And we boast in the hope of the glory of God. Not only so, but we also glory in our sufferings, because we know that suffering produces perseverance; perseverance, character; and character, hope. And hope does not put us to shame, because God's love has been poured out into our hearts through the Holy Spirit, who has been given to us.

You see, at just the right time, when we were still powerless, Christ died for the ungodly. Very rarely will anyone die for a righteous person, though for a good person someone might possibly dare to die. But God demonstrates his own love for us in this: While we were still sinners, Christ died for us.

Since we have now been justified by his blood, how much more shall we be saved from God's wrath through him! For if, while we were God's enemies, we were reconciled to him through the death of his Son, how much more, having been reconciled, shall we be saved through his life! Not only is this so, but we also boast in God through our Lord Jesus Christ, through whom we have now received reconciliation.   [Rom 5:1-11]

Submit to one another out of reverence for Christ. Wives, submit yourselves to your own husbands as you do to the Lord. For the husband is the head of the wife as Christ is the head of the church, his body, of which he is the Savior. Now as the church submits to Christ, so also wives should submit to their husbands in everything.

Husbands, love your wives, just as Christ loved the church and gave himself up for her to make her holy, cleansing her by the washing with water through the word, and to present her to himself as a radiant church, without stain or wrinkle or any other blemish, but holy and blameless. In this same way, husbands ought to love their wives as their own bodies. He who loves his wife loves himself. After all, no one ever hated their own body, but they feed and care for their body, just as Christ does the church—for we are members of his body. "For this reason a man will leave his father and mother and be united to his wife, and the two will become one flesh." This is a profound mystery—but I am talking about Christ and the church. [Ephesians 5:21-32]

Wives, submit yourselves to your husbands, as is fitting in the Lord. Husbands, love your wives and do not be harsh with them. Children, obey your parents in everything, for this pleases the Lord. Fathers, do not embitter your children, or they will become discouraged. [Colossians 3:18-21]

He even wrote of activity in the daily lives of Christians. Two particularly apt segments are in his letter to the Ephesians.

Therefore each of you must put off falsehood and speak truthfully to your neighbor, for we are all members of one body. In your anger do not sin. Do not let the sun go down while you are still angry, and do not give the devil a foothold. Anyone who has been stealing must steal no longer, but must work, doing something useful with their own hands, that they may have something to share with those in need. Do not let any unwholesome talk come out of your mouths, but only what is helpful for building others up according to their needs, that it may benefit those who listen. And do not grieve the Holy Spirit of God, with whom you were sealed for the day of redemption. Get rid of all bitterness, rage and anger, brawling and slander, along with every form of malice. Be kind and compassionate to one another, forgiving each other, just as in Christ God forgave you. [Ephesians 4:25-32]

Follow God's example, therefore, as dearly loved children and walk in the way of love, just as Christ loved us and gave himself up for us as a fragrant offering and sacrifice to God.
But among you there must not be even a hint of sexual immorality, or of any kind of impurity, or of greed, because these are improper for God's holy people. Nor should there be obscenity, foolish talk or coarse joking, which are out of place, but rather thanksgiving. For of this you can be sure: No immoral, impure or greedy person—such a person is an idolater—has any inheritance in the kingdom of Christ and of God. [Ephesians 5:1-5]

152

"He rebuked pride in his first letter to Timothy."

O Timothy, guard what has been entrusted to you, avoiding   worldly *and* empty   chatter *and* the opposing arguments of what is falsely called knowledge, which   some   have   professed   and thus gone astray [a]from the faith. Grace be with you.
[1 Tim 6:20-21]

"He repeatedly wrote about prayer, and its importance and value. I found his words in his second letter to the Thessalonians symptomatic of his writings."

As for other matters, brothers and sisters, pray for us that the message of the Lord may spread rapidly and be honored, just as it was with you. And pray that we may be delivered from wicked and evil people, for not everyone has faith. But the Lord is faithful, and he will strengthen you and protect you from the evil one. We have confidence in the Lord that you are doing and will continue to do the things we command. May the Lord direct your hearts into God's love and Christ's perseverance.
[2 Thessalonians 3:1-5]

"But most of all, I found the writings of Paul directed universally to all. He made no distinctions of race or economic status. His brilliant letter to the Romans directed his message, and indeed all his writings and sermons, even if specific to status in life, to everyone."

For I am not ashamed of the gospel, because it is the power of God that brings salvation to everyone who believes: first to the Jew, then to the Gentile. For in the gospel the righteousness of God is revealed—a righteousness that is by faith from first to last, just as it is written: "The righteous will live by faith." [Romans 1:16-17]

"He also issued repeated warnings about false doctrines."

As I urged you when I went into Macedonia, stay there in Ephesus so that you may command certain people not to teach false doctrines any longer or to devote themselves to myths and endless genealogies. Such things promote controversial speculations rather than advancing God's work—which is by faith. The goal of this command is love, which comes from a pure heart and a good conscience and a sincere faith. Some have departed from these and have turned to meaningless talk. They want to be teachers of the law, but they do not know what they are talking about or what they so confidently affirm. We know that the law is good if one uses it properly. We also know that the law is made not for the righteous but for lawbreakers and rebels, the ungodly and sinful, the unholy and irreligious, for those who kill their fathers or mothers, for murderers, for the sexually immoral, for those practicing homosexuality, for slave traders and liars and perjurers—and for whatever else is contrary to the sound doctrine that conforms to the gospel concerning the glory of the blessed God, which he entrusted to me. [1 Timothy 1:3-11]

"From my perspective, I found his reference to the relationship with governing bodies particularly apt."

Let everyone be subject to the governing authorities, for there is no authority except that which God has established. The authorities that exist have been established by God. Consequently, whoever rebels against the authority is rebelling against what God has instituted, and those who do so will bring judgment on themselves. For rulers hold no terror for those who do right, but for those who do wrong. Do you want to be free from fear of the one in authority? Then do what is right and you will be commended. For the one in authority is God's servant for your good. But if you do wrong, be afraid, for rulers do not bear the sword for no reason. They are God's servants, agents of wrath to bring punishment on the wrongdoer. Therefore, it is necessary to submit to the authorities, not only because of possible punishment but also as a matter of conscience. This is also why you pay taxes, for the authorities are God's servants, who give their full time to governing. Give to everyone what you owe them: If you owe taxes, pay taxes; if revenue, then revenue; if respect, then respect; if honor, then honor. [Romans 13:1-7]

Quintus paused. Looking at Luke and Marcus, he said. "I hope I have not bored you with these recitations of some of Paul's writings. Everything he wrote was powerful and important. What I quoted are only a small segment of the thought of this great man. I was impressed when I read in his letters, impressed when I met him, and impressed by what you are telling me of his life. Please continue Luke."

Luke and Marcus smiled in appreciation of these remarks by Quintus. "Thank you, Tribune," said Luke, "we are never bored with any readings from Paul's letters." After a short pause, he continued with his recitation of Paul's missionary activities.

"Barnabas traveled to Tarsus in order to have Paul establish a program utilizing his talents in missionary efforts. With Barnabas they proceed to Antioch. This was the start to Paul's missionary activity that would continue for some twenty years until he was executed by beheading upon the order of The Emperor Nero during his last days as Emperor of Rome."

Luke thought for a moment and continued "Paul embarked on three separate voyages, fraught with peril and difficulty. As he described it in his second letter to the Corinthians:

Are they servants of Christ? (I am out of my mind to talk like this.) I am more. I have worked much harder, been in prison more frequently, been flogged more severely, and been exposed to death again and again. Five times I received from the Jews the forty lashes minus one. Three times I was beaten with rods, once I was pelted with stones, three times I was shipwrecked, I spent a night and a day in the open sea, I have been constantly on the move. I have been in danger from rivers, in danger from bandits, in danger from my fellow Jews, in danger from Gentiles; in danger in the city, in danger in the country, in danger at sea; and in danger from false believers. I have labored and toiled and have often gone without sleep; I have

known hunger and thirst and have often gone without food; I have been cold and naked. Besides everything else, I face daily the pressure of my concern for all the churches. Who is weak, and I do not feel weak? Who is led into sin, and I do not inwardly burn? If I must boast, I will boast of the things that show my weakness. The God and Father of the Lord Jesus, who is to be praised forever, knows that I am not lying.
[2 Corinthians 11:23-31]

Luke continued, "Paul told it as it was. His travels are documented in his various letters. The quotation from his second letter to the Corinthians summarized some of the travails of his travels and missionary activities."

Luke went onto to discuss Paul's travels from Antioch to Seleucia, from Seleucia to Cyprus, and from Cyprus to Salamis, to Paphos, and then to Perga of Pamphylia, then back to Antioch, then to Iconium. And finally to Lystra and Derbe. In Lystra Paul and Barnabas were mistaken for gods, and then stoned. Paul was left for dead but recovered consciousness, and then departed for Derbe. Continuing his journeys and missionary effort, preaching all the way, and writing his letters, Paul returned to Antioch and then from there to Jerusalem for a council meeting with the apostles, including Peter, on the subject of Gentiles as followers of Jesus. At this point, Luke interjected that "more will be said concerning Paul and his mission to the Gentiles after I have completed my outline of his travels."

Looking directly at Quintus, Luke added with a smile, "You see, Tribune, as you suggested to Marcus, I am working on a history of Jesus and his apostles. I fully intend to document the life of Jesus in one volume and the life of Paul and that of the other apostles in another."

After a short pause Luke continued his narration of Paul's travels. Following the Council in Jerusalem, Paul set sail to Neapolis, and to Philippi. There Paul, who had been accompanied by Silas, was in prison for casting out a demon from a slave girl. He was freed miraculous from the prison as the doors swung open, and Paul departed. Paul journeyed from Philippi to Anphipolis, then to Thessaolonica. In this later city after preaching about Christ he was forced to flee. Paul then returned to Antioch and continued through Croatia on his way to Ephesus, where he stayed for some three years. It was there that he wrote his first letter to the Corinthians.

Paul then traveled extensively through Macedonia and Greece arriving ultimately at Caesarea where he was arrested for causing a riot with his preaching. There were various plots associated with the assassination of Paul as he remained in prison for some two years. Claiming Roman citizenship, Paul was freed from possible execution in Caesarea, and dispatched to Rome. On the way he was shipwrecked but finally arrived in Rome a year later. There as a Roman citizen, he was placed under house arrest for some two years before being released. He then spent four years in missionary work in Rome and elsewhere, most especially in Gaul and Britannica. During the persecution initiated by Emperor Nero, he was arrested and once again imprisoned. While there he wrote his second letter to Timothy in which he gave his final summary of his life, a prayer of hope.

> For I am already being poured out like a drink offering, and the time for my departure is near. I have fought the good fight, I have finished the

race, I have kept the faith. Now there is in store for me the crown of righteousness, which the Lord, the righteous Judge, will award to me on that day—and not only to me, but also to all who have longed for his appearing.
[2 Timothy 4:6-8]

The three became silent as they all considered the needless execution of Paul. Quintus broke the silence. "The Centurion Julius was in command of the unit that executed Paul. I have asked him to come and report on Paul's last days. I expect him shortly."

Luke acknowledged this and continued. "Tribune, as you can see, Paul initiated many churches in various parts of the world prior to arriving in Rome. Even then, freed from prison, he continued on with his travels and missionary efforts.

"How do you assess the results of Paul's travels?" asked Quintus.

Luke hesitated for a moment and looked up at Marcus for any cooperation, before continuing. "Paul had a magnetic affect on people. He either influenced them to the point of conversion, or created tremendous consternation. His Jewish brothers in particular wanted to become incensed with Paul. It must be remembered that Paul was a Rabbi, a Pharisee, one well versed in all aspects of the Judaic religion and law. He was well aware of the 613 Rules of the Mitzvot. Hence, when he spoke before the Jews, preaching on the nature of God, he would meet with acceptance. But when he preached on the divinity of Jesus, his resurrection from the dead, and his message of love, quite often it met with hostility and disbelief. Paul reiterated over and over that without the resurrection, the set of religious beliefs commonly referred to as Christianity would have no basis in fact. Without the resurrection, Christianity was a fraud. Hence, the resurrection was the cornerstone upon which the edifice of Christianity was built. Christians accepted this. The opponents of Christianity did not. If they felt that this was critique of their own beliefs, they might even become violent in their rejection of the Christians. Hence mutual respect and understanding was vital even if beliefs were different. Often those differences of belief were based on terminology or customary practices."

"Paul sought to create in his letters a guide to life as a follower of Christ that would replace the Mitzvot for Christians. He concentrated on belief in the one true God, and the love that linked that God and the people. Paul considered all aspects of human life in that relationship. His letter to the Romans, as we have previously quoted, spelled out many of these practices, including the relationship with governance."

"As you already know Paul was also a leading supporter of the move to expand the invitation to baptism to Gentiles, without the need for Gentiles to be circumcised. He saw circumcision as an unnecessary requirement for religious observances. Peter too supported this."

"Yes" said Quintus. "We have already considered that aspect of Peter's growth and confirmation of the role of Gentiles within the Christian community. We are also well aware of Paul's support for this, leading to the conclusions of the Council in Jerusalem where this principle was adopted by the church fathers."

"The opening of Christianity to Gentiles without the need for circumcision vastly expanded the numbers of those baptized and vastly spread the reach of Christianity throughout the world," stated Luke, himself a Gentile.

"What were the main principles in Paul's preaching and writing?" asked Quintus.

Luke remained silent for some time, obviously in deep thought. Then he looked directly at Quintus and began, "Paul did have a basic message, and that was that we are all redeemed and saved through the sacrifice of Jesus. The resurrection of Jesus proved his divinity, and showed beyond all doubt that God loved mankind, and wanted only love in return. Paul's message was that love was confirmed by repentance and gratitude for the munificence of God. His message, of course, had many branches. In a sense, then, in Paul's philosophy Christianity can be thought of as a large tree. The roots of this tree are the mutual love of God and mankind for each other. The trunk of the tree is truth and forgiveness and repentance from sin. All the branches of the tree were like arms raised in prayer to the one God - prayers of praise, petition, contrition, and thanksgiving. And the leaves were the acts of good will of Christians. The sap that made the whole tree grow and carrying the nutrients to the farthest corner of the tree was the Holy Spirit. The bark of the tree was Jesus."

"How apt," said Quintus. "How truly descriptive. In my own reading of the letters, I was impressed by the number of times the word God appeared throughout the writings of Paul. Over and over Paul insisted that God is one. How different from my religion where we have many gods, some of whom we must appease, some of whom we must thank, some of whom we fear, some of whom we can assume will help us. It was impressive to me that the Christianity of Paul, and, as I have come to learn, that of Christians, is built upon one God. Is that not so, Luke?"

Luke answered immediately. "Yes it is so, Tribune. But we do not deny that evil exists. Men have free wills, and can exercise it in any direction they so choose. They may choose evil, or they may choose good. If they choose evil, they can also repent and beg forgiveness. On the other hand, they may not repent, and continue in the path of evil. Evil, then, is real and influential, as Paul wrote in his letter to the Ephesians. But it is fleeting, and in the end will not triumph. As Paul said in his letter to the Romans, "The God of peace will soon crush Satan under your feet".

"But it is in Jesus that Paul places the emphasis in his writings, as he did in his teaching. For Paul, as for all Christians, Jesus was the embodiment of the fulfillment of the covenant of the past. He was the Messiah, who would lead all people to the promise land, the salvation of their souls and internal rest in heaven."

"Was Paul's life successful?" asked Quintus.

Both Luke and Marcus appeared stunned. Luke became speechless. "But I must ask the question, was this all worthwhile? What did he accomplish?"

After a long silence, Luke attempted to answer Quintus. "Paul was a leader who pointed the way for Christians to follow. He pointed the way with logic, with examples, and with his life. As he himself summarized his whole life, he 'kept the faith' and let his own life serve as a living testimony of the truth of Christianity. Jesus called him. Paul answered. It is as simple as that. In my mind, and I believe in that of Marcus, Paul was an outstanding success. I hope that you too will come to that conclusion."

Looking directly at Quintus Luke continued "Well, Tribune, yes or no?" Quintus laughed. A smile suffused his face. "Luke, my friend, and you have become my friend over this short period of time, I baited you to see your reaction." Quintus paused and a very serious look came across his face, before he continued. "I am sure the history will assess Paul as one of the great figures of all time. Christianity has been well served by two remarkable men, Peter and Paul. They were different, but both great leaders. They led differently. Peter lead by an appeal to the heart, to the emotions, and was followed because he could say 'I am human. I'm a sinner. I ask forgiveness. It was given to me. The same can be true for you. Come follow me to Jesus."

"Paul, on the other hand, with great talent and emotion, appealed to the intellect, he logically battered away at your mind, explaining everything, justifying everything, proving everything, and then saying 'I showed you the way, now take it. Follow me.'"

"A very clear distinction between these two," said Quintus.

At that moment the guard entered with the Centurion Julius. The guard departed, and Julius was invited to join the group.

"Julius, you were present at the execution of Paul. As matter of fact you commanded the squad who beheaded him. Can you tell us what happened that day?" said Quintus.

"As you know, Tribune, I was commanded to execute Paul on orders of the Emperor Nero. He was executing Christians indiscriminately, but I believe he executed Paul from a point a view that he was a major leader in this movement. I know that Peter was executed shortly before hand. Peter was crucified, upside at his own request, but Paul, as a Roman citizen, was beheaded upon orders from the Emperor."

"And what was his demeanor as he was executed?" asked Quintus.

Julius was immediate in his reply. "Tribune, he was remarkable. He was calm, he prayed and asked forgiveness of his God for all of us and even The Emperor Nero. There was a twinkle in his eye which I remember to this day, as he said before he placed his head on the block, 'Now I meet Jesus again.' I can almost remember his tone of voice as he said it.

"To this day I can remember this as not so much an execution, an end, but a beginning. I had a sense that this was totally different from other executions I commanded or attended. He was a remarkable man."

"Centurion, are you a Christian?" asks Quintus.

"No" said Julius. "I have considered becoming a Christian, very heavily from observing Paul during the execution. I also knew him to some extent during his final imprisonment when it was also our duty to guard him. We found him to be a model, never complaining, and always gracious to all of us. To answer your question another way, Tribune, I am impressed with Christianity, and I have seen it, and I have been involved in the execution of Christians. I understand, but I do not believe. I respect them, and I know they respect us, and me." Then almost in a tone of regret, Julius added, in a voice that almost faded to a whisper, "No, I'm not a Christian."

Seeing the look on the face of Julius, and hearing his last words, the thought went through Quintus' mind, as he was sure it went through that of Luke and Marcus, which Julius had left out two very important words "Not yet!"

Looking directly at Julius, Quintus asked "Centurion, is there anything else you can add concerning the execution of Paul? Or, for that matter, anything else you can add concerning Paul."

"No, Tribune. I can only add he was a great man." said Julius.

Quintus looked quizzically at Luke and Marcus in the event that they had anything to ask of the Centurion.

Seeing no response, Quintus thanked the Centurion, who then left the council chamber.

Quintus, Luke, and Marcus continued their discussion for a short period of time. Quintus then thanked them, and especially Luke, for providing this additional information and insight into Paul. After they left, Quintus remained in the room for some time in deep thought. In assessing Paul he could understand the reaction of Orthodox Jews towards him. Paul was one of them. He turned. Now he was a Christian. Some found this a major element of their acceptance of Jesus and his resurrection, looking forward to their baptism. Others rejected, fuming that they were equally correct in doing so. On the whole, it was not so much those who heard Paul that would define his life so much as those who would read what he had written in the years and centuries to come. Quintus looked once more at the scrolls that had been left for him by Marcus, and which he had read. He would have to reread them. These were the sort of letters that could be read many times. They were certainly remarkable documents, written by a remarkable man. Saul, Paul, Tent Maker, Zealous Opponent of Christianity, Missionary for Christianity, Rabbi, Pharisee, Orthodox Jew, World Traveler, and Martyr for his belief in the resurrection of Jesus. Quintus quietly nodded. A remarkable man!

Chapter Eight

Daily Life in Rome

Quintus was inundated with information he had received from the Legionaries and from the Centurions. In addition, he was digesting information received from Longinus, Marcus, and Luke concerning Peter and Paul. To this was added what he had learned from Cornelius and his conversion experience. It was a significant amount of information, both necessary and valuable in formulating his recommendations for the Emperor. As he weighed everything, a consolidated pattern began to emerge. Essentially, he was finding:

I.   Christianity was a religion and not a subterfuge for sedition. None of the information he received from anyone, in any form, pointed in any way that the ultimate purpose of Christianity was to overthrow the Emperor, or the Empire. In fact, the opposite was true. The Christians wanted to be left totally alone. They wanted the state to govern and leave them in peace to practice their religion and grow in spirituality. Their objective was the kingdom of heaven. That was their goal for the future. In their prayer meetings, where the central point was the breaking of bread, they prayed that the government would proceed with the grace of God that they would be forgiven for their sins, that the sick would receive the blessings to prevail, and that the dead would rest in the peace of God. In none of their prayers was there any hint whatsoever that they sought power to become rulers.

II.	Christianity was becoming an established religion with succession continuity. It was not just a temporary movement. From the manner in which they were handling the succession, and he intended to verify this, it had all of the appearances of being permanent. That was certainly the belief of Christians, based upon what they had heard from Jesus that the Holy Spirit would be with them for all time. Quintus wasn't sure if he totally understood the meaning of Holy Spirit, or accepted it, but the Christians did. In their philosophy, God was the Holy Spirit, and it was God that was infusing them with the courage and strength to withstand all persecution. They were prepared to die for their beliefs. This was certainly consistent with everything that he had heard directly from Peter, Cornelius, and from all of his associates in the investigation he was conducting.

III.   Quintus expected to meet with Linus, the successor of Peter, and the current leader of the Christians. Then he would form his final assessment as to whether or not there truly was structure and continuity of leadership to the Christian movement. He was assuming that this was so. The fact that a leader had been selected to succeed Peter was evident there was some structure. He had been told in many ways that there was a structure. He wished to verify this for himself. He would.

IV.   Everything he had learned indicated that followers of Christianity truly believed that Jesus had risen from the dead, and was God. He truly believed that they had been commanded by God himself to love God above all else, and to love their neighbor as themselves. They were motivated by a spirit of love. Love permeated their entire philosophy and way of life. He found that those who became Christians, were devoted in their belief, were sincere in their performance in following the structure of loving their neighbors, and by and large followed the beatitudes laid down by Jesus. This was not to say that they were not exceptions, where some became Christians in the hope of achieving power, influence, or wealth. But this, so far as Quintus could establish, was only a minor aspect of Christianity. By and large, from the information he had been given up to the present, Christianity attracted those who were interested in doing good for the sake of others, and not for their own benefit. Any benefit that they would receive, according to the Christian belief, would be their reward in heaven.

These were some of the conclusions to which Quintus had arrived. He wanted to confirm these conclusions from first hand observation. Despite the potential danger, he decided that he would dress in ordinary street clothes, and attended by Luke alone, would circulate himself amongst the populace of Rome, concentrating upon Christianity. He would do this a number of times until he was satisfied that he had the basic information to corroborate or modify the findings of others. He had to be certain of his facts for the report to the Emperor. Any guards accompanying them would be at a discrete distance. He would hope, with Luke directing him, to attend a prayer service so he could see for himself how Christians broke bread. Having made this decision, he summoned the guard and commanded him to send a messenger to Luke to come meet with him.

After the guard left, while waiting for Luke, Quintus continued studying the letters Marcus had brought him, those written by Peter, Paul and some of the apostles. He found them edifying. While he believed in his own gods, the more he read, especially the letters of Paul, the more he began to see the thrust of the instruction Paul was giving to all of the followers who had been baptized as Christians. He was impressed by the universality of the message both in content, and to whom it was addressed. Paul's writings in particular amplified the thoughts and teachings of Jesus. The message was directed to people in many different parts of the world, and to all levels of social status and wealth. Jesus made no distinctions whatsoever.

Paul's letters, and indeed all of the other letters that he had studied, stressed that universality. All of the letters would apply equally to slaves, as to free men. And the freed men would be those who were poverty stricken as well as those extremely wealthy. As he read them, he could see that it could apply to all the members of the Senate, as well as to the Emperor himself. It was this universality that became both apparent and impressive to him.

He mused for some period of time over that conclusion. He was still pondering that significant aspect of Christianity when the guard entered accompanied by Luke. He decided to query Luke on that very point.

Luke confirmed these conclusions by Quintus. He related many conversations with Peter, Paul and the other Apostles, especially during the long periods of time he spent traveling with them. He not only had an opportunity to catalogue their travels, but also to assess their teachings and memories of the direct teachings of Jesus. From this perspective Luke could confirm the important fact that Christianity was practiced universally by many different people, regardless of race, social status, or wealth. Christianity was universal.

The more this point was discussed, the more impressed Quintus became of the potential wide-ranging appeal of such a religion. The religion he practiced was one of belief in many gods, gods he sought to mollify or appease, gods whose anger he averted, and gods whose favor he sought. He was coming to believe that his gods were in great likelihood different from the gods of the average man or woman. On the other hand, Christianity had a universal God to whom all could appeal, and of whom none would fear. In his discussions with Luke, it became also apparent, that this god, this universal god of the Christians was one of love, and not of fear. This was unique. In his mind he was rapidly assimilating the impact of a universal god, with universal appeal and for all social levels, for all races, based upon the principle of love, and not of fear. This god would be thanked, but it would not be the case of cringing in fear before this god seeking to mollify and avert anger of such a god. How different from his own beliefs!

It was time he saw and heard for himself.

"Luke," he began, "what has been said and what we have discussed is completely consistent with everything I have been told by all those associated with this investigation. Now I would like to see for myself. I would like to visit various homes in Rome, the homes of Christians, and attend a prayer meeting where you have the breaking of the bread. Would you guide me in this?"

"Of course", said Luke. With a great broad smile he added "I think it will be very instructive for you to talk directly with Christians, and to see the breaking of bread." Luke paused, and then he added with a wry smile, "You might even become a Christian yourself, Tribune."

Luke laughed. It was not a derisive laugh, but one pointing to the humorous aspect of such an occurrence.

Quintus was startled. He was very attracted to Christianity, but he was still not convinced. He was not ready to accept, but he certainly respected everything he had learned about Christianity. He could see it as a great force for encouraging people to help each other. Quietly he said to Luke "From everything that I have learned to date, remembering my own direct association with Peter and the other apostles many years ago, I have great admiration and respect for those who call themselves Christians." He paused, and then continued. "I have not considered becoming a Christian myself, but I can see where you may

171

have mistaken my respect and understanding as acceptance."

After a short pause he continued "Come, let us see for ourselves, let us visit Christian's homes, and let us, especially me, observe the breaking of bread."

******

Dressed as ordinary citizens, Quintus and Luke walked the streets of Rome for many days and nights. Well aware of the hazards from brigands and robbers, and cognizant of the warning of Acquinas, Quintus had arranged his guard of Legionaries also to be dressed as normal Romans, and to follow them at a safe distance.

The sights, sounds, and smells were appalling. The streets were very narrow. All manner of refuse was thrown into the streets. It was even thrown out windows as they walked. As they proceeded, it became important not to have any of this fall upon them. As they passed one hovel, they came upon a cripple reclining on the stoop of his residence. Spotting them, he immediately starting wailing and begging for alms. They stopped. Quintus asked him about his malady. The cripple said that he'd been deformed since birth. Luke further questioned if there was any hope that his affliction might be corrected. With tears in his eyes the cripple looked at Luke and said "If only Jesus were alive and would pass by I would be cured!" Quintus asked "Are you then a Christian?" The beggar looking suspiciously at Quintus, then answered guardedly. "Yes, I am. I pray every day that I may be relieved of my affliction."

"That must challenge your faith in being a Christian," said Quintus.

"No, it does not" said the beggar. "Being afflicted in this fashion has nothing to do with my belief in the teachings of Jesus."

It was Luke who then asked, "What are those beliefs?"

The beggar became very suspicious now, and remained silent for a moment. Fear of persecution still lingered. Then he spoke, calmly and quietly. "I believe in God, and I believe that he loves me. I live in hope. I live in the hope that I may be cured, but more importantly I live in the hope of my own resurrection into eternal life."

"And what is that hope based on?" asked Luke.

"It is based upon what I have been told, what I hear, and what I see," said the afflicted beggar.

It was Quintus who then asked, "Where do you hear this?"

"In our prayer meetings where we break bread together. We refer to this as the sacred ritual of the breaking of the bread. We are led by one who is anointed by our leaders to be our priest. He is learned in all of the aspects of Christianity and he answers our questions. It was he who baptized me."

"What questions do you ask him?" asked Quintus.

The beggar remained silent, and a sad look came upon his face. "I ask why I am afflicted when others are not. I ask why God who loves me leaves me like this." Then the beggar brightened and smiled "But then I realize that God loves me, and that with my affliction I am given an opportunity to be an example to others. I do not condemn my God, I do not complain, I ask to be cured, but I am not bitter if I am not. I know that when I receive my eternal reward in heaven, I will no longer be crippled." The beggar smiled. His smile broadened into a grin as he put out his hands towards Quintus and asked, "Do you have alms for me?"

Quintus too grinned. He reached into his purse and extracted a gold coin and presented it to the beggar, whose eyes lit with great appreciation. "I find your faith refreshing," said Quintus. "You truly represent everything that I have heard about Christians." Then he totally startled Luke as he added, "I pray that your God will give you peace of heart, peace of mind, and the courage to prevail with your affliction. May your God be with you."

Quietly he turned and walked away with Luke. As they walked, Quintus and Luke discussed what they had heard. "It confirms everything I've heard about the Christians," said Quintus. Then looking directly at Luke as they walked he asked, "I hope this was a common Christian and not someone whom you made arrangements to have us encounter?" said Quintus.

Luke was shocked. He was quick to answer, "Quintus, believe me when I tell you that I have never seen that man before, nor did I expect in any way that we would encounter him. You will find as we go that he is typical of all those that we will meet. Those that call themselves Christians have an abiding faith in God, and an abiding hope in the Kingdom of Heaven. It is that faith, and that hope which gives them the love which permeates their whole being and their relationship with other Christians, and others who are not Christians." They proceeded to walk further when Luke added, "Ask anyone that we meet, no matter where, and you will find the same faith, hope, and love. If you do not find that in whomever you speak to, then that person is not a Christian, even if they call themselves one. We have no control over the hearts of men. We can only bring them to the word of God, we cannot force them to obey. They are persons of free will totally.

174

They can choose for themselves. They can choose right or wrong. We know that they have the ability to know the difference between right and wrong. If they knowingly commit a wrong, then they have sinned. They can remain in that sin, but if they have remorse and repent, then they can be relieved of the guilt of that sin, and of the consequences before God. They are not relieved of the consequences before their fellow man or their governing authority, for which they must make compensation. That is our belief, and that is our practice."

They walked on with Quintus in deep silence and deep thought. As they proceeded they encountered a number of ordinary persons, merchants, travelers, and other beggars.

Quintus talked to many people as he proceeded touring the many districts of Rome. As he went through the market, he talked to many farmers, free men as well as slaves. Some were Christians and some were not. The Christians all exhibited a sense of hope, looking upon Christianity and the teachings of Jesus as hope for the future, despite the despair, poverty, and often abuse in their current lives, especially if they were slaves. For those who were not Christians, in some cases he saw a certain amount of interest as to why the Christians seemed happier than they were, with the desire to learn more so that they too might be happier. On the whole, as he toured the marketplace, and spoke to the farmers, he detected a sense of hope and happiness among the Christians, and a questioning of those who were not as to whether they too could become Christians to add hope to their lives.

As they continued, he came upon a school for gladiators and entered. He spoke to the proprietor, a retired gladiator who survived the many battles. This man was not a Christian, but wondered why so many of his gladiators were Christians. Quintus had an opportunity to meet with them. What impressed him was the sense of hope amongst the gladiators who were Christians. When Quintus questioned them as to how they could reconcile the brutality of their calling, with the center place of love in their faith, to a large extent they replied that they were gladiators through circumstances beyond their control. Either they were slaves, sent to become trained and to perform as gladiators by their master, or they were destitute and looked upon the role of gladiator as a last resort in order to survive, even if for a short period of time. He left the school of gladiators with a sense that even these men who would exhibit their skill, or perish in the act, lived with a sense of hope.

As he continued his walk about Rome, he encountered many slaves. Some had the marks of the lash upon their back, some were dressed richly indicating that they had masters who valued them as persons. Once again, some were Christians and some were not. Among the slaves, it seemed that more were Christians than otherwise. And even those who were not Christians had leanings toward becoming Christians, with open questions as to how one became a Christian in terms of what was the process, and what was the requirement.

It was Luke who would reply that in such cases there was no requirement or precondition to becoming a Christian such as position or wealth. The only requirement was one of desire to follow the path of Jesus, and to understand what this involved. When asked what this did involve, Luke answered that it involved love of God above all else, and love of the neighbor as themselves. He would go on further to explain that the God in question was the one and only God and that no other gods were to be adored. This created some puzzlement on the part of some that he

176

spoke to until he went further in explaining that the one God had created the entire universe and that religions that had a multiplicity of gods had created this assembly of deities to assuage their fear. The one God that Luke was speaking of was one of love, one who loved his creatures, and asked only that his creatures love him, and love each other. This message of love and hope as explained by Luke often created desire on the part of the listener to learn more, and even to become baptized. It was Luke's explanation of the life of Jesus, his teachings, and his resurrection from the dead that was a major factor in the desire of such people to become baptized and to become Christians.

Quintus was impressed. He was impressed by the hope that Christianity aroused in the hearts of even the most lowly and oppressed individuals that they met. He was also impressed that there seemed to be no distinction in the races of those who were interested in becoming Christians, or were Christians. This universality of membership and belief extended from the slave to the wealthy. Now he understood why Christianity was growing so rapidly. He could foresee the day when Christians might very well be a majority of the people in the Roman Empire.

It was the beggars who interested him the most. Perhaps because they were very direct in their requests. Alms! Some of the beggars were crippled, and some were not. All of them who said they were Christians provided the same verification to Quintus.

All but one man. He was richly attired. When asked why he was a Christian, he replied, "It is a necessary aspect of my life. I am a merchant. Most of my clients who purchase their goods from me are Christians. I am afraid that they may seek their goods elsewhere if I were not a

Christian. I became a Christian to solidify my relationship with them," said the man with a smirk.

Luke looked at him and said nothing. Quintus could not help saying "You are not a Christian!" and walked on.

One of the most telling encounters during one of these explorations was with a poorly dressed man who was begging for alms. He seemed in robust health. Quintus wondered why he was not employed. He asked him "Why are you begging for alms? You seem to be the kind of man who would be able to earn without having to beg. So why do you beg?"

The beggar smiled and looked at him, "I beg not for myself, sir, but for those that are needy and cannot beg for themselves. I have sold everything I have and given it to the poor, I am dedicating my life to helping others. I beg of you, sir, to give me whatever you can to help many who are in great need."

Quintus asked, "Are you a Christian?"

"Of course," said the beggar. "I was told by the priest who baptized me of the encounter our founder Jesus had with a rich man who asked what he must do to achieve heaven. Jesus told him to go and sell everything he had and give it to the poor and then to follow him. That rich man did not, and turned away in sadness. Jesus too was sad when that happened." The beggar paused and then continued, "When I heard that story, I knew that I had to follow Jesus. I heard in my mind the words of Jesus to follow him. I decided to do that. I became a Christian, sold everything I had, distributed it to the poor, and now I work for them, begging for them in order to help them. Will you help me help them?" said the beggar, extending his open hands to Quintus.

Quintus looked at Luke. "Rome is full of scoundrels who tell the same story to hide their guile in seeking alms or robbing others. How do I know if this man is telling the truth?"

Luke looked at the beggar. The beggar smiled, and with his hands made the sign of the cross. Then he extended his hands again and said "Sir, in the name of God, I beg you to help me help others."

Once again, Quintus reached into his purse and extended a gold coin to the beggar. A deep smile crossed the face of the beggar as he lowered his hands and said, "God bless you, sir. I don't know if you are a Christian or not, but you have a heart blessed with the grace of God. Go in peace," he said as he turned and walked away.

Once again Quintus was deeply impressed. They walked on and met others. Some in truth were charlatans and scoundrels. Others were Christians. With Luke's help, they rapidly discerned the difference. They also encountered other men acclaimed to be Christians, but just as the well dressed merchant who did so for purposes of enriching himself, they truly were not. It rapidly became apparent to Quintus that Christianity was a movement of the heart and spirit, and not one of ambition for power, wealth, or the trappings of success of this world. Those who sought such rewards, even if they called themselves Christians, even if they had been baptized, in the opinion of Quintus were not Christians.

They witnessed one ugly incident in the late afternoon on one of their tours. A group of rowdy youths dressed in sackcloth and shouting Christian slogans came upon them in a narrow street. Quintus, remembering the warning of Acquinas, reached inside his robe for his sword. The ever attendant Legionaries detecting the potential attack, rushed in and engaged the youths in a brawl. It was over almost immediately as the youths broke off and dispersed. Quintus looked at Luke and very quietly said,

"Senator Acquinas was right. We must weigh very carefully any reports we receive that seem to cast Christians in a rebellious mood."

They walked on.

Finally they decided they had enough information and were on the last day of their excursions. After a journey that took them through many different parts of Rome, lasting most of the afternoon, they came upon a home of modest circumstances. Luke spoke to the resident of the home who asked them to enter. They came into the central atrium of the home and found a number of people gathered. They were seated around a table upon which a goblet and a loaf of bread were placed. A man stood behind a table and addressed Luke. "Luke, thank you for coming. We welcome your associate. Is he a Christian?"

"No," said Luke. "I brought him to attend our prayer meeting, our breaking of the bread, so he could see for himself how we practice our religion."

The priest extended his hand toward Luke and said, "You are most welcome to be with us as we break bread. Please be seated." Both Quintus and Luke took their place amongst the others and waited in expectation for the priest to begin. They were all seated around a large table. Some others came in and joined the group and then the priest began. He prayed to God in thanksgiving for all that had been done to them and for them. He praised God as their benefactor, and as the true God who had made heaven and earth, and sent his son Jesus to Earth to instruct them. The priest referred to the death and the resurrection of Jesus; and to his ascension into heaven as testimony of their faith, and their hope, and their motive in life as one of love, loving God above all else, and loving their neighbor as themselves.

All present prayed as well, praying for the leaders of the empire, that they would have the wisdom and grace to rule beneficially for all. They prayed for the sick; and they prayed for the faithfully departed, that they would rest in peace. Then they prayed for forgiveness for their sins, and the grace and strength to forgive all those who had harmed them. Finally they prayed for special intentions of their own.

Quintus was deeply impressed with the continual request for forgiveness. This correlated with the Christians who recognized the frailty of humanity and that the commission of a sin, or the omission when given the opportunity to do something good and noble, often created a sense of guilt and a fear of punishment. In Christianity, there was a mechanism of forgiveness, repentance, and where needed, remission or compensation for the evil that was committed. For example, in the event of theft, then the penance was directed to make restitution. In cases such as adultery, the penance was directed to cease from such illicit behavior. The concept and invocation of the process of forgiveness was very impressive to Quintus.

Then they sang hymns to their God.

Quintus was vastly impressed at the devout nature of the meeting. These were people in love, in love with their God, and in love with each other. It was when the priest went through the ceremony of the breaking of the bread that he suddenly realized that something different was occurring. The room was suddenly hushed. A sense of awe and reverence seemed to fill the room. Quintus realized that this was different than anything in which he had ever participated. The sense of something different intensified. The priest intoned the words, "This is my body" and held aloft a loaf of bread. Then he elevated a goblet filled with wine and intoned the words, "This is my blood." The priest had created the body and blood of Jesus from the bread and wine. These people truly believed this. They felt that God was with them. Even though Quintus did not believe, he felt a presence he could not explain. As each Christian went forward and partook of the bread and wine, he saw the expression on their faces. They truly believed!

There was a silence, an awe, a sense of reverence, which Quintus found absolutely refreshing, and stimulating. This service was invigorating for the Christians. Now he began to understand the source of the courage they evidenced when they would rather face death than disown their beliefs. The thought crossed his mind that this was the fundamental tenant of their religion. He was beginning to understand that Christianity was a religion of love. This love was universal. It had no basis in nationality or wealth. It had an appeal for all. It provided all who embraced it with a sense of hope that transcended any misery in which they were engulfed.

The rest of the meeting concluded with the priest asking God to bless all those that were present with grace and strength to follow their faith.

As the prayer service concluded, everyone seemed to be in a happy frame of mind, talking with each other as old friends. Many came to Quintus and welcomed him into their midst as if they've known him forever. This too impressed Quintus, significantly. After some time, he and Luke left.

"Luke, thank you for taking me to this prayer service. I was very impressed. To be quite honest with you, I have a sense of awe that I cannot explain, I felt a presence during your ritual of breaking the bread that I found significant, and uplifting. I have a sense of well being that is rare. I have faced so many difficult situations in my life, just as now I face a challenge from the Emperor that has far

182

reaching consequences. Yet, just as when I investigated the mysterious disappearance of the body of Jesus, I feel that I am doing something that will have lasting impact in the future of the Empire and the world."

With that, Quintus became very silent and said nothing as he and Luke proceeded to the villa of Quintus. When they arrived, Quintus asked Luke if he wished to discuss anything further with him on this day. Luke declined, leaving further discussion to the next day. He departed for his own residence, and the Praetorian Legionaries now closed in around him in tight formation as they proceeded to Quintus' villa.

Quintus entered his home and proceeded to his study. There he pondered everything that he had observed on his tour of Rome with Luke. In his mind he equated what he had seen with everything he had heard from the Legionaries, Centurions, from Marcus and Luke, and from the apostles. In particular, he dwelt upon Peter.

Peter was certainly the leader of the Christians. So was Paul. How did he distinguish between the types of leadership each provided, as opposed to that of the Emperor?

The more he thought about the question of leadership, the more Quintus zeroed in on a very simple concept. Leadership was the ability to establish the objective, and attain it. Attaining the objective required the support of others, and leadership was that quality which caused others to support the effort to achieve the objective. In that regard, the leader had to be sufficiently wise to select an objective that could be achieved, establish a strategy of achievement, and then convince others that the strategy was sound and could be successful. Hence, leadership called for much more than merely leading a charge. The leader also had a responsibility to those who followed not to waste their time, nor at times not to waste their lives. In summary then leadership included:

I. Setting the objective
II. Determining the best plan and strategy to achieve the objective
III. Pointing the way for others to follow
IV. Encourage and enlist followers
V. A moral obligation to lead to success and not to failure.

With that concept of leadership, how would he judge Peter and Paul? Both were very human persons - Peter especially so. From first hand observation, Quintus knew this to be so, having seen Peter's behavior in difficult circumstances; and by what Quintus had heard about him. Quintus also had an opportunity first hand to meet Peter and was impressed. With regard to Paul, his great legacy was more with regard to his writings than perhaps with his personal leadership as in the case of Peter.

Peter was a fisherman, a common man, quite physical, impetuous, and prone to error. He was courageous, and yet dedicated and determined. Despite of all of this he was a humble man, very loveable, and willing to be corrected without taking offense. He had studied under Jesus, and was buttressed in courage and faith by the Holy Spirit. The fact that he stumbled and erred made him all the more human and loveable as a leader. He was someone that the average person could equate to. He had no exalted demeanor. He was the common man. And yet, there was a nobility of purpose in Peter. It was evidenced more in how he died, perhaps, than in his everyday life. His command to those executing him to crucify him upside down because he was not worthy of being crucified as was

Christ was a sign of his true humble nature. In one sense, Peter was a leader by default. He did not seek the position for power or honor, but executed the position because he was appointed by Jesus to that task. The more Quintus thought about Peter, the more he smiled. Peter was a leader who cared for people, and who loved God. He was the epitome of what Quintus was beginning to understand Christians to be: persons for others who love God above all else, and love their neighbor as themselves. Christianity was a faith and a religion where love was the glue that held people together, and cemented their relationship with their God. Peter symbolized that love.

Paul, on the other hand, while he was a tent maker, was also a very learned man. He was a Pharisee and a scribe. He studied under the greatest Hebrew scholar of the time, Gameliel. Paul was a very zealous individual, not given to doing things in half measures. He was a highly intelligent person who initially was strongly opposed to the teachings of Jesus. He feared Jesus and his followers were creating a splinter movement within the Jewish religion. To that end, he was a zealous persecutor of the followers of Jesus until his conversion following a vision of Jesus on the way to Damascus to continue his persecution.

Paul was highly energetic, fearless, determined, admirable, prophetic, and motivated more by elements of the mind and spirit than by physical labor. Yet he earned his living as a tent maker, a significant physical endeavor. His writings were uplifting, very explicit, and quite understandable. Quintus had learned a great deal concerning Paul from the writings, and, of course, about Christianity. In many the writings Quintus could even visualize Paul dictating to the scribe, or even composing the letters himself, of which he was certainly capable.

As a leader, Paul was determined to make the teachings of Jesus available to the entire world. To him it was important to be a religion beyond nationality or sect. For that reason he strongly urged and supported the inclusion of Gentiles within those to be baptized. Paul's objective was a universal church. From what Quintus had observed in Rome, Paul was successful in that endeavor. Quintus was most impressed by the fact people of many different nationalities and different social status were Christians. This universal nature would be an important element if Christianity was to survive beyond the immediate life times of the initial leaders, Jesus, Peter, and Paul.

From what Quintus had seen, Christianity had survived beyond the deaths of these three. Indeed it was flourishing. In fact it was the death and resurrection of the founder, Jesus of Nazareth, which was the cornerstone of the religious belief of Christians. The resurrection of Jesus proved unequivocally that he was divine. Christianity was founded on that belief.

This gave added poignancy and creditability to the teachings of Jesus. Furthermore, his miracles created significant attention to his teachings. Raising people from the dead was certain to command attention.

Quintus nodded to himself as he quietly thought about these characteristics of leadership, and succession within the Christian community. It was important that he meet the new leader of the Christians. In his discussions with Luke, he had come to understand that a man called Linus was the successor of Peter. A meeting had been arranged for the following day. As Quintus contemplated this meeting, he mentally decided that the most important element of that meeting was to be his evaluation as to whether or not the process of succession had been successful, and whether or not there was a structure in place. If so, then Christianity certainly would flourish.

Quintus pondered the succession pattern of leadership. The ability of any organization to grow depended on structure and succession. This required the delegation of responsibility so that other leaders could be trained. These other leaders, or sub-leaders, or assistant leaders, however they might be designated, would then be in a position to succeed the leader. This depth of leadership would become essential in the permanence of any organization. As he contemplated the Christian community, Quintus believed that the development of these future leaders was well underway. But he would have to verify that this was so. He would make that a major point in his discussion with the successor of Peter, Linus.

Chapter Nine

Peter's Successors

Quintus dressed as a Senator and proceeded alone to a meeting with Linus. This meeting had been arranged by Luke and was to take place in the home of Linus, in the Christian quarter of Rome. A contingent of the Praetorian Guard followed at a discreet distance as protection from the brigands that frequented Rome.

When Quintus presented himself, he was immediately escorted into a small meeting room where a distinguished looking man of middle years was waiting for him. He was not tall, but had a quiet bearing, almost of nobility and yet humble. He had a white pointed beard .and piercing eyes. He was dressed humbly, with no adornments of any kind, except for a simple wooden cross on a piece of twine about his neck. His shoulders were somewhat stooped as if he had spent hours and hours poring over documents, but his face was lit with a look of benevolent kindness. There was no sternness about the man, nor anything to mark him as the leader of the Christians, and yet there seemed to be a confidence, an aura of leadership and strength that permeated his entire being. Perhaps it was the eyes, or the manner in which he held his head, but

Quintus was completely impressed with the fact that the man he was meeting was certainly a leader, and yet a very kind and considerate man.

Quintus had been ushered into the room by an attendant whom he assumed to be a Christian. He approached his host and said quietly, "I am Quintus Gaius Caesar."

His host looked very directly into his eyes and said, "I am Linus, the leader of the Christians. Welcome to my home. I am pleased to meet with you and hope that I will be able to provide any information that you require in your investigation."

Quintus was surprised. He had not explained the reason for his visit, and had asked Luke as well not to explain the purpose of seeking out Linus, but rather to indicate that Quintus had an interest in meeting with Linus in his position as the leader of the Christians. He asked Linus, "What do you know about my visit?"

"Luke asked me to see you and did not tell me anything further than that; but I had heard about who you are, and why you are seeking information about our people. I am pleased to tell you anything that will be of assistance in the investigation that you have been commanded to complete by the Emperor." Linus then turned and beckoned Quintus to be seated in one of the two chairs that were in a corner of the room. After Quintus was seated, Linus in turn seated himself and offered him wine which was already on a side table. Quintus declined and proceeded to ask Linus the first of the questions that he had decided had to be answered.

"I see that you have been well informed about my commission from the Emperor, and are prepared to assist me in gathering the information required for me to arrive at my recommendations. You must realize that I have an open

189

mind, but I am dedicated to Rome, and dedicated to the preservation of Pax Romana. If Christianity is in any way a threat, then I will so report it to the emperor. But if it is not a threat, then I will also make a recommendation that you and your people should be left in peace to continue with your religious beliefs and your religious rights, so long as they do not interfere with the civil order of Rome."

Linus smiled. "I could not ask for more than that. We seek only to live in peace and to be model citizens of the state. After all, we are citizens of Rome. I, you must know, am a Roman and proud of it. But I am also a Christian, and proud of that. I see no conflict in being both a Christian and a Roman and I hope in our discussion today to convince you that being a Christian in no way is any threat to Rome and as a matter of fact is an asset of Rome."

Quintus was relieved. He knew he was facing not only a leader, but in a few moments he had come to realize that he was speaking to a man who reminded him so much of Peter. He saw the dedication, the determination, and the faith. He was looking forward to this interview with anticipation. He decided to be very abrupt to test is initial evaluation. "Linus, I must know if Christianity is truly a religion and not merely a subterfuge for sedition. Are the Christians really interested in overthrowing the order of Rome at some future date once they have established power, or are they interested in quietly developing power until it becomes necessary for Rome to accommodate to their wishes. Or, on the other hand, in truth are you totally a religion with a creed of belief which you follow completely independent of the civil order?"

Linus seemed taken aback by the abruptness and strength of the question. His eyes took on a piercing look as he engaged those of Quintus. He replied, "Senator, while I am somewhat surprised at the abruptness of your question,

I am not concerned because I can see that it is based upon a true desire to establish the truth. You must know that our founder, Jesus of Nazareth, repeatedly said 'Render unto Caesar that which is Caesar's and unto God that which is God's.' We are a religion. We are dedicated to following the principles enunciated by Jesus of loving God above all else, and loving our neighbor as ourselves. These are our total commands. Within these commands we have certain rituals that reinforce not our strength but reinforce our commitments, our faith and our hope in the future. We strive for perfection in this life, defining perfection as avoiding all evil. We are not concerned with affairs of state unless the affairs of state impinge upon our freedom and our lives. We will defend ourselves just as you will defend Rome and have defended Rome as a soldier, as a senior member of the Praetorian Guard, and now as a Senator."

Linus paused and his look softened, but there was still a continuing determination in his features and in his speech as he continued. "Senator, I know that you have scores of Legionaries scouring Rome asking questions of both Christians and non-Christians concerning our behavior and our objectives. I will let that be a witness to what I am saying. We are citizens of Rome, as well as Christians. We find no difficulty in being both. We seek only to be left in peace to practice our religion, we seek only a continuation of civil order and the rule of law. We believe no one, even the Emperor is above the law, as we know that you in the Praetorian Guard believe as well. It was the Praetorian Guard who overthrew the tyrant Caligula, and not the people. It was the Praetorian Guard that had a leading hand in forcing the suicide of Nero who had in turn become a tyrant. As a citizen of Rome, I am well aware of the ramifications of political manipulation and political power." Linus paused then added rather strongly. "But our main concern is our souls and our salvation. All else is secondary."

Quintus was insistent. "I will accept that Christianity is truly a religion, since I am well aware of this from my own investigation of the resurrection of Jesus, and from the results of my investigation here in Rome. I am well aware of the dogma proposed by your church and of your principles of belief. However I am curious as to whether you truly believe that Christianity will prevail as a religious movement beyond the temporary attraction it has now, not just because of the proximity to the presence of Jesus. With Jesus gone, and with both Peter and Paul executed, is there continuity to this movement?"

Linus showed no emotion or reaction to the question. He merely looked directly at Quintus and began, "I am the successor of Peter. Peter was a great leader, the one who baptized many of the original followers of the principles of life enunciated by Jesus. He was also an inspiration. Peter truly believed. He received the Holy Spirit which gave him the courage to prevail no matter what opposition he encountered. As you know he was even willing to die for his principles, insisting that he was not worthy to die as Jesus died, and that he be crucified upside down." As Linus spoke, Quintus nodded in agreement, well aware of the truth of what Linus was saying. He too agreed that Peter was an outstanding leader and inspiration for those who followed him.

Linus continued. "We are not a small group of people. We now number in the thousands. Our numbers are increasing every day. The murderous persecution of the Emperor Nero had little effect on our numbers. It seemed that the blood of the martyrs spurred even greater numbers of baptisms to our beliefs. And so, Senator, I think you will agree with me that we are much more than a small group of people. We are organized. There is a line of succession already established, and I can introduce you to the man whom I believe will succeed me when I too pass on."

Quintus was impressed. Not so much by the words but by the manner in which they were spoken. "And how are you organized?"

Linus answered, "We have our priests, and we have senior priests, and we have our leader. We are rapidly coming to the point of appointing bishops who will have the power to anoint and create priests. This line of succession is important because our priests are the direct shepherds of our people in their religious observances. It was Jesus himself who created the first priests, the apostles, when he gave them the power to forgive sins, and when he asked them to create his body from bread, and his blood from wine."

Quintus probed further. "I understand that you believe that you convert bread and wine into the body and blood of Jesus. I understand that this is the central point of your meetings which you refer to as 'breaking bread together.' Is that a practice that is the cornerstone of your religious beliefs?"

"It is not the cornerstone of our belief, but rather the cornerstone of the practice of our belief which leads to the reinforcement of that belief. As part of our faith, it is our belief that through our prayer in our sacred meetings, which we call our ritual of the breaking of bread, we are thanking our God as well as asking for further blessings on causes that are worthy of being blessed. We pray for the departed, we pray for the sick, and we pray for grace that our leadership will prevail in furthering the just principles of Christianity." Linus paused for emphasis. "And we pray for forgiveness of our sins and the grace to forgive others who offend us."

"I have many more questions for you. As we speak, how do I address you," asked Quintus.

"I would be honored to be addressed by you or anyone as "Father'. As priests, we are honored to be called Father. Some Christians refer to me as their Holy Father. It is a responsibility for me to exercise that duty and a great honor which I humbly hope to be able to fulfill. It is difficult to be a successor to Peter and even more difficult to consider that in truth, that makes me a successor to Jesus. He indeed was the Son of God and demonstrated not only with his life but with his death the principles he enunciated during his mission on earth. Briefly stated, he represented the truths of God, that we should love God above all else, and love our neighbor as ourselves. That is our religious belief. We reinforce that belief, with various sacraments and rituals that provide the grace for us to prevail even in the presence of great adversity and temptation. We are human beings. As such we are subject to temptation, and to the failure of not being perfect. We are all sinners, but the distinction is that we repent, and beg forgiveness, and hope to prevail and avoid sin in the future. That is not to say that we suddenly become perfect creatures, but rather that we are cleansed and provided with a grace to prevail against adversity and temptation. Naturally and expectedly, we fail, because we are human. But we hope that our failures become smaller and smaller, that our sins as we call them become less and less critical, not only to ourselves but to those around us. That is the concept of Christianity. That is central to the manner in which we live. We live on the basis of being human. We will sin, and being Christians we will beg forgiveness and we will pursue repentance in the hope of not sinning again."

Quintus was concerned about the manner in which Christianity governed itself. He remembered the magician Simon, and of the information supplied to him that there were other instances where people became Christians seeking power from that decision as opposed to merely an exercise in becoming closer to God. He asked Linus, "How do you govern yourselves? Surely you have members who are blindly ambitious, or seek the mantle of Christianity for their own purposes, which may even be evil?"

"We hope that that is not so," said Linus. "But we know that all of us are human. Whatever lies within the heart of an individual often is hidden to the world. However, whenever an individual has, by his or her actions, shown themselves to be empty of the word of God, while still calling themselves a Christian, then we call a meeting of our elders, to decide whether or not to expel them from our meetings. We do not have the power, nor assume that we ever would have the power, to say to someone that they are not a Christian, that they are evil, but we do have the power to say that we do not welcome you into our meetings. If that person persists in coming, then so be it. We are not a political organization with the power to execute or the power to incarcerate. We do not seek such power. In years to come, as our organization becomes larger and larger, we would expect to have all manner of people claiming to be Christians. Some of these will have ideas and beliefs totally contrary to the word of God. Paul, in a number of his letters, was correcting improper practices on the part of some Christians. This may always be so. We hope not. But we do have mechanisms in the form of our own grouping of priests, presbyters, and bishops who will decide whether or not some person or some organization is acting outside the collection of beliefs that we call Christianity."

Quintus was not totally satisfied. He continued. "In the military, when someone deserts, or someone does not follow the discipline, he is punished severely, and often executed. It is that fear of execution, or the fear of punishment, that often is the difference between someone being disciplined and obeying commands, or not. How do you exercise that discipline?"

Linus smiled broadly. "Our discipline lies in the desire to be saved, to spend eternity in heaven with God, or to be condemned, never to see the face of God throughout eternity. That is the punishment, not execution, but merely the denial of the ultimate goodness of God."

"Is that enough?" asked Quintus.

"Yes," said Linus. "The ultimate punishment for anyone is the denial of the proximity and oneness with God. That is the ultimate punishment. On the other hand, the ultimate commendation, or the ultimate reward, is union with God in heaven for all eternity. That is what we strive for. That is what we call salvation. And the rituals in which we engage in life are preparation for it." Linus smiled broadly again, and his face took on a calm beatific appearance. He continued, "This may be difficult for political or military minded individuals to totally accept and understand. A political person seeks the highest office and a military person seeks the highest possible rank, and awards. You and I both know that the greatest reward a military leader can achieve is a tribute paid to him by the Emperor and the Senate. For us Christians, the reward is salvation in heaven. As our great leader Peter of fond memory was wont to quote Jesus, 'What does it profit a man to gain the whole world and suffer the loss of his soul?'"

"How appropriate," said Quintus. Then, after a short pause, and looking directly at Linus, Quintus asked, "What do Christians ultimately seek?"

Without any pause whatsoever, Linus replied, "We seek the kingdom of heaven. We seek only to do what is right so that we can rest in the bosom of our God throughout all eternity. We do not seek riches, we do not seek power, and we do not seek to be able to lord it over other people. The fundamental objective of our lives is to save our souls. It was our Lord Jesus who also said 'It is easier for a camel to thread the eye of a needle than for a rich man to attain salvation.' The honors and the wealth of this world are nothing in comparison to the rewards for the just, and the good, in the kingdom of heaven. That is the driving force of all Christians, and that is the grace that gives us the strength to suffer martyrdom for our faith."

Quintus became somewhat subdued. The sheer nobility of the reply gave him some indication of the strength which bound Christians together in their common search for goodness, and their ultimate destination, the salvation of their souls.

"Tell me, Father, what is the soul?"

"The soul is that part of the individual that truly represents the person. While the body dies, and the mind dies, the essence of the person continues beyond death. For instance, looking at Peter, we can look upon his work, we can look upon his nature, we can look upon everything he stood for, we can look upon everything that he said and did, and that represents his soul. His appearance, and his physical body, is of no consequence when we evaluate Peter. The same is true of Paul. We do not think of Paul as a tent maker, or of a writer, or as a Pharisee, but we think of Paul as the spokesman for Christianity, we think of Paul as the one who put into words the essence of the teachings

197

of Jesus. The same is true of Jesus himself. We do not think of Jesus in terms of his appearance, but rather in terms of what he did, what he said, and what he set in motion. His teachings will prevail because we do not look upon the words themselves, but upon what they mean, upon the impact they will have on us and those who follow us. That is the soul. The soul is the person. The soul transcends human life and continues for all eternity. The soul is the essence of the person and it is our belief that the soul is immortal and will continue in the afterlife, and will continue to reside, if saved, in heaven with God. That is the soul."

"Nobly said, Father. I truly begin to appreciate the distinction you make between the soul, the intellect and will, and the parts of the body and mind that terminate with death. As I listen to you, I cannot help thinking of all the people I have known and I begin to understand your meaning of the soul. I too knew Peter, if only briefly, and I was completely impressed with the essence of his personhood, or his soul. I will always remember the spirit of leadership within him, and the great courage when he looked at me and said 'Are you going to free me, or kill me?' That courage told me that there was something much more to the mystery of the disappearance of the body of Jesus than the simple explanation that the body had been stolen. I went to great lengths to examine all possibilities and came to the conclusion that Jesus truly did rise from the dead. As a result I can see that you have a fundamental cornerstone in your own faith and belief in his teachings as being a road to your own personal salvation. It is necessary for me to understand you, and to understand your motivation, even if I do not believe the same thing."

"Thank you, Senator." said Linus. "I can see that you are beginning to appreciate the driving motivation of our lives."

"Father," said Quintus, "Your people think for themselves in discerning right from wrong. Can that be interpreted by the state as a dangerous principle?"

Linus laughed. "I can see where some people would misinterpret the phrase that we think for ourselves, have free will, and can know between right and wrong. That refers to our own actions. That refers to whether or not what we do is what we consider a sin or not. If we deliberately do something that is wrong, then we call that a sin. It must be deliberate on our part, with full knowledge that it is wrong and then we still do it. Then it is our faith that we have the power of repentance. Our priests have been empowered to forgive our sins. This was the great grace given to all of us by Jesus when he was here on earth. It is a fundamental aspect of our belief."

"But," said Quintus, "no man wishes to tell another man how evil he is, or how he has erred. Don't you find that an impediment for people to seek forgiveness of their sins?"

Linus smiled. "Remember I said that the penitent had to seek forgiveness, had to have remorse for having erred, or committing a sin. There is nothing that would force anyone to seek recourse to repentance, but it is a tenet of our faith that salvation requires contrition. All of us are sinners, all of us at one time or another err, and hence it is important that we seek forgiveness, and do penance for our commission of some act that is wrong. In that sense, the confession of our sins is a form of cleansing, a form of relief, and hence is something to be sought."

Quintus was impressed. This concept of repentance and confession was truly a remarkable element of the

Christian belief. It cleansed a man's conscience, it cleansed a man's feeling of guilt. This endowed man with freedom and not with the terrible burden that would be carried throughout their life. Quintus mused on this point, recognizing one of the great strengths of Christianity.

"I have one final point I wish to discuss with you, Father," said Quintus.

"I have been studying the letters of Peter, Paul and the other writers, including John and James. I have been very impressed by them.

Quintus mused for a moment and then went on, "It is part of my analysis of Peter and Paul, both great leaders. Peter was the one who carried the flag in a sense, was the leader in the battle, creating followers by his actions and by his dedication to the principles of Christianity. Paul on the other hand, because of his training, and possibly because of his zealousness and dedication to the written word, has become your source of a permanent record of the teachings of Jesus. Paul relied on existing oral tradition of what Jesus did and said. Paul presented a theology and understanding of who Jesus was, and how his teachings are to be applied in life for our salvation."

After a short pause, Quintus continued. "Between Peter and Paul, you have a richness of those teachings which permeate, in my opinion, what you have told me concerning the belief and practices of all the followers of Christianity. You are to be commended for adhering to these principles." Quintus rose to take his leave. Bowing slightly towards Linus he said, "I commend you, as the successor of Peter, who in turn was the successor of Jesus, upon your sincerity. It is still necessary for me to answer the fundamental question posed by the Emperor: Is Christianity a threat to Rome, or is Christianity a possible ally or bulwark of Rome?"

200

Linus looked very carefully and calmly at Quintus. Then he too stood. There was a slight smile of appreciation upon his lips, and yet his eyes took on a far-reaching look, as if he were looking into the future. "Tribune, thank you for your compliments, and thank you for your understanding of our belief. I see that you have studied the matter very carefully, placing your confidence upon the information provided to you by the many investigators at your disposal. I can only give you my opinion, which I hope you will be able to confirm through all of your sources of information, and your investigation. My opinion is that Christianity will become the bulwark of the Roman Empire. We are not a threat. In fact, we strongly believe that an alliance between Rome and Christianity will lead to a long standing continuation of both the power of Rome, and the power of the word of Jesus. Our aim only is to spread the word of God, to have people love God above all else, and to love each other as they love themselves. There is no room for us to engage in political manipulation, and that is farthest from our thoughts."

Quintus became more and more satisfied that there was nothing further he would be able to discern from Linus that would help in his investigation. He considered it necessary to meet with the potential successor to Linus, a priest named Cletus. "Is your successor available to meet with me now?" asked Quintus.

"Cletus is not here now, but I can arrange for him to come to you at the Castra Praetorian tomorrow if that is suitable for you?"

Quintus agreed and so the appointment was set that Cletus would come to meet him at the headquarters of the Praetorian Guard the next day. As Quintus turned to leave, Linus quietly said to Quintus, "Senator, I know you are not a follower of our religious belief, but as an older man, I

201

hope that you will take with you my blessing that you find peace in your life, and determine all of the facts necessary for you to come to a complete set of recommendations to present to the emperor. Would you allow me to say a blessing for you?"

Quintus was agreeably surprised, and smiled broadly as he replied, "Thank you, Father. I would be privileged to receive a blessing from you."

As Quintus bowed his head, Linus blessed him, using the sign of the cross, and the words, "May God bless you in the name of the Father, and of the Son, and of the Holy Spirit. Amen."

Quintus remained standing for a moment before looking up at Linus and bowing slightly said, "Thank you for your time, Father, I wish my gods would look upon your work with favor." With that, Quintus turned and left. As he walked back to the headquarters of the Praetorian Guard, the Castra Praetorian, he remained deep in thought. He had just completed a remarkable meeting with the successor to Peter, a man who reminded him so much of Peter in some ways, but yet different. Peter was a rough-hewn fisherman selected by Jesus to be the head of his church, the rock upon which he would build his church. Peter grew in that task until he became a giant, a great leader who not only inspired followers to become followers of Jesus with his words, but also with his example. Peter indeed had been a great leader, and Quintus was not surprised to see the same elements of leadership in Peter's successor, Linus.

As he walked, he considered more and more the question of whether Christianity would survive. With leaders like Linus and his expectation that Cletus would be of similar stature, he began to believe that there was a great possibility that Christianity would prevail.

Chapter Ten

Cletus and Clementus

Quintus had just completed his meeting with the Legionaries and with the three Centurions who were engaged in scouring Rome and its environs for information about the Christians. As they were filling out of the meeting room, a guard came to Quintus and told him that two men were at the entrance asking for him. Somewhat surprised, Quintus asked who they were. The guard indicated they had given their names as Cletus and Clementus. Quintus knew of Cletus but who was Clementus? Linus must have included him along with Cletus whom he had promised to send. Quintus commanded the guard to bring them in after the Legionaries and Centurions had left.

Marcus had been in attendance taking notes of the meeting with the Centurions and Legionaries. Quintus asked him to stay for this new meeting with Cletus and Clementus.

The two men who entered were totally dissimilar. The first man was tall and had the bearing of a noble, and was dressed somewhat plainly. The second man, on the other hand, had a stooped look of a scholar. The satchel

203

over his shoulder reminded Quintus somewhat of Marcus. He was certain that the second man had the ability of a scribe and had waxed tablets in his satchel that he would use for making notes. He noticed that the vesture of the second man was even plainer in nature, and Quintus wondered if it was sack cloth.

Quintus directed a quizzical look at each in turn. As they came forward, the tall one gave Quintus a slight bow and said, "Senator, I am Anacletus, commonly known as Cletus. Linus sent me, and my associate Clementus, to accompany you to the resting place of Saint Peter."

Quintus smiled as he greeted them both. "Thank you for coming. And please upon your return extend my thanks to Linus for this courtesy of sending both of you to accompany me to the gravesite of Peter. Why do you refer to him as 'Saint' Peter?"

It was Clementus who answered. "It is our practice to address those who are with the Lord as 'Saint'. It is a designation that we are certain they have achieved salvation and reside in the presence of God, in his kingdom, in heaven."

"Ah," said Quintus. "Then you do make judgments as to the sanctity of the person and of their adherence to the principles of Christianity in their lifetime. Do you designate all Christians as 'Saint' after they die?"

It was Cletus who spoke. "Senator, it is our hope and expectation that all Christians become saints, but we designate only those who have lead exemplary lives, obviously full of sanctity and a closeness to the Lord with the title of 'Saint'. We do this not so much to call attention to our opinion concerning their salvation, but rather to point to them as examples for us to emulate. Those whom we designate as 'Saint' then become our models for our own behavior."

"I begin to understand," said Quintus. "I can understand your designation of Peter as a saint, but how do you reconcile that with the occasions in his life when he did such things as to deny knowing Jesus on the night prior to his crucifixion?"

"But that is exactly the point to be made," said Clementus. "We are all human, and prone to error, if not sin. Saint Peter erred in denying Jesus, but he was full of remorse, seeking repentance and forgiveness throughout the rest of his life. Our judgment is not whether or not someone is perfect, and totally free of sin in their entire life, but rather that they try to avoid sin; and when they fail, as we humans invariably do, that they seek forgiveness and repentance."

"Very nobly stated, Clementus." said Quintus. With that, Quintus mused for a short period of time over his personal knowledge of Peter, including what he had been told during this current investigation. Peter was certainly human in all aspects, given to his great enthusiasms, and great falls. The nobility of Peter, the courage, and the spiritual growth came to a climax when he asked to be crucified upside down. How noble, how grand, and yet, how human; how much a reflection of the person that Peter was. In his mind, Quintus was quite prepared to accept the designation of 'Saint' associated with Peter. His original assessment years ago of the leadership qualities of Peter was confirmed.

He wondered what the designation was for Paul. "And do you refer to Paul as 'Saint' Paul?"

"Of course," said Cletus. "His writings surely indicate his closeness to God. We were indeed privileged to have such a spokesman not only during his life time, but through his writings, we believe, for all time. We also believe that he was truly repentant of the days when he was an ardent pursuer of Christians. It was the vision on the road to Damascus that converted him from being a zealous persecutor of Christians to an equally zealous supporter and exponent of the teachings of Jesus. In his writings he gave a full measure of repentance for the prior errors in his pursuit of Christians. And yet, even in that role, something prevented him from being directly involved in the stoning of Saint Stephen. While he guarded the cloaks of those who did the stoning, he did not cast any stones."

"I too," said Quintus, "found that Paul had reservations even prior to his conversion. I sensed this when I met him in Tarsus on my way to Judea to investigate the mystery of the missing body of Jesus from the tomb. You know my report to the Emperor Tiberius confirms that Jesus did rise from the dead. I believe that is a very important article of faith and belief for Christians. It was during my discussion with Paul that I sensed that he was not thoroughly and solidly convinced that those who followed Jesus were wrong. I was not surprised to learn of his conversion, nor am I surprised at the zealousness with which he initially pursued those who were followers of Jesus, those we now call Christians. Paul was a remarkable man given to deep conviction. You have been fortunate to have been led by these two remarkable men, Peter and Paul. I am not surprised you refer to both of them as 'Saint'."

Quintus paused and thought for a moment before adding, "I am gratified that Linus has sent both of you to accompany me to the gravesite of Saint Peter, or Peter as I will always think of him. Will you also take me to the grave site of Paul?" Both Cletus and Clementus almost simultaneously said "Yes!"

"Before we do so," said Quintus. "I am interested in what happened to Maryam, the mother of Jesus. I met with her when I was in Judea many years ago and was quite impressed by her graciousness, sense of humor, and obvious sanctity. She was a remarkable lady. It is hard for me ever to forget the privilege I felt to have met her. I cannot fully describe the sense of complete love that seemed to emanate from her person, from her words, from her smile, from her bearing, but most importantly from her total graciousness as we spoke." Quintus paused and then asked again, "Can you tell me what happened to her?"

It was with a deep sigh that Cletus replied to Quintus, "It was John who took care of Maryam. She went to live with him after the crucifixion.

Maryam suffered greatly as she saw her son crucified and watched him die on the cross, but she was the first to know that he had risen   from the dead. He visited her before he spoke to anyone else. His love for of us all was only exceeded by his love, attachment, and reverence for his mother. We have no doubt whatsoever that Jesus deferred to his mother to the greatest extent possible. We were all well aware of his first public miracle when he changed water into wine because she asked him to intervene to do something when the wine ran out during the wedding feast at Cana."

Cletus paused in deep thought, and a sad look came across his face as he continued.

"Maryam went to sleep some fifteen years after the crucifixion. She had gone to Ephesus with John, who built a small house for her. She lived there in quiet and happy solitude until she went to sleep. A short time later her body was assumed into heaven to join her soul in union with Jesus. That is our belief, and it is evidence by the fact that her body disappeared from the tomb." With that, Cletus sighed and seemed to brace himself as he added, "We were saddened to lose her, but we are gratified in our knowledge that she is in heaven with Jesus, and acts as our intermediary for our requests. We believe she is praying for us to do what is right at all times, and that we beg for forgiveness and repentance when we sin."

Quietly Quintus asked, "And do you refer to her as Saint Maryam?"

Clementus answered, "Yes we can do that, but we prefer to address her as 'Our Lady' or 'The Blessed Virgin Maryam' or as the 'Mother of God'."

Quintus was impressed. What a suitable designation for the Mother of Jesus. In his judgment, Jesus was a deity and as such Maryam was indeed the "Mother of God".

After a short pause, Quintus abruptly changed the subject. Turning to Cletus whom he assumed to be more senior of the two, he asked, "Can we now proceed to the grave site of Peter?" Turning to Marcus he said, "Please accompany us". As he said this he noticed the satchel always at hand with Marcus, and remembered that Clementus too had such a satchel over his shoulder. He turned to Clementus and asked, "I noticed the satchel over your shoulder. Are you a scribe?

"Yes," said Clementus

Quintus smiled, and asked, "Do you write letters and reports concerning the activities and beliefs of Christians?"

"Yes," said Clementus. "I have written reports for Linus and I am currently preparing a letter which I hope will be promulgated amongst Christians concerning our beliefs."

"Before we leave," said Quintus, "I am assuming one of you gentlemen may become the successor to Linus upon his death. Am I correct of my assumptions?"

It was Clementus who spoke up. "Cletus will undoubtedly become our next leader. But we are hopeful of having Linus for many more years before that occurs." Clementus looked fondly at Cletus and then at Quintus before continuing, "Cletus is too modest to tell you of his activities but it is my privilege to know him and to express the gratitude of all Christians for the strong support he has given to many of us, and for his unrelenting support of our leader, Father Linus. While a selection of our leader is always left to the vote of the elders, it is my feeling, and hope, that Cletus will become the successor."

Very quietly Cletus added, "I do not seek to be the leader. That is a role with great responsibility. Saint Peter was superb in his role as head of the church following his selection by Jesus. Linus has succeeded Saint Peter and is leading us with the grace of God. I am hopeful that I will not be selected as the leader to replace him; but if I am, I am hopeful that I will receive all the graces necessary to perform my role of leadership for our code of beliefs, which is now categorized by the term Christianity." Cletus said all of this in a very humble tone of voice. Quintus believed that he was truly knowledgeable of the responsibility of being the leader of the Christians. His quick assessment was that Cletus, just as with his impression of Linus, would serve nobly as a successor to Peter.

Giving a perceptible nod, as if to close this direction of conversation, Cletus said, "Then let us conclude our discussion now and proceed to the gravesites of Saints Peter and Paul."

******

Accompanied by a contingent of Legionaries providing a guard against marauding brigands so common in Rome, Quintus accompanied by Cletus, Clementus, and

209

Marcus proceeded to a gravesite on Vatican Hill. There, in a simple ossuary, as Clementus indicated, reposed the bones of Peter. He and Cletus then discussed at great length the plans to build a small memorial in the guise of a workshop over the gravesite of Peter. There the Christians could meet for the ceremony of breaking of the bread, where in their belief they converted bread and wine into the body and blood of Jesus. At the present time, they normally conducted their memorial ritual in the individual homes of Christians.

They then proceeded to a gravesite outside the walls of Rome where once again Clementus directed them to an ossuary which he indicated contained the bones of Paul. As in the case of the visit of burial place of Peter, now at the burial place of Paul, both Cletus and Clementus made the sign of the cross and prayed for a few moments in silence.

Once again it was Clementus who described plans for building a memorial over the burial site of Saint Paul. This building would be referred to as Saint Paul Outside the Walls. "And how will you refer to the building over the grave of Peter?" asked Quintus.

It was Clements once again who answered, "We will refer to it as Saint Peter at the Vatican."

"How noble," said Quintus. "I foresee this effort to build such memorials in honor of these two great leaders to be an important factor in the growth of Christianity. You are wise to honor your great leaders as symbols and models for all of you to emulate. I was privileged to know them both. I was vastly impressed by both, but for different reasons. I found Peter to be a giant amongst men. Like all men, he had his faults, but was strong enough to overcome them, and to have remorse for all his errors, and at all times to act as a leader, asking only to be followed as he sought perfection and union once again with Jesus in heaven."

"And Paul?" asked Clementus.

Quintus smiled before stating, "Paul was equally a giant, but more of the mind. He was brilliant, and totally dedicated in whatever he did. He did nothing in half measures. His travels, his exhortations, his writings, and his example are well worthy of his designation of him as Saint Paul. As I said previously, you have been blessed with having two such outstanding leaders as Peter and Paul. "

Quintus paused before continuing, his brow furrowed in deep thought. "While I am not one of your believers, I am a person given to analyses leading to understanding and appreciation. I can appreciate the clarity of thought and performance as shown by Peter and Paul, and I can commend them, and you, for your adherence to the principles of Christianity. I can respect you and them, but I cannot accept. I do not question what you believe, but I do not at this time have the same belief. Perhaps that is what you call faith."

Both Cletus and Clementus smiled broadly. Even Marcus, who normally maintained a very poker expression which was impossible to discern, broke out into a broad smile. It was Clementus who spoke. "Senator, you are a brave and honest man. We would welcome you at any time as a Christian, and we pray that day may come. However, we do not hold you in any lesser esteem. We respect your beliefs, and we respect your person. We are privileged beyond measure to have a man such as you investigating Christianity and for preparing a report for the Emperor. We have suffered greatly at the hands of Emperor Nero, and we expect that we may very well suffer under leaders in the future. It is our hope that, guided by your report which we believe will be factual and very objective, Emperor Vespasian will allow us to live in peace. Our hope is to be able to practice our faith on one hand, and as citizens of Rome, to be loyal subjects and supporters of the Emperor. It is our objective, as Jesus would have us do, to 'render under Caesar that which is Caesar's, and unto God that which is God's'."

Accompanied by the Legionaries they then made their way back to the Castra Praetorian. There they parted.

Quintus and Marcus proceeded to the study within the Castra Praetoria assigned for their use. They sat quietly for an hour, mulling over all that they had learned about the Christians. Quintus was almost ready to address the Emperor. But first, after discussing it with Marcus, he decided to hold a summit meeting to consider all the information gathered about Christianity. To this he would invite Cornelius, Longinus, Senator Maxim Valerius Acquinas, Luke, and the three Centurions who had directed the activities of the one hundred Legionaries assigned to this investigation. He asked Marcus to prepare invitation notices to each of them. They decided to hold the meeting a week hence. Quintus called the guard and instructed him to send Praetorian Guards to each of them with the invitations that Marcus would provide. With that Quintus departed for his villa.

Chapter Eleven

The Mystique of Christianity

The day of the meeting dawned clear and bright. There seemed to be a crispness in the air which was a good omen for the meeting. As Quintus entered the Council Chamber of the Praetorian Guard, he saw that the three centurions were already there, as was Marcus. He noticed that the stewards had already brought wine and fruit for everyone. Marcus, he was sure, had attended to that. Shortly afterwards, Longinus entered with Luke. A few moments later, Senator Acquinas entered. After greeting everyone warmly, Quintus asked them to all be seated at the table. He took the position of Deputy Prefect

Quintus opened the meeting by thanking all them for coming, and asking them to be frank in their replies to the questions he was going to pose. He indicated his assumption that these questions were uppermost in the mind of the Emperor. By considering in full detail the answers to these questions at this session today, Quintus expected to be able to reply to any and all questions or observation posed by the Emperor.

"To begin," said Quintus, "What is Christianity?"

213

All were silent for a moment. Cornelius was the first to respond. "Christianity is a name attached to a group of people following the teachings of Jesus, carpenter from Nazareth, who was the son of God sent to earth to redeem mankind."

There was silence in the room, until gradually there were a series of nods as everyone indicated there agreement. Senator Acquinas spoke up, "That is well summarized, Cornelius" he said. "I would add that Jesus proved that he was the Son of God by rising from the dead after he was crucified, died, and buried in a tomb."

"That is very important," said Quintus. "My investigation in Judea proved without doubt that Jesus did rise from the dead, and that I believe is a fundamental cornerstone of Christianity."

"Yes," said Luke. "But the resurrection was only the final element of proof. The miracles performed by Jesus in a lifetime were more than enough to indicate his divine nature. If you will recall, he did raise three from the dead, and cured many of their various illnesses. He made the lame to walk, the blind to see, and deaf to hear. No solely human person could do that. Hence the belief in the divinity of Jesus is well founded."

"That of course gives greater credibility and emphasizes to his teachings," said Longinus. "I saw him die. In fact it was my spear thrust that did much to kill him. Yet, despite his suffering, and despite his torment as a person, in his human nature, he begged his Father in Heaven to forgive his executioners, including me. Forgiveness and love, or love and forgiveness, intertwined, were fundamental in all of his teachings." Longinus paused, and looked at Marcus, before adding, "Marcus, I am sure that you have records from your interviews of many of the miracles and teachings of Jesus. Will you

214

make these available to Luke and to others who are seeking to record these events?"

"Of course," said Marcus. "All of my notes and records are available to all those who have interest in them. As the Tribune knows, I have made copies of the findings concerning his investigation in Judea of the resurrection of Jesus. These were placed in the libraries in Rome, and are available at this time. I will also place in the library copies of my notes that have been made since then. These notes and reports will include all aspects of this investigation by the Tribune as commanded by the Emperor."

"All that is very important," said Quintus. "I will summarize it for the Emperor by stating that Christianity is a name given to the followers of the teachings of Jesus of Nazareth. I will follow that with a statement as to what are the underlying beliefs of these teachings, and what is the objective of these teachings."

"From everything that I have learned from all of you, and from the reports presented by the Legionaries, it seems to me that the objective of this religion, of Christianity, is for its members to achieve salvation, and for their souls to reside forever in heaven for all eternity. The objective, then, is salvation. Do you all agree with that?"

As Quintus let his eyes rest upon each of those in the room, he detected complete agreement. Once again it was Cornelius who spoke up. "Well and succinctly stated, Tribune. I suppose your next question has to do with the methodology, in terms of what is the road to salvation, and what are the guide posts and means of travel along the way?"

Quintus chuckled. "Cornelius, you have read my mind. Of course we have to consider the path and the means of transportation. For example, to oppose an

215

analogy, is it a straight line, a tortuous route, on foot, on horseback, or by chariot?"

It was Luke who spoke up. "The path to God is love, Tribune. It is love of God above all else, and love of one's neighbor as oneself. Those were the commandments summarized by Jesus as the roadway to salvation. As for the method of travel, and the pathway, Jesus was very clear in his insistences on repentance. He recognized, as we all do, that we are all guilty of sin. We have free wills, and also the ability to judge between right and wrong. It is when we judge something that is wrong, and still do it, that we still sin. It is a detour on the path to salvation. We can redirect ourselves to the correct and proper path by repenting of our sins, and asking for forgiveness. Jesus gave us that mechanism, by empowering us to forgive sins or retain them as we judge ourselves. In doing so, he created priests empowered to forgive sins. This is one of the mechanisms that Jesus created in his lifetime."

"Did he create any other mechanisms?" asked Quintus.

Once again it was Luke who had responded. "He created aids, which we call sacraments, which assist us on the road to salvation. Do you wish me to explain further, Tribune?"

"Please do so," said Quintus.

Luke then proceeded to detail the various sacraments instituted by Jesus. First and foremost was that of baptism, with the example of his own baptism by his cousin, John the Baptist. The next was what Christians call the sacrament of marriage, or matrimony, endorsed by Jesus with his attendance at the wedding feast of Cana; and his stress upon the union of man and woman in marriage. When he left the earth, and ascended into heaven, he promised to send the Holy Spirit to confirm with fire and

216

strength and grace our belief in his teachings. This is what Christians call the sacrament of confirmation.

Luke went on to talk about the last gathering or supper in the upper room on the night before his crucifixion. During that supper, Jesus broke bread and told his followers that they must break bread and it would become his body, and drink the wine which would become his blood. This was to be done in remembrance of him. This was not a symbol, but a true transformation of bread and wine to his body and blood. This was the institution of the Holy Eucharist which is the cornerstone of the practices of Christianity, the cornerstone of the meetings on the Lord's Day and at other times. The gathering consists of the recitation of prayers, singing of hymns, and selected readings. These all lead to the climax, which is and transformation of bread and wine into the body and blood of Jesus by their priest. Jesus created this during the last supper with the apostles.

It was after his Resurrection that Jesus also laid hands on his followers giving them the authority to forgive sins or retain sins as they decided. This is when he established the priesthood of Christianity. It is the bishops who now lay hands upon the selected followers of Christianity anointing them as priests.

Finally there is the anointing of the sick, especially those in danger of dying. In Christianity, the body is the temple of the Holy Spirit. During the lifetime of each individual, the body, and the mind, are the repositories of the soul. It is the soul that is the person. It is the soul that continues after the death of the body and the death of the mind. It is the soul that is the true essences of the person, and it is the soul that lives on in eternity.

Luke concluded by saying, "These are the sacraments that are our aid as we travel on the road to heaven." Quintus looked for agreement from those at the meeting. All of them voiced their agreement with what Luke had said. It was Marcus who had added, "Well stated, Luke. You summarized it very well."

"Assuming that everything you have said is correct, Luke, how can you be sure that everyone believes the same thing? Surely you have experienced situation where people do not understand something you have said. As a matter of fact, we all know from experience that a room full of people will have somewhat different interpretations of anything we say. How can you, then, be sure that Christians have the same set of beliefs? More importantly, how do you handle the situation where there is conflict between what two groups may believe or even teach?"

"When there is disagreement," said Luke, "we try to resolve the conflict by calling a meeting with all of the senior elders, and bishops. One good example of this is the Council of Jerusalem. There was some disagreement as to whether those who wished to be baptized as Christians had also to be circumcised. There were many who believed that circumcision was necessary. At the Council of Jerusalem, Peter and Paul spoke up very strongly in favor of allowing Gentiles to become Christians without the need for circumcision. James became convinced and supported this recommendation. There was a unanimous support at the Council of Jerusalem, and thereafter it was an article of faith and practice that circumcision was not a necessary requisite for baptism. It is expected that in the future other Councils will be called to consider similar questions concerning faith and practice within Christianity."

"It was Senator Acquinas who spoke up, "But don't you have heresy now, don't you have some Christians now who do not believe that there is a true transformation of bread and wine into the body and blood of Jesus?"

"Yes," said Luke. "Paul addressed this in his letters, and this is still being addressed by our bishops wherever there is such contrary belief. Another contrary question raised, another heresy as such, is that some believe that Jesus was not divine. That seems rather difficult to imagine in light of the resurrection, and in the light of the miracles performed by Jesus; but there are some that still do not believe in the divinity of Jesus."

"Then you have some methodology of policing errant beliefs," said Quintus.

"Yes," said Luke. "People who are heretics are instructed concerning the error of their beliefs. They have free wills. They can accept that they have been wrong, or they can continue in their error. If they continue in their error, then they must separate themselves from the practice of Christianity. One such example, of course, was the magician, Simon. His heresy was he believed that he had inherited and had the powers of Jesus, and could fly. That heresy cost him his life when he crashed to earth as he attempted to fly from a high pole." Luke paused and then continued, "We pray and grieve for them. We hope they will see the light and return. Our whole belief structure is based upon providing aids on the path to salvation, and helping all to achieve salvation. If it is their choice to detour from that path, no matter how we may extort them to come back, it is their decision finally."

"That is very significant to me," said Quintus. "Christianity, then, may be compared to a roadway. Only one road leads to the objective. There are many side roads that do not lead to the destination desired. You believe that you are establishing the guideposts to achieve the objective, the objective being salvation, and repose of the soul in heaven. There are those who may chose to take a side road in the belief that that is a better path to heaven, even if it is not so. If they realized the error of their ways, they can seek forgiveness and be placed on the correct path. It is that element of forgiveness that makes the belief of Christians credible," said Quintus.

"Yes," said Longinus. "Like most soldiers, I found it difficult to reconcile my calling with my religious belief. It was continual attendance at our sacred ritual of the breaking of the bread, and reception of the body and blood of Jesus, that gave me the courage to prevail. I am sure the same is true of those who chose death no matter how painful rather than to deny their faith."

Gazing around those in attendance, Quintus detected approval of what had been stated. There were no dissenters. In fact he verified that by asking, "Does anyone disagree with anything said up to this point?" No one did. Quintus found this very significant in his study, but he also found it significant in his own heart as he began to understand the depth of faith of the Christians. He commented upon this. "I am highly impressed by the faith of the Christians that I have encountered. I am assuming that that faith permeates all those who call themselves Christians. I am further impressed by their feelings of hope. No matter how miserable their current lives are, they have hope of redemption and happiness in the next world. It is that hope that fuels their love of their neighbor, showing itself in many ways as they help each other. This I found to be very impressive."

Looking about the room, Quintus asked, "Why is Christianity growing? In fact, how did it come to Rome, and why is it growing so quickly in Rome?"

There was a heated discussion with all taking part in answer to the question posed by Quintus, as to why Christianity grew so quickly throughout the world, and why it grew so quickly in Rome.

It was Luke who began with, "Christianity initially grew in the Jewish community because it offered a continuation of the traditional Jewish religion, while still encompassing the teachings of Jesus. There had been many predictions by the prophets of the arrival of a messiah, and those who followed Jesus believed that he was the messiah. They referred to him as the Christ, or the Anointed One - the Savior. He became known as the Jesus the Christ, or a shortened up form Jesus Christ."

Luke paused, seemed to collect his thoughts, and continued. "His teachings were not in conflict with the teachings of Judaism, but were often in conflict with the practitioners and the priests, most especially the High Priest. To some extent, they looked upon him as a usurper, and a threat to their power base. Not all of them felt that way, but the High Priests, Caiaphas, was determined to stop him. At the time of his arrest and crucifixion, Caiaphas was quoted to have said 'better to sacrifice one person then to lose a nation'".

Luke looked around at everyone present to give emphasis to his next statement. "While the miracles of Jesus called attention to his teachings, especially the raising of at least three persons from the dead, it was his own resurrection from the dead that punctuated and solidified everything he had taught. It was his message of hope, his message of love, and his emphasis upon repentances and forgiveness that attracted many to follow him. I might summarize, just as you have already agreed, that Christianity is a religion of hope, dedicated to charity, or love of God and of our fellow man. We have faith in our belief buttressed by the fact of the life of Jesus. That support is enhanced significantly by the fact of his resurrection after he was crucified, died, and was buried."

Once again looking at the assembled group, one at a time, Luke continued, "It was this message of hope that attracted many to follow Jesus, and to become what we call today Christians. When the Council of Jerusalem, composed of the leaders of the movement met and decided that circumcision and conversion to Judaism was not necessary to become a Christian, then the number of Christians expanded dramatically. It was not only Paul teaching to the Gentiles, but it was everyone who converted also preaching to their fellow men in an expanding fashion. Just as a stone creates a ripple in the water which extends on and on, just so the word of Jesus created a ripple which expanded on and on. It was that effect that lead to the vast increase in numbers of Christians. This expansion factor, coupled with the appeal to all levels of society, from slave to freed men to the wealthy, independent of any race or nation, which also served as a catalyst in the expansion of the numbers of Christians."

Looking directly at Cornelius Luke continued, "Cornelius, you can attest to the fact to even as a Centurion in Roman Legion in Caesarea you learned of the teachings of Jesus, but it was only after a vision that you prevailed when Peter came and visited. The teachings of Jesus were not unknown to you, and the existence of Jesus was not unknown to you, but the actual teachings that lead to your baptism came from Peter's visit. Is that not so?"

"Yes," said Cornelius. "While I knew, I did not have the faith to proceed. That came with Peter. Suddenly I not only knew, but I understood and accepted. That with the element of faith which led to my baptism."

"Cornelius," asked Luke, "Was not your conversion a factor in Christianity spreading to the Roman Legions?"

"Yes, it most certainly was" replied Cornelius. "Many of my centurion comrades, as well as Legionaries,

222

hearing of my conversion, proceeded to investigate and some were baptized. If you will recall, my household and many of my friends were also baptized when Peter came. Some of these friends were members of the Roman Legion as I was." Glancing at Longinus, and then addressing Luke, Cornelius added. "Luke, the conversion of Longinus also induced other members of the Legions to consider being baptized."

"Yes, Luke," said Longinus, "I too was attracted to the teachings of Jesus when I saw his behavior and his prayer for those who were crucifying him on the day of execution. I asked further. That was the path which led me to being baptized. So to emphasize what Cornelius has said, Christianity was known within the Roman Legions. They in turn, whether baptized or not, carried this knowledge throughout the Roman Legions in Judea and as they moved to other parts of the Roman world, to other Legions, and to Rome."

"As the center of the world," said Quintus, "I can understand how the message of Christianity could spread very quickly not only throughout the Roman Empire, but within Rome itself. I can also understand that the universal appeal to all nations, and to all levels of society would in turn amplify the spread of the knowledge of Christianity, and thereby increase the numbers of the followers." Turning to the three Centurions, he brought them into the discussion "Antinus, as one who directed the execution of Peter, were you attracted to Christianity? Did you ultimately become a Christian yourself?"

"Yes," said Antinus. "Seeing Peter die, and hearing how he wanted to be crucified upside down so as not to imitate Jesus caused me to desire to learn more about the teachings of this man Jesus. The more I inquired, the more I became attracted to these teachings, and ultimately was baptized. I might add that the persecution of the Christians by Nero was a deciding factor for me. I saw on one hand so many people of good will being persecuted, condemned, and executed, often in a horrible fashion, merely for the diversion of a despot. Nero was insane. Any man who would murder his mother and wife cannot be considered of any sound mind. While I was concerned that being a Christian might lead to my own execution, I was not afraid. Had I been arrested, I was quite prepared to go to my death rather than to denounce my beliefs."

Julius spoke up next. "I too was attracted by the execution of Paul. I was present and commanded the squad and carried out Nero's orders. While I was attracted to Christianity by seeing how Paul conducted himself, and having to come to know Paul during his captivity, I still did not have the faith to become a Christian. That may well happen, but I am still debating in my mind. I am not quite ready to accept, even though I understand." said Julius.

It was Paulucci who then added, "I am a Christian. Many of my fellow Legionaries are Christians as well."

"I am not a Christian," said Quintus "From everything that I have learned, I have great respect for them, and for their beliefs. I have great admiration for Jesus. I am willing to accept that Jesus was a deity, but in my religion we have many deities so I have no difficulty with continuing in my beliefs while still respecting the beliefs of Christians."

Quintus looked about him and looked at each of those present. After a few moments of silence, Quintus went on to say, "I believe that Christianity has a universal appeal to all people, of all races, and to all social status. I also believe that Christianity poses no threat to Pax Romana because Christians by and large are supportive of law and order. They are not supportive, just as non-

Christians would be non-supportive, of a tyrant and despot. The Praetorian Guard could never be accused of being a hot bed of Christianity. But it was the Praetorian Guard that had a leading hand in removing Caligula and Nero from their office of Emperor. It was not the Christians. This is not a criticism of the Christians, but rather an evaluation of the impact of Christianity upon Pax Romana. It would appear Christians are supporters of peace, tranquility, and law and order. As such, they are an asset to Pax Romana, and not a threat."

Quintus then looked at each, and in particular upon Senator Acquinas, as he added, "Do all of you agree with that assessment?"

After a few moments of silence, it was Senator Acquinas who spoke up. "Quintus, you have said it very well. Those who claim that Christians are a threat because they can discern between right and wrong make a fundamental error. The distinction between right and wrong has to do with the spiritual essence of an act, rather than political consequences. The consequences of evil may be the same in both insistences, but a Christian thinks first of the spiritual aspect of an act before thinking of the political consequences. For example, all citizens, except those who would benefit by the evil, know very well the arrests and execution of innocent people merely for their religious belief, is an evil act. For the Christian this is also a sin. How the Christian acts in a political sense has no connection to their religious evaluation. As a Senator, I abhorred Nero's actions in the arrest and executions of Christians. As a Senator I did everything that I could to oppose him and stop him. I am not a Christian. Even if I was a Christian my actions would not be any different. I acted as I did because it was incumbent upon me as a Senator to act in the best interests of Rome. What Nero was doing was not in the best interests of Rome, and so I opposed him. Had I been a Christian, I would have also opposed him because it was an evil act, and contrary to the teachings of Jesus."

After a moment Senator Acquinas continued, "You are right, Quintus. Christianity is not a threat to Pax Romana, but rather a bulwark. I believe the day will come when Christianity and Rome may unite, but that is not for today, nor for your report."

Quintus was startled by this comment by his good friend Senator Maxim Acquinas. It offered a new direction of thought. He would have to pursue it. He wasn't sure how he would present it to the Emperor but the thought expanded in his mind.

After a moment of silence, Quintus asked those assembled, "Does anyone have anything else to offer?"

With a broad smile, Marcus removed a scroll from his satchel and handed it to Quintus. His smile deepened even more as he added, "Tribune, I have completed the history you asked for. You may find it of interest with facts about the life of Jesus of which you may not be aware."

Quintus was moved. He grinned as he accepted the scroll and said, "Thank you Marcus for this. I will read it carefully and then return it to you. I am sure that this will become a historical document for years to come for both Christians and non-Christians alike." Looking around he repeated, "Is there anything else?"

It was Longinus who spoke up. "Tribune I wish to thank you for your many courtesies and the opportunity to work with you on these investigations. After the presentation to the Emperor, I intend to return to Caesarea and spend the rest of my year se with friends of the Roma Legion who have retired there. This may be my last opportunity to wish you all well."

Everyone present thanked Longinus for his help and all spent a few moments in conversation. Then Quintus thanked them all and brought the meeting to an end and they all left.

Quintus remained in the counselor chamber for a few moments, deep in thought. His report to the Emperor was forming in his mind. Sarto was wrong. People who thought for themselves were not necessarily a threat to Pax Romana. In fact, they were probably a major asset. Christianity was expanding through the force of ideas and through the power of love. The Roman Empire was expanding through the force of arms, and through the draining of blood with the sword. Could the Empire of Rome expand without the sword, and through the power of the word? That was a question that had to be examined.

Chapter Twelve

Report to the Emperor

Quintus was finally satisfied that the investigation was complete. He had received information from the enumerable reports by the Legionaries, coordinated and summarized through the Centurions; as well as his own observations and discussions with Marcus, Longinus, Cornelius, Luke, Linus, Cletus and Clementus. As he thought of the leaders of the Christians, he mentally thought of them as representing the universal nature of the members of the sect. All were citizens of Rome. Cletus, however, was the son of Greek slaves; and Clementus was a Jew.

He decided to concentrate on consolidating all the information he had received and to work with Marcus to prepare his report for the Emperor. He isolated the two of them in a room in his villa and they worked assiduously for a number of days. During one of these sessions, he returned the history Marcus had prepared. He was very complimentary, praising the work as being one of the great historical documents for the future.

Marcus was pleased and promised to share his document with Luke.

228

They continued preparing the report for the Emperor. When they were ready, Quintus sent a message to the Emperor that he was prepared to present his report whenever the Emperor was pleased to receive it.

A short time later, a message came from the Imperial Palace that the Emperor was prepared to receive the report by Quintus the following day at the sixth hour.

The next day, shortly before the sixth hour, Quintus proceeded to the palace accompanied by Marcus bringing with them a scroll for the Emperor containing the final report. As usual, they were accompanied by a contingent of Praetorian Guards.

As they walked, they discussed the full scope of the study, and how it could serve as a history of these times. Quintus challenged Marcus to prepare a detailed report of everything that he knew about Jesus, Peter and Paul, and the other apostles, together with what had been discovered in the investigations in Judea and in Rome. He strongly urged Marcus to have Luke do the same thing. Marcus agreed that he would do so, and also that he would place the completed documents by himself and by Luke in the Library of Rome. Quintus was pleased that the history of these events and times would become available for the study of people in the future.

Upon their arrival at the palace, they were shown into the Emperor's Council Hall by the palace guards. Quintus was surprised, but not totally, to find that Titus and his younger brother Domitian, and Senators Servo and Acquinas were also in attendance in the Emperor's Council Hall. All stood in front of the raised dais containing the throne-like chair for the Emperor. Quintus entered the room and greeted the four dignitaries who were awaiting the entrance of the Emperor. Marcus walked to the far side and then stood well away from the group of five.

The Emperor entered, walking rapidly, and took his place at his throne-like chair and sat down. He calmly reached into the bowl of fruit on the table to his right. He nodded to each of the dignitaries in turn before looking at Quintus and, munching on a grape, the Emperor said "Quintus my good friend, what have you discovered in your criminal investigation of these Christians?"

Munching on fruit, the Emperor obviously meant to indicate that the matter today was not one of extreme importance affecting the fate of the state, as would be the case of declaration of military action to be taken. The Emperor telegraphed a relaxed approach, an atmosphere that while important, important enough for the Emperor to be involved, it was not a situation affecting any major element in the state. This was certainly a gibe at Sarto who was seeking to make the matter his road to power. Inwardly, Quintus wondered if Senator Acquinas had very quietly sent a message or given a message to the Emperor of Sarto's belligerence on this point. Consciously or unconsciously, the atmosphere being created by the Emperor was one that would deflate any of the bombast that might come from Senator Sarto. Quintus was pleased.

"Sire, I am grateful to you for asking me to conduct this criminal investigation. I looked upon this assignment as another opportunity to be of service to Rome. I wish to thank Prefect Titus for his assistance in so many ways during this investigation. Because of this assistance, the investigation has been very thorough. Three Centurions and 100 Legionaries of the Praetorian Guard conducted interviews and investigations throughout Rome and environs. I verified their findings by my own personal tours over numerous days. I was also greatly assisted in my overall plan and activity of this investigation by Senators Sarto and Acquinas, Tribune Cornelius, Centurion

Longinus, the Physician Luke, and my good friend the scribe Marcus."

After a short pause, he continued. "In addition to personal interviews with many diverse elements of the population of Rome, Christian or not, I also interviewed extensively the Tribune Cornelius, and the current leader of the Christians, Bishop Linus. Through him, I also met with his two deputies, Cletus and Clementus, one of whom may well be his successor. Finally, guided by the physician Luke, I examined the letters and writings of some of the founders of the Christian sect. The two major leaders of the Christians were Peter and Paul, both of whom were executed on command of the Emperor Nero. These readings were confirmatory of our conclusions as to the motivation and life objectives of Christians. I will summarize these shortly."

Again a short pause for emphasis before continuing.

"Most of our interviews and investigatory procedures were without incident. However, I must report that on numerous occasions, rowdies chanting or shouting Christian expressions interfered. On one occasion, when I was conducting interviews in the streets of Rome dressed in normal citizen clothing, I suspected that I was about to be assaulted. The Legionaries accompanying me, also in street clothes, dispersed the potential attack."

Quintus noticed the frown on the face of the Emperor. After a very short pause, Quintus continued. "Upon our investigation, we concluded that these rowdies, and those in other instances, were not Christians but either brigands seeking to blame the Christians for their actions, or hired thugs intending to discredit the Christians by their actions. Hence, while these incidents are reported, they were given no credibility or weight in our analysis and recommendations."

Sarto stepped forward as if to speak, but, perhaps thinking better of it, stepped back. Quintus was tempted to look at Sarto, whom he was convinced was guilty of instigating these attacks. Quintus was certain that everyone in the room would assume this to be the case, so he remained silent.

Quintus paused to give emphasis to the change of direction with his report. He continued. "Sire, during the analysis of our findings, it became apparent that the major factor in projecting the behavior of Christians was their set of beliefs. The objectives for their actions and their lives were intimately intertwined with the teachings of Jesus which they follow. That was the main consideration, supported by all the evidence gathered throughout this intensive investigation that has led to the recommendations which I am making."

Once again, Quintus paused to give emphasis to the recommendations that would follow.

Quintus began. "Sire", he said, "The Christians are not criminals of any kind. I found them to be worthy citizens of Rome. From my findings, and in my opinion, Christians are not a threat to Rome, but rather an asset." Quintus heard an audible gasp which he knew came from Sarto. A smile seemed to curl above the lips of the Emperor as has he too noticed the gasp, but gave no indication of this. Quintus continued.

"Sire, Christians come from all races and from all economic backgrounds. Their creed of hope attracts members universally. They will grow in numbers without cease. They are like a tidal wave after a great storm. In my opinion, nothing will stop this growth." Quintus paused to give time for his remarks to take effect. Then he went on. "Christians are dedicated to leading their lives as citizens while still maintaining a code of conduct consistent with their desire to separate the right from wrong; and always to follow a life of doing good for others. Their creed is to love God above all else, and to love others as they love themselves. What they seek is salvation in the afterlife in heaven."

Quintus paused for his words to take effect. Then he continued.

"While they pursue their lives as soldiers, merchants, tradesmen, artisans, or whatever it may be, it is not great power or great wealth that they espouse to achieve, but rather salvation of their souls to reside for all eternity in what they call heaven."

"And what is heaven?" asked the Emperor.

"It is the spirit world, Sire, where the souls of Christians who have led exemplary lives reside throughout all time, and beyond, or eternally, with God who created the whole universe. Unlike us, Sire, they believe in only one God, a God of love."

"Are they organized, Quintus?" asked the Emperor. "Do they have a structure that can survive death of their leaders, growth in numbers, and time?"

"Yes they do, Sire." answered Quintus, who then proceeded to describe the structure of the Christians with priests and bishops, and with a new leader selected by the bishops. As he did so, he saw a smile creep across the face of the Emperor. Quintus must have shown his surprise.

The Emperor suddenly grinned and said, "Let us hope the structure does not stifle the good men." Then becoming serious again, he added, "How do the Christians exercise some balance in the control of their members?"

Quintus described the Council structure and the example of its use on the very important question of circumcision for gentiles who wished to become Christians.

"What are their immediate plans for the future?" asked the Emperor.

Quintus then described his meetings with Linus, Cletus and Clementus, and the discussions concerning the growth of their members. He then went on to outline their plans for churches over the gravesites of Peter and of Paul.

"You have been very thorough, Quintus" praised the Emperor. Then he asked, "Can you tell me about the origin of the Christians and why they have flourished so rapidly in Rome?"

Quintus then proceeded to describe the life of Jesus, his death and resurrection, and the lives of Peter and Paul. The Emperor became very engrossed in his portrayal of these three great leaders. He seemed to accept Quintus' decision on the deity of Jesus.

It was when Quintus linked the widespread nature of the Roman Empire with the widespread growth of Christianity that the Emperor sat up in great interest.

"It would seem to me." the Emperor stated, "that the interests of Rome and of Christianity are identical in a common desire, if not need, to support Pax Romana. Christianity has seemed to flourish because of Pax Romana despite their persecution by Nero. Do you agree, Quintus?"

"Yes, Sire."

The Emperor went on. "Furthermore, their creed suggests they would be a stabilizing influence in Rome and our subject territories. Do you agree, Quintus?"

"Yes, of course, Sire." answered the beaming Quintus. "That is exactly the conclusion I arrived at. Hence my recommendation to leave them in peace."

The Emperor smiled. Then he said, "Senator Sarto. What do you think of this?" Sarto abruptly took a step forward. So did Titus, Domitian, and Senator Acquinas. The discussion seemed to have broadened to all in the room. Sarto abruptly stated, "What nonsense!" Sarto laughed. "Heaven?" he derided. This is merely a subterfuge for them to hide their true motivation." Looking directly at the Emperor Sarto continued, "Sire, these people think for themselves. They are a threat to any structure of governance. If they deem any civil order to be wrong, then they can ignore it and do everything they can to change it. As such, they are a threat to the status quo, perennially a threat to the power of those who govern. No governing organization, and certainly not you the Emperor, Sire, can afford to have subjects who think. Your subjects must act in support of whatever you wish or do. That means they must make no judgment whatsoever. Their role is to support you and just to enjoy whatever largesse which you may distribute to them." Then, almost as an afterthought, he added, "They will appear to support Pax Romana when in truth they are working to use it to cover their nefarious plans for power."

With a smile, the Emperor asked, "Then Senator Sarto you think that we should continue our policy of games and grain as a means of insuring popular support?"

"Yes, Sire. The people must not be allowed to question whatever the rulers decide. They must follow and support; never oppose!"

"I can see that you feel strongly about the Christians," said the Emperor. "But what about the Praetorian Guard? Are they to blindly support the Emperor? Is the Emperor always to be considered above the law?" There was great silence in the room. Everyone immediately thought of the horrific reigns of Caligula and Nero; and of the role of the Equestrian Guard in deposing them both. Supporters such as Sarto were especially suspect with their personal agendas and activities at the present time and had to be controlled. Men such as Sarto seeking power had to be controlled.

It was Titus who broke the silence. While the Emperor was his father, he deferred to him as the Emperor rather than as his father. "Sire, what you are implying is absolutely true. We must not confuse the ability to think and equate it with the ability to revolt. Pressed enough, harassed enough, anyone will revolt against vile treatment. The slaves in the galleys certainly think often of revolt, but do not have the means. There are those in our captive lands who I am certain think of revolt, just as the Jews in Judea not only thought of revolt, but did indeed revolt against Rome, and fought nobly in their cause. Our policy, throughout the Empire, has been to eliminate revolt by having our captured citizenry become part of Rome. They are members of our Legions, they fight side by side with us on behalf of Rome. In the captured lands, we allow them to proceed with their own religious beliefs, and with their own government, subject of course, to the power of Rome. It is only through this mutual sharing of power and responsibility that we have been able to extend our domain throughout the known world."

Looking directly at Sarto, Titus continued, "Senator you are terribly mistaken. We should not fear people who think, but rather embrace them. In the battlefield we insist upon discipline, we insist upon the following of orders. Only by rigid discipline can we have each Legionary work with a Legionary on each side, together, in attempting to achieve the objectives of the leaders, the Centurion's and the Tribune's. The discipline is direct and harsh but, any leader will listen to suggestions made by any Legionary at anytime. Quite often it is these suggestions that lead to victory. We want our Legionaries to think for themselves; but we insist on rigid discipline. Once a decision is made, and orders are issued, then they are followed without question. It is discipline that we demand, but we also demand Legionaries to think. The ones who think best yet follow commands are the ones we promote. We are not interested in coarse persons of no intellect as our leaders. No-one will follow an automaton. Our strength lies in working with people who think for themselves, and through this joint endeavor, extending Pax Romana throughout the known world. So it has always been with Rome, so it is my hope that it will always be."

Titus became silent, and slowly turned and directed a piercing look at Sarto. His look hardened dramatically. After a few seconds, he turned and looked directly at the Emperor and said, "Sire, as Prefect of the Praetorian Guard, and as your designated heir to become Emperor, it is my opinion that we should have no concern or fear from the Christians because they think for themselves. So long as they remain peaceful, and continue in their support, I see no reason to persecute them merely because they are Christians. However, whether Christians or not, I do strongly recommend the rule of law. If they break the law, then they must be prosecuted to the full extent indicated by that law. No matter who they are. This must also apply to all those who masquerade as Christians and attempt to foment dissension and riot." Titus once again paused and turned slowly towards Sarto. He directed a stern look at him before once more looking back to the Emperor and continuing. "It was that sense of Roman law that led the Praetorian Guard to assassinate Caligula when he trampled the laws of Rome. Even though an Emperor, he was not above the law. The Praetorian Guard executed him. And so, Sire, my opinion is that the Christians should not be persecuted merely because they think for themselves. If, on the other hand, they ever changed their approach, and begin to conspire to revolt against Rome, or against you, the Emperor, then we certainly have the ability to exterminate them immediately."

Sarto seemed to be shrinking in stature, as if deflated. His most important sally in attacking the Christians had been totally destroyed. Hiding his absolute chagrin, and attempting to retain some measure of dignity and the appearance of power, Senator Sarto quietly, and almost meekly, stated, "Prefect, I cannot criticize what you have said. Upon further reflection, I support your position." As he completed his statement, Senator Sarto seemed to shrink within himself. He wrung his hands briefly before dropping them to his side. He surreptitiously glanced at the Emperor before casting his eyes once again towards the floor of the room. That one glance told him that The Emperor was totally in agreement with what Titus had said, as evidenced by the broad smile on his face.

The Emperor spoke up. "Thank you Titus, and thank you Senator Sarto. I think that Prefect Titus has stated the position quite clearly. As Emperor, I rely heavily upon the strength and support of the Praetorian Guard." Looking at Quintus the Emperor added, "Quintus, what do you think of this?"

Agreeably surprised at what Titus had said, Quintus said, "I endorse what Prefect Titus had said. In my position as Deputy Prefect, I came to share the same opinion. As one charged by you to investigate the nature and potential role of the Christians in our society, I came to appreciate the very important fact that the Christians can become an outstanding asset for Rome. Dedicated as they are to what is right, they can become a bulwark of support in furthering the interests of Rome. After all, we can all decry the extreme behavior of Caligula and Nero, just as we can praise the wise actions of Augustus Caesar, Tiberius, and

Claudius. It is in the best interests of the Emperor to have strong support from the citizenry of the empire. The Emperor should be the leader in the full sense of the word leadership. As the greatest military leader of our time, Sire, I know you will agree. Leadership requires the ability to define the objective and to have others follow as you strive to achieve that objective. Leadership can never survive when there is significant difference of objective between the leader and those who are led. All must have the same objective. True Christians all have the same objective. That is not to say that some who seek power or wealth may pretend to be Christians to gain an advantage; but they are ultimately uncovered for what they really are. Hence, Sire, I recommend that we leave the Christians in peace, allowing them to follow their religious beliefs, just as we allow everyone else to follow their religious beliefs, so as long as they obey the law of Rome. As we have discussed, their interests lie in strong support and even enlargement of Pax Romana. This recommendation is reinforced by all of my findings, which I have included in my report which my associate Marcus has written on a papyrus which we can leave to be included in the archives of Rome."

With that, Quintus turned and walked over to Marcus with his hand outstretched to receive the papyrus which Marcus presented to him. Quintus then turned and walked to the Emperor and handed him the papyrus. Standing back respectfully, Quintus added, "Here is the papyrus with the details of all of our findings, Sire. It supports the conclusion which I have presented to you today."

"Thank you, Quintus. I am truly appreciative of the effort expended, and gratified that I have nothing to fear from the Christians, but only an expectation of their continued support in my role as Emperor. As you know, I became Emperor because of the support from the Germanic Legions which I led to victory in so many battles. I agree with you that leadership requires the support of those who are led." After a short pause, the Emperor added, a broad enigmatic smile on his lips. "That requires judgment!"

Looking about the room the Emperor asked "Senator Acquinas, do have anything to add?"

Acquinas was beaming. "No, Sire I have nothing to add. I am completely in support of the report which has been presented by my good friend Senator Quintus Gaius Caesar. I also am strongly in support of the remarks made by Perfect Titus."

Acquinas paused and seemed to be in deep thought for a moment. Then he added, "I cannot help thinking to the history of Rome. As all of you know, Cicero is one of the great leaders in our history, and reputed to be the greatest orator Rome ever produced. If you will recall there was at one at time a conspiracy to overthrow the rulers of Rome by Cataline. It was Cicero who exposed the Cataline conspiracy leading to the condemnation and ultimate execution of all those who sought to overthrow the rule of law at that time. As you spoke, Sire, I was reminded of this important element associated with the history of Rome and its very foundation. Rome is based on the rule of law. Pax Romana is our attempt and our methodology for enforcing the rule of law and guaranteeing it to all of our subjects, whether born as Romans, or as conquered peoples who are now part of Rome. Our whole approach is one of granting to all the right to live in peace under Roman law, protected by Pax Romana, the peace of Rome. I see no distinction between that concept and the endorsement of Christians as being subjects under Roman law. As long as they obey the law, they should be allowed to practice their religion   in peace." After a moment's

240

apparent deep reflection Acquinas added "I too foresee the day when Christianity will be a major asset to Rome." Then he added in a soft tone of voice. "That may even be now!"

The Emperor turned to his younger son Domitian and asked "Domitian, what do you think?"

"Sire," answered Domitian "I am a great believer in the status quo. I look with suspicion on anything that differs from what we should expect. I have some deep suspicion of Christians because they are different; but I have no evidence that this difference poses any risk to Rome or to the Emperor. Until I sense that there is a risk, then I too would accept that Christians should be left in peace. But," he added sternly, "if there is the least suspicion that this is not so, then I think we should act sternly and persecute them aggressively, if not exterminate them. I also believe, if anything, we should act on the side of caution and perhaps treat them more sternly than that we might treat others who believe in the same gods as we do."

The emperor was not surprised at the conservative statement of his son Domitian. He knew the difference between his two sons. Titus had fought by his side, and proven himself time and again as a great leader. He knew Titus to be fearless, looking not with suspicion upon those who might be different from himself but looking rather on how to have them follow him in his role as leaders. Because of this, Titus had been a very successful leader in battle; and his Legions strongly supported him. Titus, in his opinion, would do well as Emperor. Domitian, on the other hand, had never led in battle. As the much younger son, he had not developed the same experience level as Titus. If Domitian ever succeeded Titus to become emperor, then Vespasian was concerned as to whether he would have the

241

same approach towards the Christians. In any event, that likelihood was remote.

Vespasian cast his gaze about the room, before resting his eyes on Quintus. He smiled broadly. "Quintus, thank you very much for your report. You have examined Christianity and evaluated its potential threat to Rome. You have found, to the contrary, that Christianity is not a current threat to Rome. Rather, it is an asset. Your logic and your facts have convinced me." The Emperor paused to give great weight to his next words. In a voice full of command authority, the Emperor announced: "I endorse your recommendations, Quintus. Let the Christians live in peace!"

With that the Emperor nodded briefly to each dignitary present, then rose and strode briskly from the room. Without a word or looking at anyone, Senator Sarto drew his cloak around himself and left with his head held high, looking straight ahead and leaving without any parting remark to those in the room.

The others gathered and spoke briefly for a few moments, exchanging pleasantries, until they left individually. Longinus took his leave once again commenting upon his imminent departure for Caesarea.

Finally, only Quintus and Marcus remained. As they left the room together, Quintus let his thoughts extend back to Judea with his investigation of the mysterious disappearance of the body of Jesus. That effort had now been extended to this new investigation of Christianity, the movement founded by Jesus. In his lifetime to date, Quintus had seen this significant growth of the followers of Jesus. As he walked quietly with Marcus, the thought entered his mind that the ranks of the Christians would swell and grow until one day they would become an all encompassing force throughout the known, and the unknown, world. Quintus smiled. He was grateful to the Emperor for this opportunity to study in detail what it meant to be a Christian. He had nothing but admiration for them. He smiled ruefully. Quintus wondered if he was becoming a Christian.

About the Author
Dr. Rocco Leonard Martino

Dr. Rocco Leonard Martino is Founder and Chairman of the Board of the Cyber Technology Group, Inc. and of CyberFone Technologies, Inc. Previously, he was Founder, Chairman and CEO of XRT, Inc., the world leader in providing complete global treasury, cash and banking relationship management solutions for many of the world's largest corporations and government entities. Treasury systems designed by Dr. Martino are integrated and operate in real-time in a fault-tolerant, disaster-tolerant, on-line environment in major organizations around the world. Dr. Martino has patented and is the inventor of the CyberFone - the first Smart Phone - and the driving force behind the software systems that unite communication and computer power. The CyberFone Smart Phone provides real-time video, voice and data linkages, in personal and corporate use, anywhere.

Dr. Martino is a pioneer and international authority in the planning and use of computers systems within Cyber-Security, and originated many of the methods in use today. Dr. Martino served in various high-level positions prior to XRT and CyberFone Technologies, Inc. He was EVP of Mauchly Associates created in partnership with Dr. John Mauchly, the co-inventor of electronic computers. He allied with Rear Admiral Grace Hopper USN, on Automatic Programming techniques, which were the forerunner of COBOL. As Director of the Computer Division for Adalia Limited, a consulting firm headed by Sir Robert Watson-Watt, the inventor of radar, Dr. Martino participated in the extensive development of wireless navigation systems.

Dr. Martino graduated Summa Cum Laude from the University of Toronto in Mathematics and Finance. He earned a Ph.D. from the Institute of Aerospace Studies for work in the re-entry of Space Vehicles, specifically in heat transfer requirements for heat shields. In 1993 he was awarded an honorary Doctor of Science degree from Neumann University for his contributions in Information Technology. In 2000, he received Honorary Degrees from Chestnut Hill College in Philadelphia and from Gonzaga University in Spokane, Washington. Both degrees were awarded for his humanitarian and charitable activities, as well as for his scientific achievements.

The National Italian American Foundation honored Dr. Martino for Lifetime Achievement in 1992, as did the Monte Jade Society in 1999, and the CYO in 2000. In this latter award he was chosen as a symbol for Youth. In 2011 he was awarded The Order of the Golden Palm by the Equestrian Order of the Holy Sepulchre. He also received the Order of Merit by the Order of Malta in 2011.

Dr. Martino served as Professor of Mathematics and Engineering at the University of Waterloo and at New York University. His graduate and senior undergraduate lectures included such topics as Artificial Intelligence, Space Flight, Information Systems, Economics, and Financial Modeling Systems. He continues to lecture at numerous Universities throughout the World.

Dr. Martino has been knighted five times. Most significant is his Papal Knighthood in the Order of St. Gregory the Great awarded by Pope John Paul II in 1991. Dr. Martino has served on various Public Service, Charitable, and Church Organizations. He served as Vice Chair of the Board of the Gregorian University Consortium Foundation and as a member of various public service Boards, including: St. Joseph's University; Equestrian Order of the Holy Sepulchre; Order of Malta; Vatican Observatory Foundation; and Founding Chairman of the

245

MBF Foundation dedicated to applying computer technology for those with severe physical and/or mental handicaps. Dr. Martino has also served on various Corporate Boards over the past fifty years.

Dr. Martino has been a guest speaker at many functions in the United States, Canada, Mexico, Europe and Asia. He has taken part in scores of radio and video broadcasts speaking on Foreign Affairs, Information Technology, Innovation, and National Security. He is a Senior Fellow of the Foreign Policy Research Institute.

Dr. Martino is also a lifetime member of the Union League of Philadelphia, of Overbrook Golf Club in Bryn Mawr, PA and of the Yacht Club of Sea Isle City. He is an avid sailor, and a Past Commodore of the Yacht Club. He also served as a member of their Board for twenty years, including seven years as their Chairman. He has served as Commodore of the Mid-Atlantic Yacht Racing Association, and as their Secretary for eight years.

Dr. Martino is the author of twenty-four published works including this book, his fourth novel, as well as scores of papers, and numerous corporate monographs. He is listed in various biographical anthologies.

Reviews of
The Resurrection: A Criminal Investigation . . .

"So yesterday I finally had time to pick up your book and the only problem was I couldn't stop reading it. Congratulations and thanks for my wonderful experience. You really captured the essence of our faith in a manner easy for all to follow. Your book is an excellent tool for the Year of Faith.......Your summary of leadership was also right on target!"
> *-Tim Flanagan, Founder and Chair, Catholic Leadership Institute*

"This book brings commonality to theology."
> *-Dr. Patrick McCarthy, KMOb*

"Dr. Martino paints Tribune Quintus as a savvy detective assigned by the Roman Emperor to undertake seriously the apparent disappearance of the body of the crucified criminal Jesus of Nazareth. Filled with tension and mysterious details, the book locks our attention. I found it hard to put the book aside....the story finally shines into the face, and the soul, of us readers an important serious question....does that reveal the crucified Criminal Jesus of Nazareth as ALIVE? And if so, how important is that to all of us?....The novel, breathless at times, rings with the Good News of the Risen Jesus."
> *-Fr. George Aschenbrenner, SJ, Jesuit Center, Wernersville, Pennsylvania; Rector Emeritus, Scranton University*

"Throughout history many have attempted, well intentioned or otherwise, to augment or rewrite the gospel record of the life, death and resurrection of Jesus Christ: Gnostics in the early centuries of Christianity and modern movie producers being two examples. In most cases artistic license, or worse deliberate theological distortion, trumped truth and accuracy. A clear exception is "The Resurrection: A Criminal Investigation..." Faith is not being challenged; it is enhanced. Doctor Martino has expertly crafted an imaginary scenario of the events not recorded in Scripture of the happenings surrounding the death and resurrection of Jesus. The story is not only plausible but compelling. The characters with familiar names are vividly portrayed. The reader easily is carried back two thousand years to contemplate, through the eyes of a Roman Tribune, the Paschal Mystery, and become better for the experience."

-Paul Peterson, Professor of Theology, Archdiocese of Philadelphia

"Believe it! For 99 cents, I was able to read, perhaps, one of the most important books I will ever read! Once I started, I couldn't stop until finished, less than a day! For me personally, it seemed to give me what I had been searching for all my life!....This is a must-read for anybody who would like to learn how the investigation of an individual should be conducted...before...they were crucified....Thank you Dr. Martino for satisfying my personal need for closure...and for justice to prevail, at least legally..."

-Glenda A. Bixler, Editor, GABixlerReviews

"Leaving to others the subtleties of biblical criticism, Dr. Martino leads us through an engaging series of interviews conducted by a persistent but sensitive Roman tribune seeking the answer to why the tomb of Jesus was empty. The author gives expression to his vivid faith and his taste for logic and reasoning, treating us to a couple of imaginative surprises at the end."

-Peter Kearney, Biblical Scholar

248

"I am reading your book myself and find it thoroughly gripping and very well researched....your book is a real page turner....it is a deeply inspirational work."
> *-Gerard O'Sullivan, PhD, Vice President for Academic Affairs, Neumann University*

"A vivid portrayal of the most time-less events of our salvation history... the empty tomb elicits gripping attention, lingering wonderment and thanksgiving."
> *-Dr. Robert Capizzi, FACP, FASCO, Co-Founder, President, Chief Medical Officer, CharlestonPharma, LLC*

"I wanted to let you know that I just finished your latest book, The Resurrection. I thought it would be a fitting read for Holy Week. Thank you for writing it! Even though I'm a believer, it always helps to have my beliefs reinforced, and your wonderful book certainly did that for me. I enjoyed your creative approach and liked the way you brought the characters to life. Every doubter of Christ's life, death and resurrection should read this book."
> *-Stafford Worley, Co-Founder, Worens Group*

"THE RESURRECTION. What a marvelous experience. Congratulations! I thoroughly enjoyed it. You really integrated everything in a most engaging way."
> *-Rev. Fr. Dominic Maruca, S.J., Professor Emeritus, Pontifical Gregorian University of Rome*

"I read your book, 'Resurrection', and it is the best yet. It's fascinating to see how one uses logic to arrive at the same conclusions that the rest of us arrive at by faith."
-Dr. Stephen Schuster, University of Pennsylvania Health Systems.

"I enjoyed reading it very much. The way the author told the story kept my interest in the factual details of what really happened to our crucified Lord. I learned so much of why Jesus was unjustly murdered. Reading your book strengthens me in my own fundamental faith and beliefs in the agony and suffering of Jesus."
-John Snyder, S.J.

"...just as Mel Gibson's movie The Passion has forever changed how I feel about the ministry and painful death of Christ...The Resurrection has changed how I...feel about the politics behind Christ's conviction to death...I really enjoyed this...and foresee a film version..."
-James Longon, Entrepreneur

"I must congratulate you on your page-turner THE RESURRECTION. It is fascinating, beautifully written and – well brilliant! I enjoyed every minute of it. It deserves a wide readership...a potent force for evangelization. Thanks for writing it..."
-Patricia Lynch

Reviews of
9-11-11: The Tenth Anniversary Attack

"Drawing on his vast expertise in national security, defense and the internet, Rocco Martino has done it again. 9/11/11 is a fascinating read that is a product of our time depicting the dangerous world in which we live. I foresee a future big screen Harrison Ford blockbuster!"
-Rear Admiral Thomas Lynch, United States Navy (Retired)

"Dr. Martino lays out a credible Al Qaeda sponsored plot to cripple the "American Satan" on the anniversary of 9/11... The theme of the book is apparently that cyber warfare particularly focused on finances is the way we can successfully combat terrorism."
-Clifford Wilson, Former Member New York Assembly

"Timely plot, well-developed characters...and a truly engrossing explication of the complexities of international money laundering and the fearsome dangers facing western civilization from fanatics wielding weapons of mass destruction."
- Dr. Rosalie Pedalino Porter, Author of "American Immigrant: My Life in Three Languages"

"The story accurately illustrates the complex and abstract world of cyber security and constant vigilance needed for tracking terrorist plots, including their planning, correspondence and financial movements."
- Dr. James F. Peters, NASA Engineer and Vice President of Technology for Quasar Data Center

"The man behind this political thriller is extremely knowledgeable about the world of computers. Dr. Martino wrote the fictional story to stress the need for America to stay vigilant and fight terrorism with Cyber Warfare."

-Jean-Bernard Hyppolite, Chestnut Hill Local

Reviews of
The Plot to Cancel Christmas!

"Rocky Martino is like Rocky Balboa. His book is a punch in the heart and a hug at the same time. So hold on – don't just read it – pray it!"
-Jim Murray, Co-Founder, Ronald MacDonald House

"A timeless tale that speaks volumes...a modern Christmas Carol."
-Joe Looby, Voice Actor

"A book that gives you pause – could this really happen? An engaging story of what greed can lead you to do."
-Patricia Parisano, Legal Secretary

"Rocky gives us a snapshot of how powerful individuals, organizations and institutions can use politicians as pawns and puppets in an attempt to enrich themselves. We are reminded that the 'Greed is Good' philosophy needs our vigilance in a world that should care for the needs and rights of the individual. He offers hope in a distressed world."
-Jim Fitzsimmons, President, Malvern Retreat House

"Reading this book is an experience in theater. Martino limns his two-dimensional characters with the skill of an artisan bringing them to the third dimension with extraordinary color. They literally dance from the page to the stage."
-Sister Marianne Postiglione, RSM, ITEST

"It's delightful – a modern day Dickensesque Christmas Carol!"
-Dr. Joseph Holland, President, Pax Romana

253

"This book is a gift that will put your life in perspective."
-Tim Flanagan, Founder and Chair, Catholic Leadership Institute

"A Classic Battle between might & right!"
-Jim White, CEO, JJ White, Inc.

"Martino's story reveals the human spirit and all of its wonderful contradictions through one man's campaign to cancel Christmas. A miser who believes happiness is only found in money just might find true happiness accidentally in his quest for riches & power."
-Joseph J. McLaughlin, Jr., President, Haverford Trust